D0921984

THE ODDFITS

THE ODDFITS

TIFFANY TSAO

amazon crossing

This is a work of fiction. Names, characters, organizations, places, events, and incidents are either products of the author's imagination or are used fictitiously.

Text copyright © 2016 Tiffany Tsao

All rights reserved.

No part of this book may be reproduced, or stored in a retrieval system, or transmitted in any form or by any means, electronic, mechanical, photocopying, recording, or otherwise, without express written permission of the publisher.

Published by AmazonCrossing, Seattle

www.apub.com

Amazon, the Amazon logo, and AmazonCrossing are trademarks of Amazon.com, Inc., or its affiliates.

ISBN-13: 9781503952621
ISBN-10: 1503952622

Cover design by David Drummond

Printed in the United States of America

for Justin and Zephyr

CHAPTER 1

When Yusuf bin Hassim disappeared from Singapore in 1939, it baffled everyone. The slim, bright-eyed lad of nineteen had just started what looked to be a promising life. He had procured a job as an ice cream vendor with Magnolia, Singapore's very first ice cream company. His parents were in the process of finding him a suitable wife from the daughters of families they knew. He had great hair—full, lustrous, glossy, as if his head were crowned with a dollop of jet-black whipped cream. Everything seemed to be falling into place. And then he had vanished.

He had left a note for his mother and father, his brothers and sisters, his grandmother and grandfather, his uncles and aunts, and all his cousins, addressing each by name and explaining the situation. The note was immensely long—thirty-seven pages of letter paper, each page crammed full of handwriting so small that the only way to make out the words was to squint. The note was so long, in fact, that only his youngest sister Aminah had actually finished it; the rest having given up only part way through. But when the rest of the family asked Aminah for a summary, she couldn't remember the contents. "Oh, same as the first few pages," she told them. "How much he loves us, memories of this good thing or that good time, something about a Quest he must go on. Not very coherent. I've forgotten most of it, actually. Sorry."

In response, they nodded sadly. They had loved Yusuf dearly, but the letter was just so . . . long. And they took some comfort in knowing that at least something terrible hadn't befallen him. Still, his cousins and younger siblings did miss the prestige of having an ice cream man in the family—the occasional free treats and getting to try on the smart white pith helmet he'd worn as part of his uniform just couldn't be beat. In the turbulent years that followed, his family would reflect on how perhaps Yusuf had left at a good time. He had missed the Japanese invasion, the terrible war years, the riots and political chaos of the independence and post-independence period. They hoped that wherever he was in the world, he was doing all right, *insha'Allah*.

So when Yusuf bin Hassim reappeared in Singapore in 1985, it baffled everyone. Well, everyone who was left to be baffled. All those in the generations above him, including his parents, had died. Two cousins had been killed in the 1964 race riots, and most of the other cousins and all his siblings save one had emigrated to Malaysia, Australia, or the UK. In the end, Yusuf's sudden return only had an audience of four: three cousins and Aminah—not counting the families they'd gone on to have after Yusuf had vanished. Though to these two wives, two husbands, fifteen fully grown children, and twelve grandchildren, Yusuf was only a name they seldom heard, and it was difficult for them to understand the magnitude of his homecoming and the excitement it generated.

"It's like having someone come back from the grave," Cousin Fatimah explained to one of her granddaughters.

"Yuck," the granddaughter replied.

Aminah, who had received Yusuf's telephone call and spread the news of his return, arranged for a celebratory dinner to be held that very Saturday, hosted by her and her husband Hassan at their new government-built Housing and Development Board flat in Tampines.

Hassan borrowed woven straw mats from various neighbours to provide extra sitting space. Aminah's children, under their mother's supervision, helped prepare enormous pots of beef rendang, vegetable curry, and rice. One of the cousins brought soft drinks, another sweet kuih-kuih, and another fried corn fritters. Crammed in Aminah's tiny living room, elbow to elbow and ear to ear, they ate, chatted, and celebrated the return of one of their own. Everyone, of course, was genuinely happy that Yusuf had come back, and they genuinely tried to keep the happiness running at full speed throughout the evening. But there remained the undeniable fact that they didn't really know him anymore, and that he didn't really know them. Try as they might, they couldn't help feeling that the wizened, frail wisp of a man sitting among them was a complete stranger.

After the family had eaten their fill, chorused their disbelief and joy at his return multiple times, and eaten still more, the atmosphere of collective jubilation began to deflate ever so slightly, like a day-old balloon. It didn't help that the children had left and taken with them their shrieks of merriment. After receiving permission from the adults to leave, they had scrambled over each other into the open-air corridor and down four flights of stairs to play imaginative variations of hide-and-seek and tag among the open grassy spaces and sheltered void decks of the HDB blocks. In the children's absence, the lively chatter was exhibiting signs of audible strain. The spirit of the evening was on the verge of collapsing entirely when Cousin Khalid, realizing that Yusuf had been relatively quiet all evening and that they all still had no idea where he had been those forty-six years, thought it a good idea to ask. With the same unassuming smile that he had worn all evening while peacefully basking in the boisterousness of a family gathering for the first time in a long time, Yusuf told them.

It was almost midnight by the time Yusuf finished and everyone left to go home. Bundling groggy babies and toddlers into strollers and over shoulders, and conducting several head counts to make sure that all the children were present and accounted for, the cousins and their families departed into the cool darkness of a night on the cusp of turning into morning. Before they went their separate ways, they tried briefly to speak together of the fantastic things that the long-lost Yusuf had just told them about. However, try as they might, they couldn't. All that remained in their memories were the fierce, bright, flashing black eyes of Yusuf as he had recounted to them the frightening, dazzling, and extraordinary events of his forty-six-year-long absence. But even that impression was beginning to fade, like a water stain on fabric, drying imperceptibly into invisibility.

Back at the flat, Aminah and Yusuf, at his own insistence, worked alongside each other in the kitchen, washing and drying the dishes. Even she, with her brother standing right next to her, was beginning to forget what he had recounted that enthralled them all so. What exactly had he been through all those years that had whitened and thinned his hair? What had wrinkled his skin and deepened its colour? And what had put that black fire in his eyes? He had just told them, hadn't he? But the knowledge was dwindling with every passing second, even as she looked sidelong at him from the sink. The magnificent richness of his eyes was fading too, and by the time the last dish had been put away, there was nothing special left in them—just the washed-out, watery colour of all old eyes. Her husband came in after seeing the last of their children and grandchildren off, and insisted that Yusuf stay the night. It was far too late for him to go home and it would be no trouble at all. Yusuf, however, was determined to leave. Embracing his newly discovered brother-in-law and his dear sister, and accepting three containers of leftover food neatly stacked and tied up in a blue plastic bundle, he said goodbye and promised that he would call soon.

This dinner was the last time Yusuf saw any of his extended family. The morning after, everyone woke with no memory of where Yusuf had been and what Yusuf had done. They only recalled the unfamiliarity of that stranger, surprisingly ancient-looking and withered for a man of sixty-five. Not only that, but a bad, bloated feeling had settled around the memory of him and the prospect of having anything to do with him. They politely stayed away. Aminah's reaction wasn't so severe, but her head did ache a bit the day after. She was diligent in keeping up communications with him, though, for he was her brother, and she loved him. Or at least, she felt that she wanted to get close with him, but couldn't quite. She made sure that they met up at least once every few weeks, and she felt guilty that they didn't meet up more. Always, Aminah's head felt a bit achy afterwards. Who knew why?

So in the end, Yusuf returned to his former life, only to find it a solitary one—a room that he had left behind filled with beloved and familiar objects. He had returned after a lifetime to find it waiting for him still, but empty. He accepted this placidly and without surprise, as if he'd been expecting it all along. He made no attempt to contact his cousins, and only spoke to Aminah occasionally. He seemed to have money enough, and upon his sudden reappearance, he had managed to procure a small one-bedroom flat, very similar in design to that of his sister's, in Ang Mo Kio. He cooked all his own meals and did all his own housekeeping. Although he was always polite to the neighbours, he was too reserved to ever become familiar with them, and every other evening, he could be seen in the large community park nearby, ambling on the winding paths and steps around and up the hillock, always by himself.

In one respect, he did attempt to pick up his old life from where he had left off. He went into the ice cream business again, opening a small ice cream parlour in a row of rather dilapidated shophouses, a ten-minute walk from his flat. Except for the rental price, there had been little to recommend the space. All four of the existing businesses appeared to be on the verge of extinction—or had already expired without realizing it. When the Hoh Heng Coffee Powder Trading Company Pte. Ltd. stopped turning a profit, they had ceased turning the great roasting drums as well, and now their income appeared to be wholly derived from the occasional sale of plain cream crackers and brightly iced fancy gem biscuits, weighed by the gram on an old-fashioned brass scale. The contents of the ABC Typewriter and Stationery Shop were all coated in a fine layer of dust, including the proprietor—a spindly, hollow-eyed ancient who sat motionless behind the counter day after day. Double Swan Tailoring on the far end hadn't been doing well since the resident seamstress went blind in one eye. And on the far end of the row, Fun-Fun's House of Board Games seemed to have undergone an unofficial conversion into a Bible and Christian pamphlet storage facility.

Such neighbours would have depressed a lesser man, but Yusuf remained undeterred. Clearing his newly acquired space of the remains of paper lanterns (and illegal firecrackers) left over from the previous tenant, he set to work fixing the place up.

In three months, the Tutti-Frutti Ice Cream Shop was open for business. It was a humble affair, small but well lit and clean, with pastel orange walls and light-blue Formica tables and plastic stools. All the ice cream—well, all seven flavours—was made by Yusuf himself, though for some reason, he never really thought to advertise the fact. Gradually, he built up a small but loyal customer base from the local resident community. The ice cream was absolutely delicious, his admirers said—the richest, most flavourful, most wonderful that they'd ever had.

Unfortunately, his ice cream wasn't to everyone's taste. Some complained that it left a mild sour aftertaste at the back of their throats. Those who did like the ice cream, however, were passionate about it, and asked Yusuf why he didn't expand—add new flavours, make the place bigger, more modern, do more advertising? Yusuf simply smiled and shrugged. He'd had his adventure and he was content, he would say.

"Uncle got no ambition, is it?" asked one customer who was particularly frustrated at Yusuf's complacency. The man came in to the Tutti-Frutti at least twice a week, wore a big gold watch and a big ruby ring, and patent black leather shoes polished to a high shine.

His hair was slicked back and he was always checking his pager. He came from a self-made merchant family—recent immigrants from China who worked hard and smart and made good for themselves. Entrepreneurship coursed red through his veins and he saw the world and its unfolding events as a collection of ever-changing, shimmering opportunities. He liked Yusuf and wanted to see the old Malay man make something of his life.

"Uncle may be old, but what for just wait around to die? What for, lah?"

Shocked at the rudeness of the words that had just tumbled from his mouth, the man was on the verge of uttering an apology, but decided instead to see what effect his question would have. Perhaps it would goad the old man into action.

Yusuf was immovable. He smiled that maddeningly contented smile of his. "No, boy. I'm waiting for other things, but if death comes first, then so be it."

The man shook his head uncomprehendingly and proceeded to order his usual: two-scoop sundae, one scoop chocolate, one scoop red bean, extra whipped cream. *Odd old man*, he thought to himself. *Very odd.*

CHAPTER 2

Very odd. Those were the exact same words that Yusuf bin Hassim was to mutter to himself some years later, right after he had discovered the boy. The boy was, in fact, the very type of "other thing" that Yusuf had been waiting for since his return to Singapore. He hadn't been certain that an "other thing" was going to show up, not by a long shot. In fact, he would have been almost as content if he had left this earth without encountering one of the "other things" he'd had a hunch would one day cross his life's path. But it turned out that his hunch had been right, and now he was fully content. Very odd the boy was, and therefore, just right. Yet to Yusuf's profound embarrassment, he hadn't noticed what the boy truly was right away. In fact, the boy's oddness, or rather, his oddfittingness, was only the third peculiarity Yusuf had noticed when the boy had wandered wide-eyed into the Tutti-Frutti Ice Cream Shop.

The very first peculiar thing Yusuf had noticed about the boy was, frankly speaking, the fact that he was as blonde-haired and blue-eyed as the weather in Singapore was hot and muggy. Almost all of the Tutti-Frutti clientele were Chinese, Malays, or Indians—identifiably local. The Tutti-Frutti wasn't much to look at—hardly worth a mention in any of the tourist guidebooks, and too out of the way for anyone who didn't live nearby. Certainly, no westerners ever came: not tourists, nor the well-paid foreign expatriates who had been sent to represent their companies' interests in Singapore. Ang Mo Kio wasn't that kind of neighbourhood.

It was far away from the major attractions, a little too modern to be quaint, and a little too authentic to be comfortable. Business was conducted gruffly and conversation loudly in Hokkien, Teochew, and Hakka. Cheap clothes and bed sheets adorned with Japanese cartoon characters and bad floral prints hung from bamboo poles outside HDB slab blocks. Multicoloured fairy lights were considered tasteful shop and restaurant decor. Here and there blew the ashen flakes of spirit money—burnt offerings for the ancestral dead—and the sickly strong odour of incense wafted around corners and through alleyways, emanating from tiny, garish Buddhist shrines that were tucked in enclaves underfoot and overhead. The bakeries sold pandan bread of suspicious green hues; the "medicine" stores stocked dubious-looking dried herbs and animal parts; the jewellery stores displayed gaudy gold and jade wares against garish red cloth backing; and while the produce and meat sold in the wet markets were undeniably fresh, the floors were, well, suspiciously wet. No, westerners did not venture into these parts. And yet, one day, there came the boy, appearing suddenly and silently and pale as a ghost. Yusuf had been absentmindedly polishing ice cream spoons with a dish-cloth, surveying the empty parlour. He had stooped down to put them away underneath the counter. And he had risen to find a boy pressing his little face against the glass of the ice cream case, staring with amazement at the seven different flavours on display.

"Hello, boy," Yusuf had said by way of greeting. The boy looked up at him with the same wide-eyed gaze, as if Yusuf himself had been a variety of ice cream. Smiling a small, uncertain smile, the boy resumed staring at the tubs of ice cream, the blueness of his eyes intense with longing.

The second peculiar thing Yusuf noticed about the boy was that he was alone. In his experience, westerners living in Singapore tended to be notoriously protective of their offspring, sending them to private schools and keeping them within the confines of the exclusive clubs that defined themselves by country: one for the Americans, one for the British, one for the Germans, one for the Dutch . . . When the children did venture out into the "local" areas of Singapore, they were always accompanied by their mothers, or by diminutive dark-skinned maids, or both. And yet, here was this little chap, wandering in without any sign of a mother or father or a maid, or any guardian of any sort.

"Boy, are you lost?"

The boy shook his head, his eyes still riveted by the ice cream.

"Where are your parents?"

"At work," the boy replied softly.

Very strange, Yusuf thought to himself. Leaning over the counter, he regarded the boy. And then he noticed the third peculiar thing.

The boy was clearly and unmistakably oddfitting. Oddfittingness emanated from his every pore; it enveloped him like a cloud; it hung on him and exceeded him as if it were a baggy, oversized T-shirt that came all the way down to his scrawny little ankles. The oddfittingness was so obvious that Yusuf was ashamed to admit that he hadn't seen it until now. He was obviously out of practice.

"Boy, would you like an ice cream?"

The boy looked up at him with an expression that could only be described as mournful. "I don't have enough." He stretched out his palm and, lifting it to Yusuf's gaze, showed him the tarnished pale gold of a five-cent coin.

"Never mind, boy. Choose which flavour you want."

The boy's face lit up with delight. After another bout of contemplation in front of the ice cream, he made his choice: yam. Yusuf piled a cone high with two purple scoops and handed it to the boy. In a matter of minutes, the boy had lapped and crunched the entire thing into oblivion.

"Did you like it, boy?"

The boy nodded, licking his fingers to make sure none of the sticky sweetness went to waste.

"Secret recipe." Yusuf tapped his chest proudly. "Came up with it myself. You see these flavours?" Yusuf said as he gestured at the case. "Yam, chocolate, sweet corn, red bean, strawberry, vanilla, durian . . . you can get these flavours from any ice cream shop in Singapore, right?"

As the Tutti-Frutti was the first ice cream shop the boy had ever been to, he couldn't say. He looked confused.

"Well, you can," Yusuf affirmed. "But *this* ice cream here . . . the ice cream in *this* shop, your Uncle Yusuf makes them all from recipes he came up with himself. That's what you call me, okay, boy? 'Uncle Yusuf.'"

The boy nodded.

That night, Yusuf wrote a letter to his colleagues from his former line of work—a past existence, a different life altogether, it seemed now—notifying them about the boy. He hadn't written to them since he had retired. He dusted off the lid of the box where he kept his professional writing implements, took out a single sheet of red paper, a magnificent fountain pen, and a pot of peacock-blue ink, and proceeded to tell them of the news:

Dear Former Colleagues,
I hope this finds you well.
Found: One Oddfit.
Age: Estimated eight to nine years old.
Will act when time is right.
Regards, Yusuf

From that day onwards, the boy became a regular visitor to the Tutti-Frutti, and a friendship developed between him and Yusuf. He came in almost every day, and in exchange for ice cream, the boy would help polish spoons, or put glasses away, or wipe the counters, or whatever other chore Yusuf needed help doing. Every now and then, Yusuf would present him with a special sundae—three scoops of any flavour, whipped cream, raspberry syrup, chocolate sprinkles, cookie wafers, a neon-red maraschino cherry, festooned with the brightly coloured paper parasols in which the boy seemed to take a particular delight.

Despite the frequency of these visits, they hardly ever exchanged a word. The boy was naturally quiet, and gave only the most minimal of answers to any questions asked of him. Yusuf was also naturally quiet, and although he was mildly curious about many things concerning the boy, he also felt that there would be plenty of time for such things to be made known. Why did the boy's parents let him roam unsupervised? Did they know he came here every day? Why wasn't the boy in school? Yusuf wondered these things every now and then, but he was also a very patient man. There was a right time for everything. It simply wasn't important to know these things now. Although the way his former colleagues had been pestering him since he'd told them about the boy, one would think that there was no time to lose. They had always been in a hurry. The latest letter he'd received had read, all in capital letters:

INFORM BOY OF THE QUEST.
WHY WASTE TIME?

Yusuf had actually been so offended by this last one that instead of storing it in the bottom drawer of his desk where he had stored all the previous letters, he had crumpled this one up and thrown it into the rubbish bin.

"'Why waste time?'" Yusuf had repeated angrily. "I don't waste time. I wait till the time is right. I always did." Why did nobody else understand that important matters *had* to be handled deliberately and carefully, and therefore, slowly?

Weeks turned into months—one month, then two; three months, then four. The boy still visited almost every day, and each visit was spent in happy silence and the briefest of conversations. After six months, Yusuf finally decided that the time was ripe. It was time to show the boy the Great Freezer. And then it would be time to write to his former colleagues, setting in motion the steps that needed to be taken to secure the boy's safety and future.

To celebrate the special day (the specialness of which the boy was still ignorant), Yusuf presented the boy with one of the signature Tutti-Frutti three-scoop sundaes, extra sprinkles, extra parasols. After the boy had licked the bowl clean and lovingly tucked the parasols away in his left hip pocket, as was his habit, Yusuf made his move.

"Boy. Want to see where I keep the ice cream?"

The boy nodded.

"Follow me."

And the boy, full of ice cream and curiosity, followed Yusuf through the wall in the shop's corner to the Great Freezer.

The Great Freezer would come to be the stuff of legend in the More Known World, where news—fact, fiction, or combinations thereof—was necessarily circulated across the settlements and among the Territories by letters delivered hand to hand and by word of mouth. They would say that the exact dimensions of the Great Freezer were never known, that it had flummoxed all the dimension-measuring specialists, who could only come to one maddeningly imprecise conclusion: that the Great Freezer was, at the very least, magnificently expansive, if not downright preposterously gigantic. Possibly the biggest freezer ever to exist in the entire history of both the Known and More Known Worlds. It was also said that those who had discovered it had found it filled with ice cream—shelves and shelves and shelves and shelves and more shelves of it. And not just any ice cream—it was full of the same ice cream that had been appearing inexplicably every now and then all over the More Known World ever since the first settlements were established. A newcomer would find a small case of it left at his or her front door, or a crate of it would arrive at a provisions store in one of the more out-of-the-way Territories. Sometimes containers of it would appear underneath cots in a poorly supplied sick ward. This, it was said, was the source: the Great Freezer.

What people said had been true, for the truth was so fantastic that it was impossible to exaggerate it. Anyone who would hear these tales in the future would have drooled over the prospect of standing where the boy was standing now. Of all this ice cream, the Known World had only sampled seven flavours—the seven sold in the Tutti-Frutti. In total, there were seven hundred and thirty-six different flavours of ice cream, all concocted by Yusuf himself and lovingly stored here, awaiting their unexpected and irregular distribution throughout the Territories. At this point in time, only three beings had ever seen the interior of the Great Freezer, and two of them were inside it right now.

The boy was always quiet. This time, he was speechless.

The freezer was, predictably enough, freezing. As the boy walked alongside Yusuf through the aisles of the Great Freezer, he marvelled at the white puffs of air coming from his mouth. He had never experienced cold weather before. Goosebumps sprung up all over his shivering arms and legs. Yet he felt the blood circulating inside him warmer, thicker, stronger.

They stopped at the foot of a shaky metal ladder, and Yusuf clambered up its rungs slowly and carefully, retrieved two small tubs of ice cream, and even more slowly and carefully clambered back down. "Look, boy. This one is your favourite." He pried open the lid of the one marked "Y" to reveal the lavender-hued contents. "See? Yam!"

Yusuf set the tub down and opened the other, marked "SnR." The colour from the tub bathed their faces in a soft orange, red, and purple light. "This flavour is Sunrise. A lot like Sunset, but backwards and with coffee beans added."

They continued on, and the boy saw and sometimes sampled a flavour here and there. There was Quiet (translucent but wondrously rich), Darkness (so intensely black it hurt his eyes), Rainbow (colourful and maddeningly elusive), Chocolate (just for familiarity's sake), Toasty Toes (as implied, warm in the toes, no sensation in the mouth), and Yusuf's Super-Duper Taste Sensation (hard to describe: bubbly, tangy, zippy). Just as they were about to exit the freezer, Yusuf stopped at one more shelf, opened one last tub, and held it out.

"Boy, this is your Uncle Yusuf's favourite: Stars. Try it."

The boy dipped a finger into the container, scooping out a small blob of velvety dark blue and, atop it, a tiny, twinkling, sparkling shard.

As the ice cream melted in his mouth, the boy felt violets and chocolate and warm honeyed peaches and coconut milk and the spine-tingling sensation that the universe was a very, very vast place indeed. As he bit into the shard, it exploded and he felt his eyes and ears and throat aglow with firelight.

"Wow," the boy whispered. He was quite overcome.

"Not bad, eh?" Yusuf grinned.

"Do *you* make all this ice cream, Uncle Yusuf?"

Yusuf grinned proudly and his eyes flashed. "Yes. All of it."

Once they were outside, Yusuf brushed the frost off the boy's head and shoulders and told him, "Boy, that's just a little bit of what's to come. I'm sending word tonight. Don't worry. Things are underway!"

The boy, still dazzled from the experience of the Great Freezer, nodded. He had no idea what Uncle Yusuf was talking about. But it sounded very exciting.

"What's your name, boy?" Yusuf asked. He had never asked before. It hadn't been important before now. "I'll need to include it to send word."

The boy uttered something unintelligible.

"Eh? Come again?"

"Murgatroyd. Murgatroyd Floyd."

Yusuf frowned in perplexity. "Are you sure?"

Murgatroyd nodded.

"How do you spell that?"

Murgatroyd stared at him in panic.

"Oh, sorry. Uncle forgot you haven't learned to spell. Never mind." He gave the boy a pat on the head and chuckled. Don't look so worried, boy. Uncle Yusuf will take care of everything."

***

Later that evening, after a simple dinner of curried vegetables and rice, Yusuf made his way to his desk. His sat down and took out a sheet of red paper. He stared at the blank red sheet for a while as he composed the letter in its entirety in his head. Then, dipping his pen nib in the inkwell, he began to write:

> *Dear Former Colleagues,*
>
> *The time has come.*
>
> *Please be informed of one Oddfit, ready for retrieval.*
>
> *Name: Murgatroyd Floyd*
>
> *Location: Singapore*
>
> *Course of Action: We will be waiting at the corner of*

Yusuf put down the pen. He felt very tired all of a sudden. Positively sleepy. But this was very important business. It was time, and it was one of those rare occasions when it couldn't wait until tomorrow morning. He made his way to the kitchen to make himself a cup of instant coffee. After he put the kettle on the stove, he sat at the kitchen table, leaned forward, and rested his head on his folded hands. Just for a little while. The water was almost boiling . . .

***

Two days later, a little yellow-haired boy ran towards the Tutti-Frutti, crying and bleeding profusely from the nose. It was Murgatroyd Floyd, and he had just experienced his first day at school. To be fair, his schoolmates hadn't intended to shed any blood, just rough him up a little. But in such situations, things get out of hand, and when the *ang moh* (as they called him) curled up into a ball on the ground for self-defence, what was meant to be a harmless foot tap in the face turned into a mighty, bloodletting kick. Being obedient, studious, timid children in all other respects, they promptly fled the scene, leaving their victim to pick himself up and run to the one place he felt most at home in the world: Uncle Yusuf's Tutti-Frutti Ice Cream Shop.

The interior was dark. The "closed" sign was hanging in the window. Murgatroyd tugged on the doors. They were locked. He peered inside. The stools and tables had been taken away. Big cardboard boxes were strewn here and there. The ice cream display case was lightless and empty. There was a handwritten sign pasted to the right of the front doors, which Murgatroyd peered at uncomprehendingly, for he didn't know how to read:

> *Dear Respected Loyal Customers,*
> *We regret to inform that Yusuf bin Hassim, owner of the Tutti-Frutti Ice Cream Shop, has passed away.*

Murgatroyd didn't need to know the meaning of the words in order to know that something terrible had happened. He collapsed in front of the shop, sobbing uncontrollably. He thumped his fists on the concrete until they were sore and bruised. He let loose a cry of anguish and sorrow and pain—the soul-chilling, excruciating cries that only children are capable of giving shape and sound. And when there were no more tears left, no more strength left, nothing left but the bitter dullness of having had a good cry, he took a deep breath, picked himself up and trudged back to his home. His "real" home.

CHAPTER 3

Before Murgatroyd had experienced that terrible first day, it actually had long been his dream that he would one day have the privilege of going to school. In all of his nine years of existence, he had never even so much as stepped foot inside a classroom. He harboured the sneaking suspicion that, like other children his age, he should be wearing a uniform, toting around a knapsack and water bottle, and hanging around bus stops. School uniforms, school chums, knapsacks, and water bottles were conspicuously absent from his own life, he had no idea how to ride the bus, and he was never given money, so he couldn't take the bus even if he wanted to.

So disturbed had he been by this disparity between his life and that of other children that one morning, when he was eight, he had dared to break the cardinal rule his family lived by—"Children, especially you, should be seen and not heard." He approached the dining table where his mother sat drinking a cup of tea and reading the newspaper.

"Mum," he had begun tentatively. "Why don't I go to school like all the other children?"

Mrs. Floyd had turned to him with a sleepy, weary sort of motion, and regarded her son with a sleepy, weary sort of gaze before answering him.

"Because you're too stupid, my darling," she had said, ruffling his blonde hair in a cautiously affectionate-like way before turning her attention back to the news story she had been reading.

And so Murgatroyd's life had continued the way it had ever since he could remember. Every morning, after his parents left for work, he would tidy up the flat as he'd been taught, making the beds, cleaning the bathrooms, sweeping the floors, putting away the clean dishes and washing the dirty ones. For lunch, he would eat a slice of bread with butter or jam and then, more often than not, he would go wandering outside in the wide world of Singapore. He would go as far as his own little legs could carry him and as far as he dared to go. He meandered past community centres and schools and through endless HDB blocks. He strolled through public gardens and parks, and sometimes visited the giant lake near the flat. He often visited a sprawling building complex with gaily painted roofs topped with dragons and many rooms housing great golden statues of seated, serene men. All he carried on these excursions were the coins he would occasionally discover on the street and the key to let himself in and out of the flat.

But now, at the age of nine years, four months, and three days, he had at long last attained a measure of intelligence deemed sufficient by his mother and father to begin his education. In honour of this momentous and glorious occasion, his father had even given him a haircut the night before, though it had turned out to be a very peculiar one. The fringe on the left side of his forehead remained long and had been combed straight so it nearly covered his left eye, while the fringe on the right side of his forehead had been lopped so short that it jutted out of his scalp like a partial crew cut. While holding the electric razor, his father's hand had slipped and accidentally shaved off all the hair in the middle of his crown in a neat, circular patch, leaving Murgatroyd looking very much like a juvenile monk who had been attacked by a blind sheep shearer. Murgatroyd's father had also accidentally shaved off half of one eyebrow.

"I look funny," he said, staring at his reflection in the bathroom mirror.

"Well, nothing can help that but plastic surgery later in life," his father had answered cheerfully. He gave his son a manly slap on the back before accidentally sprinkling a liberal fistful of hair down the back of his son's shirt.

The next morning, his mother laid out a frilly pink girl's blouse and woollen dress trousers for him to wear.

"Where's my uniform?" Murgatroyd asked.

"We'll get one for you later," she said.

"Can't I just wear my regular clothes?" he asked.

"Out of the question," she replied. She opened her mouth as if to explain why, but instead gave a great yawn.

Murgatroyd tried one more time. "It's too hot to wear these trousers."

"Why are you always complaining?" his mother snapped. "If they're too hot, just don't wear any trousers at all."

Even without proper schooling, Murgatroyd knew that to go around in one's underpants was simply unacceptable. With great reluctance, he got dressed.

Murgatroyd's first day at school was not actually the first day of the school year. School had been in session for seven weeks, and all the boys had already formed their particular friendships and cliques. But Mr. and Mrs. Floyd had managed to pull a few strings to get their son admitted a little late into the school year at Da Qiao Primary School.

"I'm sorry, we really didn't know. We do things a bit differently in England, you see," his father had explained to the principal in a charming drawl.

"We do things a bit differently in England" had always been a winning excuse for the Floyds. So when the charming, lanky Mr. Floyd flashed his charming, lanky British smile and explained the misunderstanding in his charming, lanky British accent, what could the principal do but shake her head at these clueless British expatriates and make an allowance?

"Okay, lah. We'll make an exception this time." Privately, the principal of Da Qiao Primary had her doubts about whether the Floyds' decision to enrol their child in a local Singaporean school was a wise decision, even though the child was technically a citizen. But who was she to meddle in others' affairs?

Not only had Murgatroyd's parents decided that their son should enter school seven weeks into the school year, but they had also decided that he should make his first appearance at school well into the school day. It was half an hour before lunch break when the principal strode into the classroom, ushering in a blonde-haired, blue-eyed boy—an *ang moh*—who looked older than all of them by at least two years. He had a funny haircut. He wore pink lace.

The principal, remembering the instructions she had received from Mr. and Mrs. Floyd ("Don't give him any special treatment.") announced to the class, "This is a new student. His name is . . ." And here, she paused not so much for dramatic effect as to concentrate on the pronunciation of his name.

"Murgatoy Froy."

This pronouncement sealed little Murgatroyd's fate. For the twenty-five children staring at him from their desks, Murgatroyd, taken as a whole, was simply unforgiveable.

Needless to say, Murgatroyd's first day went very badly. The worst of the bad events of the day were as follows:

- Three attempts to pull down his trousers. All three of which were successful.

- The bestowal of several derogatory nicknames. Among them: "girly-girl," "big nose," "*xiaojie*" (which means "Miss" in Mandarin), and of course "little *ang moh*."
- The hurling of his shoes high into the big tree behind the school.
- The dunking of his head into a toilet bowl.
- The physical beating of his person, including a kick to the face, resulting in a bloody nose.

Murgatroyd's mother returned home from the office that day and found her son curled up into a ball on the living room sofa, his face stained with dried blood and tears. She was, of course, thoroughly outraged—so outraged, in fact, that she apparently lost all control of her facial muscles. Strangely enough, her expression involuntarily contorted into a broad grin suggestive of mirth or amusement.

"Oh no!" she exclaimed, thoroughly outraged with a big smile on her face. "Poor dear, what in heaven's name did they do to you?"

Murgatroyd burst into tears and ran into his mother's arms. And as any loving mother would do, Mrs. Floyd patted her son on the head, sat him at the dining table, and went into the kitchen to fix him a hot cup of Milo. So distressed was she over Murgatroyd's predicament that instead of sugar, she absentmindedly added two heaping spoonfuls of salt to the chocolate malt drink. Such mistakes were not uncommon for Mrs. Floyd. She was always making silly mistakes when it came to preparing her son's food—mistakes that anybody could have made, really. Like sprinkling chilli powder instead of cinnamon into his birthday cake batter every year, or accidentally spreading crushed cockroaches instead of tuna onto his tuna sandwiches.

"Now," she began tenderly, sitting next to him at the dining table. "Why do you suppose they were so nasty to you?"

Murgatroyd sniffled and thought hard before finally arriving at an answer. "Because I'm different. I'm not like them and so they think it gives them the right to bully me."

The innocent and childish truth of his answer hung in the air above their heads for one brief, shining moment before Mrs. Floyd shot it down with a metaphorical rifle.

"Wrong. They wouldn't be so nasty to you if they didn't have a very good reason. It must be because there is something wrong with *you*."

Murgatroyd stared into his mug of salty, hot Milo and felt thoroughly ashamed of himself.

His mother continued. "Now you must try very hard tomorrow to be a better boy and get them to like you. Try to make yourself more agreeable, all right? There's my brave boy!"

She gave Murgatroyd a light squeeze on the arm and lovingly stirred more salt into his drink. Murgatroyd supposed that he felt a little less miserable, but he also felt a little guilty, for he hadn't told his mother the other reason for his misery: the mysterious closure of the Tutti-Frutti and the disappearance of Uncle Yusuf. In fact, Mum and Dad knew nothing about his home away from home. He hadn't spoken a word to them about Uncle Yusuf, the ice cream, and certainly not about his recent visit to that glorious Great Freezer or what Uncle Yusuf told him about things being underway. Some inexplicable child's instinct had always prevented him from telling them, and not telling them had been made easier by their never asking him how he had spent each day.

That night, before Murgatroyd went to bed, he stepped out onto the balcony of their flat and stared long and hard up at the heavens above. They lived in a well-to-do neighbourhood flanking a large nature reserve, and it was as quiet as anywhere in the rapidly developing city could be. But even at that distance and that height, the collective illumination from faraway high rises and shopping hubs tinted the dark sky purple and lessened the radiance of any visible stars. By squinting very hard, Murgatroyd could make out a few of them scattered here and there in the great expanse of the universe. Stars—Uncle Yusuf's favourite flavour. So powerful was the memory that he could still taste the fiery explosion of that twinkling shard on his tongue, and felt—as he had at that moment in the Great Freezer—the magnificence of the universe unfurled before him, fluttering proudly on the mast of the great night sky.

For a moment, he imagined himself up there wandering among the stars, and he had the strange sense that the far, unknown reaches of space were where he truly belonged and where he would feel at home. This feeling came as a surprise to young Murgatroyd: his home was here, with Mum and Dad, wasn't it? He reflected on this new feeling and whether it had any connection with the recent and strange developments of his life. Uncle Yusuf had said that there was more to come, that things were underway. What things? What was there to come? And what had happened to Uncle Yusuf? Would he ever see him again? What would life be like now that there was no ice cream shop, no Uncle? Now that he had to go to school? What was to become of him? *Things are underway!* The echo of Uncle Yusuf's words still reverberated within Murgatroyd's person. It made his heart tremble with joy.

Something was underway, it would seem. Or at least that's what Uncle had said. Murgatroyd wasn't sure what it was, but he felt sure that it was something very extraordinary. Something extraordinarily stupendous. Standing in the humid night air, eleven storeys above the hustle and bustle of the city, timid little Murgatroyd dared to take all of the emotions and feelings swimming around inside him and form them into a single, very bold thought: *Something extraordinarily stupendous is waiting for me*. This sudden and stubborn conviction first planted itself, then snuggled itself in the depths of his nine-year-old heart. There it would remain until some day in the future when Murgatroyd's prediction eventually came true. What Murgatroyd didn't know, and had no way of knowing, was that the extraordinarily stupendous Something had been interrupted with Yusuf's death. It was not until much later in his life, long after the visit to the Great Freezer had been swept underneath the rug of memory, remembered only dimly as a strange childhood dream long past, that the Something would finally find him.

CHAPTER 4

"Mr. and Mrs. Froy, it has come to my attention," said the principal of Da Qiao Primary School, "that your son does not fit in so well here." The principal had a reputation for being extremely straightforward. And for having perfectly manicured fingernails. Resting her elbows on her desk and folding her hands in front of her, she appraised her nails with a barely noticeable downward glance and smiled to herself before turning her attention once again to what she privately called "the *ang moh* problem."

"Really?" said Mr. Floyd with an astonished look on his face. "I had no idea. He's never told us!"

It was the principal's turn to be astonished. "Hah? He never said anything?"

"No," Mrs. Floyd confirmed. "When we ask him how school is, he tells us that he absolutely *adores* it. He seems as happy as the proverbial clam. When he came home after that first day of school, I'd never seen such a wide grin."

The principal sighed. "I am terribly sorry to be saying this, but I think he has been lying to you."

The Floyds looked aghast. Mr. Floyd even gasped.

"Murgatroyd? Lie to us?"

"Why would he lie about such a thing?"

"Oh, dear me. If only we had known."

"What is wrong, exactly?"

The principal elaborated. Murgatroyd had been attending Da Qiao Primary for one month now, and while he was doing passably in his classes, he had no friends and kept getting picked on by the other children, even when he finally started showing up in a white and green school uniform instead of girls' clothes, and even when his hair started growing back. During recess, he would hide in the toilet stalls or hang around the teachers who had to pry him off their persons before they could retreat to the safety of the teachers' lounge.

The principal spared no grim detail, pulled no punches. And after she had given her frank account of the situation, the principal leaned back in her chair, quickly admired her fingernails again, and waited for the Floyds' response, which she hoped would involve taking the poor little *ang moh* boy out of Da Qiao Primary and putting him in a school where he might stand a better chance of being happy—perhaps one of the well-funded, well-maintained private schools where foreigners usually enrolled their children.

The news of their son's extreme unhappiness had evidently come as a shock to them. The father appeared to even be clutching his chest as if he were experiencing a heart attack.

"Are you . . . feeling all right, Mr. Froy?" the principal asked, leaning forward in her chair.

He didn't appear to have heard her. "That's terrible. Absolutely terrible," he muttered. The principal nodded gravely in assent. James Floyd took a deep breath. He took three more deep breaths, placing his hands on his knees as if to steady himself. He looked at his wife, who had been sobbing silently all the while into several tissues, which now lay crumpled in a soggy heap on her lap. He looked at the principal. He opened his mouth to speak.

"So, what can we do to help him fit in at Da Qiao Primary?"

Flabbergasted, the principal peered at him through her wire-rimmed spectacles. She had heard wrongly. She inclined her head towards him and cupped one hand over her ear. "Excuse me?"

Mr. Floyd repeated himself. "How can we help him fit in?"

"Say again?"

Mr. Floyd said again, "How can we help him fit in?"

She stared in disbelief at the British couple sitting in front of her, looking so pathetically earnest.

"Maybe I'm not making myself clear." The principal of Da Qiao Primary cleared her throat and addressed the Floyds in a very slow, very loud voice. "Mr. and Mrs. Froy, your son does not belong here."

The words seemed to have no effect on the Floyds' blinking, expectant gaze. She decided to try pleading with them. "Please, for his sake, find another school for him. There are many other places where you can send him. How about the British school or American school where he can be with other children like him?"

At the suggestion of a British or American school, Mr. Floyd's naturally good-natured brow furrowed. "Other children *like him*?" he repeated coldly. "You mean other *ang moh* like him?"

The principal grew quiet.

"That is precisely what I would *detest* the most!" he thundered. "Madam, we are not aliens, nor are we foreigners. As you well know from all those forms we had to fill out, I am a naturalized Singaporean citizen, and my son is a citizen by birth. The farthest out of the country he has ever been is Malaysia. He has never been to England, and I daresay he would not recognize a picture of the Queen if it came to life, bit him in the buttocks, and introduced itself. His skin may be white and pasty and prone to redness if overexposed to the sun, and it is entirely possible that one of his distant relatives might have helped undertake the colonization of this island. Nevertheless, he has just as much of a right to attend a local school as your own son or daughter. I will not take my son out of this school just because he *does not fit in*."

The principal accepted the reprimand and sighed. "You're right, Mr. Froy, I misspoke. But please, for the sake of your son, be practical. Murgatoy is very unhappy here. This is the fact of the matter."

"Give him time," Mrs. Floyd said. "They'll learn to accept him eventually. He'll learn to fit in."

The principal gave one last desperate try, "Half of them cannot even pronounce his name correctly." She paused. "*I* cannot even pronounce his name correctly."

"Then we'll give him another name," Mr. Floyd promptly replied. "We'll give him a Chinese name to help him fit in, see?"

"Oh, I see," the principal said sarcastically. "What will his name be?" she asked with a challenging smirk.

There was silence. Then, all of a sudden, Mrs. Floyd decided to stop sobbing long enough to offer a suggestion. "His name will be Shwet Foo."

James Floyd turned to his wife, his face radiant with adoration. "Olivia, darling, you're a genius."

"Murgatroyd Floyd Shwet Foo." Olivia Floyd uttered the entirety of their son's new name for full effect.

The principal of Da Qiao Primary reacted somewhat curiously to Mrs. Floyd's solemn pronouncement. Torn between profound pity for the little *ang moh* boy and the uncontrollable urge to giggle at his nonsensical new "Chinese" name, she did both. As snorts of laughter shook her small frame, the edges of her mouth also curved downwards in a sympathetic grimace for the fate of Murgatroyd Floyd Shwet Foo.

Poor little Murgatroyd Floyd Shwet Foo.

Having made "the *ang moh* problem" a little bit worse instead of solving it, the principal concluded the meeting, and resigned herself and little Shwet Foo to the unhappy circumstances at hand. After Mr. and

Mrs. Floyd had left, she pulled out a nail file from her desk and began doing what she did whenever she needed to decompress. *Why would they do such a terrible thing?* she asked herself, working furiously at an irregularity in the curve of her left thumbnail.

Why indeed would Mr. and Mrs. Floyd do such a terrible thing? Of course, the Floyds' behaviour towards their son had always been slightly peculiar. Those who could call themselves friends of the Floyd family had always noticed as much, but could never quite place their finger on it.

Despite James and Olivia's supposed best intentions in Chinese-ifying their son, the children's behaviour towards their *ang moh* class-mate remained much the same: abusive, with a slight swelling of even more abuse when they found out about Murgatroyd's ridiculous-sounding "Chinese" name. The newly christened Shwet Foo never did assimilate into life at Da Qiao Primary. In fact, he never really assimilated into life in general. Part of it had to do with his initial ostracism at Da Qiao Primary, which set the pattern for the rest of his student life: fearful of his schoolmates, he avoided their company, and they in turn continued to ignore him, or occasionally, to torment and tease him. Part of it had to do with his personality, which was naturally quiet and withdrawn. Part of it, sadly, did have to do with his blonde hair and blue eyes, which were a superficial difference, yes, but inalterable nonetheless. And despite Murgatroyd's increasingly Singaporean accent and his growing familiarity with local life, his unhappy days continued. A large part of it had to do with something else entirely—something that was not only imperceptible to the overwhelming majority of the population, but to their knowledge, simply didn't exist. Murgatroyd would discover what that something was much later in his life, and to his surprise, it would be intimately connected with the hope for the extraordinarily stupendous Something that would, every now and then for the next sixteen years, drift momentarily to the surface of his consciousness before submerging itself once more.

Murgatroyd's life did not turn out to be an entirely solitary one, though. In fact, he emerged from his otherwise painful six years at Da Qiao Primary with a friend by the name of Seng Kay Huat—a boy older than him by two years who was to remain Murgatroyd's closest companion for many years to come, even after their lives had diverged to follow very separate paths. Even at a very young age, it was clear that Kay Huat was destined for great things. Endowed with great intelligence, clean-cut good looks, and an affable personality, Kay Huat's natural abilities paved over the rockiness of life's path, turning it into a veritable freeway of easy success down which he could cruise in a silver Porsche. His high examination marks upon leaving Da Qiao Primary earned him a scholarship to attend the elite Raffles Institution, where he completed his secondary and pre-university education. After serving his mandatory two years' national service in the Singaporean army, Kay Huat won a full scholarship from Stanford University in the United States. He graduated *summa cum laude* with a BA in economics and philosophy, and a minor in art history. He had then returned home to take his place in Singaporean society as a highly paid, highly ambitious, and highly successful private banker.

In contrast, it was clear from a very early age that Murgatroyd Floyd Shwet Foo was not destined for anything involving high pay, ambition, or success. Murgatroyd had never been very good at studying, and chose to end his education after graduating from a low-ranking secondary school. After scraping through his two years of national service, he went through a number of odd jobs, all of which he was fired from, until he found employment as the top waiter of a wildly successful restaurant. Surprisingly enough, Murgatroyd was very good at this job.

SINGAPORE

2004

CHAPTER 5

A mysterious figure crept cautiously from his corner into the open space, enshrouded by a turbid murkiness thick and dense as pea soup. Tilting his head to one side, he appeared to be listening for something in particular: a signal or a warning perhaps. Tonight, he felt instinctively that something was wrong, but he wasn't quite sure what it was. The area in which he stood was usually terribly packed, with hardly any room to move or space to breathe. But over time, the crowds had thinned, and now he found himself solitary, and actually, a little lonely as well. He would have never called himself a social butterfly, but the sight of the desolate square (well, what he could see of it through the gloom) filled him with sadness. Sadness? Was it sadness? Never having been much of an orator or writer either, he racked his brains for the proper words to describe his feelings. After a while, they came to him. It was not sadness or loneliness that so gripped his heart. It was a feeling of mild terror—not enough to send him screaming into the night, but enough to make the very hairs on his legs quiver ever so slightly in alertness. He must be on his guard.

He stood now before the Great Screen, claiming an enviable spot directly in front of it—a spot which, in the past, he would have never been able to obtain without a great deal of pushing and shoving, and even then he would have been able to hold his position for a few minutes at the most. Long gone were those days, and long gone were the multitudes jostling with each other for the privilege of a glimpse into that other world; although on a night like this, one could only make out their immense figures if one really squinted. That other world would never change. He felt sure of it. Its cycles of alternating illumination and darkness, activity and quietude, would never cease. They would continue long after his own demise, into the far reaches of eternity.

It was the figures' aura of immortality that had the power to draw the crowds, to hold them mesmerized until they forgot the existence of anything apart from the magnificent creatures before their eyes: strange-looking gods and goddesses who congregated regularly to feast and celebrate, and their servants clad in white and black who spent their lives perpetually setting up and dismantling banquet after banquet after banquet. The lives of these immortals were so vastly different from their own; it helped them to escape their cramped existence spent in the confines of this prison. Even now, he felt a wave of calm washing over him—a wave so strong that he felt as if he were being lifted slowly off his feet and out of the water. He waved his eight legs as frantically as he could, but he was weak from hunger. Summoning the last dregs of his energy, he strained convulsively against the restraints that bound his pincers shut, but to no avail. So this is what happened to the others, he thought sluggishly to himself as he was removed from the tank. Still, he couldn't tear his eyes away from the Great Screen.

***

"My apologies, madam, but this is the last lobster we have left. If you find him unsuitable, perhaps you would like to choose something else for your main course this evening?"

Murgatroyd held the lobster aloft before the guest so that she could inspect it. He held it firmly so the lobster wouldn't flick water onto her clothes, but elegantly too, to maintain the ambience of fine dining so assiduously maintained at L'Abattoir. He held it not so close that the guest would be subjected to the fishy stench, but not so far away that the guest couldn't easily spot any defects that might prompt her to reject the lobster in favour of something else.

Mrs. Tan was a regular patron of L'Abattoir. She took lemon and lime in her water and wore a rouge too pink for her age. She examined the lobster in front of her.

"He looks a bit listless, don't you think?"

Murgatroyd sensed that this was an opportune time for a light joke.

"He's resigned to his fate, madam."

Mrs. Tan laughed and turned to her husband. "Aloysius, what do you think?"

Her husband—a short, plump man who was disconcertingly similar to his wife in appearance and who couldn't resist a good crème brûlée—peered at the proffered lobster through his spectacles and nodded. "He'll do, lah."

"As you may have read in tonight's menu, madam and sir, the chef will be searing the lobster lightly and serving it over a bed of risotto made from sushi rice and enoki mushrooms, with a dollop of our signature sesame sauce on the side."

"Yes, that's fine."

Murgatroyd bowed slightly and lingered, sensing that Mrs. Tan had something else to say.

"You've been working here for quite some time already, is it?" she asked in a friendly tone of voice.

She had acknowledged that she recognized him. Now he could address her with more familiarity to demonstrate his skill and experience on the waitstaff of L'Abattoir.

"Three years now, Mrs. Tan."

"You're quite young. How old are you?"

"Twenty-five, madam."

"Your accent is like a local," she observed. "But you're obviously not from here."

Such observations were not new to Murgatroyd. "I'm a citizen, Mrs. Tan. My parents are originally from England."

"Ah, I see. Both of them are Caucasian? You don't look mixed."

"No, no. Not mixed."

Mr. Tan ceased peering at the lobster to peer at Murgatroyd. "Wah. Very interesting, I must say."

"Thank you, Mr. Tan."

"Which part of England are they from?"

"I think they both grew up in London."

"Have you ever been there?" Mr. Tan asked.

Murgatroyd shook his head.

"London's a lovely city," Mrs. Tan said, taking a sip of water. "We stayed there for a few days when looking at schools for our son."

"Oh?"

"He's at Oxford now. Studying mathematics at St. Peter's College."

"You must be very proud of him."

"We are," Mr. Tan confirmed. The mobile phone lying next to his dinner plate began to vibrate. As Mr. Tan picked it up, and as Mrs. Tan let her gaze fall abstractedly on the family dining at the next table, Murgatroyd knew that he had become a nonentity once again, and it was time for him to bow and bear the lobster off to the kitchen for its execution. Keeping the lobster a crooked-arm's length away from his body, he glided away, past the glass-panelled arena at the centre of the restaurant, through the silver swinging doors of the kitchen, and handed the victim over to his fate: to be laid belly-up on a wooden chopping block, to have the point of a knife inserted into its middle to sever its ventral nerve cord, and to have its head and brain split in two. A fast death, and arguably the kindest one possible, but not nearly spectacular enough to merit public viewing in the infamous L'Abattoir arena.

Of course, the Tans never took the arena into consideration when they came to L'Abattoir to dine. They were regular patrons only because they thought the chef a wizard and his food exquisite. In fact, one could say that they came *despite* what L'Abattoir had become famous for. They always requested the worst table in the house—"the worst" insofar as it was the sole table that offered almost no view of the arena. All the other tables had been positioned so that its occupants could enjoy the spectacle to its fullest, with a few choice seats positioned only metres away from the glass-panelled enclosure. The Tans' aversion to the spectacle that drew almost all the other clientele made them truly exceptional. Everyone else was out for blood and was willing to pay to see it.

The various bribes that the staff members of L'Abattoir had been offered in exchange for a seating at one of the closer tables bordered on the absurd: sums of money up to thousands of dollars, designer bags and watches, stocks and bonds, fine wines, antiques and artwork. The headwaiter could even boast of having been offered a herd of llamas by the erstwhile dictator of some small Latin American country who had been passing through Singapore on the way to his summer mansion in the Philippines. Almost none of these bribes had been taken, and when they had been, the accepting party had always been fired. Shakti Vithani stood for no such shenanigans among the staff of any of her restaurants. Apart from the fact that bribery was unprofessional, allowing them to supplement their incomes in this way would have undermined her control over them. Discipline had to be maintained. Besides, such bribes rightfully belonged to the restaurant owner, not to mere employees. After all, how could *they* properly appreciate the exquisite

Sung Dynasty vase that had added such class to her guest bathroom? And where would they find the means to build the kind of stable she had just commissioned to comfortably house her newly acquired trio of beautiful show-quality llamas?

From her position at the far end of the bar, her customary glass of Coca-Cola Light in her hand, Shakti Vithani lovingly surveyed her establishment—the jewel in the crown of her small but successful restaurant empire—and sighed with contentment. At long last, she had finally arrived. Of course, business at L'Abattoir hadn't always been this good. In fact, there had been a time—an exceptionally dark time—when it had been in very real danger of closing, dragging down with it Shakti's hopes of becoming a world-famous restaurateur.

She smiled and shook her head at the memory. She could smile now. What a long way she had come since then! How young and inexperienced she had been! The surprisingly easy success of her very first restaurant—an upscale Northern Indian bistro called the Spice Larder—had deceived her into thinking that all a restaurant needed was good ambience and good food. The struggle she'd had with getting her subsequent two restaurants to follow suit had taught her the hard way that eating may have been the national pastime, but winning over the hearts, stomachs, and wallets of the Singaporean people was extraordinarily difficult and took exhaustive amounts of energy, skill, and cunning.

Singaporeans loved food, and Singapore was the right place to love it. Food of every variety and suited to any budget was to be found everywhere. Local cuisine was the cheapest, its quality practically guaranteed, and in itself was endlessly diverse. There were noodles any way you wanted them, flat and thick, thin and translucent, yellow and chewy, hand-pulled or knife-cut, in any liquid medium your heart desired—fragrant prawn-pork broth; rich brown sauce; curried coconut gravy; soup bright with tamarind and lime; fish stock, singing sweet and pure, made creamy with a touch of milk. How about rice? Rice flavoured with broth and garlic and ginger served with delicately poached chicken and three sauces—beige ginger, black soy, and red-orange chilli; rich rice boiled in coconut milk and scented with the clean green of pandan leaves; biryani rice flecked yellow and orange with saffron and turmeric, glinting with ghee, disappearing down your gullet and leaving a faint spice trail behind it of cardamom and coriander, cinnamon and ginger. Carnivorous cravings? Duck with skin roasted red-brown and crisp, or stewed pork belly, black and velvety; beef or lamb or chicken slow-cooked in curry, tender meat melting off the bones. Seafood? Brilliant, blushing steamed prawns the size of a grown man's fist; crab chunks in black pepper gravy or a sweetish chilli sauce that left you licking the bowls and plates clean; whole grouper fish, fried to crunchy perfection on the outside, white flesh delicate and flaky on the inside. Vegetarian? Tofu and boiled eggs deep-fried in shrimp-chilli paste; sweet potato leaves stewed in spicy coconut cream; a salad of pineapple, turnip, water-apple, green mango, and cucumber doused in a spicy-sweet black sauce and christened with crushed peanuts. Snack? Bright yellow egg-custard tarts; flaky pastry puffs stuffed with your choice of curried chicken, curried sardine, apple, yam, pineapple, or durian paste; toast slices spread with butter and glistening green coconut jam. Dessert? Mounds of shaved ice flavoured with rose syrup and condensed milk, concealing a treasure pile of jelly, red beans, and corn kernels; plump glutinous rice balls floating in clear, sweet liquid, waiting for you to sink your teeth into them and release a gushing ooze of buttery peanut or black sesame paste; chewy, porous pancakes rolled around sweet bean filling, gooey chocolate, or strands of orange-dyed grated coconut. Thirsty? Tea or coffee with condensed milk, or the fresh juice of a gingerroot; white milk of the soya bean, green juice of the sugar cane; liquid blends of carrot, pineapple, apple, dragon fruit, mango, cucumber, rose apple, and guava made to your exact specifications.

Those were just a few of the local options. And what about the foreign ones? British and American and Italian and French; Indonesian and Thai and Vietnamese; Northern Indian and Pakistani; Japanese and Korean and Taiwanese: their cuisines flooded the Singaporean marketplace too. From the west: English-style pubs selling fish and chips, bangers and mash; fifties-style diners serving cheeseburgers, hot dogs, and pancakes and waffles; patisseries filled with croissants and pains au chocolat, madeleines and éclairs, and gorgeous macarons in all the colours of the rainbow; trattorias turning out thin-crust pizzas and mounds of delicate house-made orecchiette. From East Asia: ramen noodles and tonkatsu and sushi; kimchi fried rice and bibimbap and soondubu; dim sum and Shanghainese soup dumplings; Taiwanese beef noodle soup and pearl milk tea. From South and Southeast Asian neighbours: steaming hot bowls of pho, shrimp on skewers of sugarcane, fluffy naan bread and chicken vindaloo, green papaya salad and pad thai, gado-gado and otak-otak. Add the food chains that had sprung up all over. Fast food: McDonald's, Burger King, KFC, and Subway. Coffee: Starbucks, Spinelli's, Ya Kun Kaya Toast, the Coffee Bean & Tea Leaf. Bread and pastries: Breadtalk, Four Leaves, Prima Deli, Délifrance.

As if the number of competitors wasn't enough, there was also the problem of Singaporean stinginess. Ready-made food could be gotten so cheaply that many Singaporeans had stopped cooking all together, preferring to head to the hawker centres for all the family's meals. If you knew the right places to go, you could pay as little as forty cents for a gloriously greasy prata with curry on the side; eighty cents for a fat popiah roll stuffed with radish, shrimp, egg, and lap cheong sausage; and two dollars for a giant bowl of fish-ball noodle soup. The older and wiser Shakti Vithani now knew that even though Singapore was a nation of food-obsessed individuals, it took something really special to convince the average Singaporean to go for the pricier option—to whip out the credit card rather than the change purse. Even the wealthiest CEO could be found boasting of the tasty bargain he'd just discovered hidden away in the corner of a dingy, no-name hawker centre.

The Spice Larder had been lucky. Shakti's next restaurant attempt had been disastrous. In all probability, it was the most infamous restaurant in the entirety of Singaporean culinary history. Like its older sibling, the Colonial Table served Indian cuisine, but attempted to add a historical dimension to its diners' experience by recreating the atmosphere of colonial India during the height of the British Raj. This involved all the waiters not only wearing the garb of Indian servants and addressing the patrons as "sahib" and "memsahib," but also, if they weren't naturally of a brownish hue, having their skin painted so from head to toe. Shakti *might* have been able to get away with even that, but applying white powder to the patrons' faces upon their entrance into the restaurant sent the whole establishment tumbling into the abyss. The restaurant had been roundly condemned from all quarters as "insensitive," "bigoted," and "in poor taste." She'd merely intended the restaurant to be "kitsch-chic" and hadn't meant to offend anyone.

"I don't see what the bloody fuss is all about," she had said angrily to her husband over breakfast. She had just finished reading an article in the op-ed section of the paper about all the kerfuffle that the Colonial Table was causing. "You'd think we'd all be able to have a good laugh about colonization by now, *yaar*? After all, the sun *has* bloody well set on the bloody British Empire."

Sweeping the pages of the newspaper off the table onto the floor, along with her teacup and saucer, she crossed her arms and sulked.

Mr. Vithani looked up from his breakfast. "Well, dear, I *told* you that the whole concept might be a bit insensitive."

"Oh, shut up."

Years later, Shakti still winced at the memory. She had dared to walk the fine line between tastelessness and fashionably risqué, and, with the Colonial Table, she had fallen on the side of tastelessness. A year later, she had attempted to play it safe with another restaurant venture—the Phoenix—only to produce a thoroughly insipid dining experience. The Phoenix was really nothing special: just one more unremarkable

East-meets-West fusion restaurant among the many others. Like so many of its kind, its attempt to blend the wonderful, distinctive flavours of both worlds resulted in a mediocre mish-mash of taste that was neither here nor there. *The Straits Times* reviewer gave it three stars out of five, which wasn't bad at all, considering the positively scathing review that appeared in the Singaporean high-society magazine, *Prestige*. "One can only hope," concluded the *Prestige* reviewer, "that after its imminent closure, this Phoenix will not be rising from the ashes anytime soon." It seemed inevitable that the reviewer's prediction would come to pass: after taking a nasty tumble from its nest, the fledgling fine-dining establishment was barely clinging to life, fading further with each passing week. The poor thing was only being kept in existence by a twice-weekly busload of unwitting Japanese and German tourists—the victims of a deal Shakti had struck with a local tour-group company in exchange for a small share of the profits.

At the time, Shakti Vithani had been distressed beyond measure. But with the prospect of a second failure looming on the horizon, Mrs. Vithani had summoned all her energy and courage to yet again walk that fine line, and this time, found that it was indeed possible to find her balance. The idea for L'Abattoir's signature arena had come to Mrs. Vithani as she was sitting at the sushi counter of a Japanese restaurant at the Fullerton Hotel. Watching the sushi chef at work, deftly slicing up sea creatures, shaping rice, and rolling maki, it dawned on her that the Japanese were very clever people indeed—perhaps it was all the fish they ate, fish being good for the brain and all that. Instead of hiding the workings of food preparation away in a back kitchen, they had managed to make it an integral part of the dining experience. Not just the maki-rolling sushi chefs! Think of the knife-juggling, steak-dicing culinary acrobats of the teppanyaki grills! Chefs who could dice a carrot in midair and toss spatulafuls of fried rice into bowls blindfolded without spilling a single grain! The wheels of her mind began to turn. Then again, why resort to cheap circus tricks? Shouldn't the diner rest easy about the freshness not only of his seafood, but of his poultry and red meat as well?

Inspiration overwhelmed her. Demanding the use of a notepad and a pen from a waiter, she began scribbling furiously, pausing only to take hurried and ferocious bites of her sashimi. Images of solemn executions flashed before her mind's eye: the grandeur of the Roman Coliseum, the terror of the guillotine, the sinister Tower of London. She scrawled down phrases and words indecipherable to anyone but her: "One at a time." "Executioners must wear black." "What to do about excessive blood?" She sketched rudimentary variations of what she had in mind: a raised wooden platform in the middle of a medieval-style banquet hall, a miniature version of a Greek amphitheatre with the stage surrounded by glass panes. Finally, she arrived at something that would eventually evolve into the final blueprints that would make L'Abattoir the preferred restaurant of the rich, the famous, the glitzy, the glamorous, and all aspirants thereto.

She had drawn that sketch six years ago. Six years before the restaurant became so adored by the crème de la crème of Singaporean high society that it became known affectionately as "L'Abs." Six years before L'Abattoir earned a place on the San Pellegrino World's Fifty Best Restaurants list. Six years before Success with a capital *S* had finally scooped up Shakti Vithani, flopping and flailing about in her little pond, and deposited her in international waters to swim with the rest of the big-fish restaurateurs. And now, this very evening, it stood gleaming in the middle of her restaurant in all its glory: a circular arena about ten metres in diameter, walled in soundproof glass, surrounded by tables at which excited patrons perched on the edges of their black velvet chairs, craning their necks in anticipation of the evening's grisly entertainment. The arena floor was covered in white sand. A heavy black curtain on one side of the arena concealed a corridor to the restaurant kitchen from which the players in the night's performance could make their entrances and exits.

Even after all this time, Mrs. Vithani had not tired of watching the spectacle for which L'Abs was so famous. And now, with her calorie-free caffeinated beverage in hand, she sauntered over from the bar to the small table that was always kept specially reserved for her. The deep, rolling rumble of Japanese *taiko* drums, one in each corner of the restaurant, swelled, announcing that it was time for the show to begin. The restaurant grew quiet, and everyone turned their hungry eyes to the entrance of the arena. The curtains parted, and a tall, bony man clad in form-fitting black clothes strode in, a long, thin sword hanging at a sheath by his side. The bottom part of his face was covered with black silk wrapped snugly around his nose, mouth, and chin. The audience murmured appreciatively. It was the restaurant's star butcher—the most infamous of L'Abattoir's meat-slaughtering fleet. And he was not alone. At arm's length, he held a flailing duck firmly by the neck. The soundproof glass rendered the whole scene mute—a silent film or a moving work of art on canvas, a visual narrative unfolding to the ominous reverberation of the drums.

For what seemed like eternity frozen, the figure stood motionless in the centre of the arena, head bowed downwards, hand outstretched. The only movements were made by the desperate duck, who was now beating her wings weakly and listlessly, as if her struggle were merely an obligatory gesture rather than an actual attempt to free herself. A few of the diners lowered their gaze or averted their heads slightly as the tension mounted. Shakti couldn't tear her eyes away.

The executioner lifted his head and assessed his victim calmly and evenly. He looked long into her wide, terror-stricken pupils, which darted every which way in a flurry of motion. Mrs. Vithani held her breath. Everybody did. The drums swelled and subsided, swelled and subsided, like a great heart heaving, pulsing, throbbing. Faster. Faster. Faster. Then silence.

In one swift, seamless movement, the executioner threw the duck upward. A sword flashed from its scabbard and swung into an arc, severing her throat before she even had time to flutter. A streak of crimson lightning split the air and scattered into droplets on the white sand. The headless body fell at his feet, the head landing a metre to his left. An attendant, also clad in black, swiftly entered the arena, bundled the head and flopping body into a black basket, and exited just as quickly to present the chef with the fresh meat.

The executioner remained for a moment longer. Wiping his sword with a black rag that he then let drop to the floor, he made one solemn bow, turned sharply, and made his exit. Over the next few minutes, the atmosphere of silent awe dissolved and the clink of silverware and light-hearted chatter prevailed once more. Or at least it would for the next fifteen minutes, until the black-clad minions now cleaning the glass panels and scooping up the bloodstained sand had prepared the arena for the next performance.

The L'Abattoir waitstaff had been trained to never *ever* serve food and drink during performances, and like most of the other waitstaff, Murgatroyd had been standing against a wall to the side of the arena, watching the performance until it was over and service was resumed. Unlike his fellow waiters, however, Murgatroyd wasn't really paying attention to what was going on in the arena. Instead, his mind was adrift somewhere else, dwelling on something that, unbeknownst to him, he spent the rest of his life forgetting: the revelation he had received at the age of nine. A period of sixteen years had made the revelation vaguer, dimmer, dustier, but it was still there, floating about like a little paper boat in the flooded subterranean caverns of his consciousness. *Something extraordinarily stupendous is waiting for me*. There it was. How could he have forgotten? Then the performance ended and life picked up where it left off. The other waiters resumed their activities, but Murgatroyd remained leaning against the wall for a few more seconds, staring abstractedly into the distance, holding the two plates of fig and rocket salad that the Tans had ordered.

A terrible screeching sound caused him to recall himself with a sudden jolt, and he looked up to see where it had come from: a Chinese woman sitting alone at a table, scraping her butter knife over her bread plate as if she were drawing a bow over the bowstring of a violin. She appeared to be completely absorbed in this activity, oblivious to everyone and everything else, including the scowling patrons around her. Yet, her other hand, as if acting with a mind of its own, pointed at him and beckoned him over with an impatient gesture.

Murgatroyd approached the table. "Yes, madam?" he asked politely, masking his shock as best he could. Only as he came closer, and only as she turned to look at him full in the face, did he see the black velvet patch covering her right eye, which seemed to accentuate rather than draw attention away from a startlingly green left eye, brilliant and garish, as if an emerald had been lodged there in place of the iris.

She put the knife down and took a sip of water. "Enjoying the show?"

There was nothing funny about the question, but he chuckled softly, as if she had made some witty joke. "Quite, madam. Can I get you anything?"

"Well, you could drop the 'polite waiter' persona."

Murgatroyd coughed. "Excuse me, madam?"

The woman took another sip of water.

"Tell me something, Murgatroyd."

He was getting a little nervous. Perhaps Shakti Vithani had told her about him. How else would she know his name? But how did she know *that* name? He was Shwet Foo to everyone except his parents. Even Shakti called him that.

"Erh. What, madam?"

"Do you belong here?"

"Where, madam?"

She fished an ice cube out of her glass with her fingers and began rolling it around between her palms. "Oh, you know. Here. Working in this restaurant. Living with your parents. Hanging out with your best friend. Every now and then, secretly dreaming that something will alter the course of your entire existence, like you were doing just now." She looked up at him again. "Is this life where you belong?"

Her intimate knowledge of his life's particulars startled Murgatroyd. "Hah? What's wrong with it?"

"Nothing's *wrong* with it, Murgatroyd." The ice cube completely melted, she wiped her hands elegantly on her serviette. "Nothing at all. And I mean that. I'm just asking you if you're happy."

"I—I suppose I am."

"Oh," the woman replied. Then, hunching over her bread plate, she turned all her attention to shredding her bread roll into a pile of crumbs. Murgatroyd was utterly bewildered.

"So . . ." he ventured.

"So what?" she replied, not bothering to look up.

"Is . . . is that all?"

"I suppose. You just told me this is where you belong, didn't you? Nothing more to say." Turning towards him, she regarded him with her good eye. "However."

"However?"

"However. Here's my card." With a quick flick of the wrist, a green card was produced out of thin air and slipped into the pocket of his waiter's jacket. The woman turned her attention to arranging the crumbs on her bread plate into a seven-pointed star. "You'd better go, Murgatroyd. I imagine those salads you're carrying are eventually meant for someone's consumption."

"Oh. Right." Still in a daze, Murgatroyd drifted over to the Tans' table to serve them their first course. On the way back to the kitchen, he felt a hand clamp down on his shoulder. It was a familiar sensation: as if a falcon had alighted there and dug its talons into his flesh. It was Shakti.

"Oi, Shwet Foo. Who was that woman?"

Murgatroyd feigned ignorance, though he wasn't sure why. "Which woman?"

"The one talking to you for so long. Chinese. All in green."

"Ah, yes. I don't know."

"What did she want?"

He hesitated. "Erh. Nothing really. Just to chat."

"Well, guess what?" Murgatroyd waited for her to continue until she burst out impatiently, "Well?! GUESS!"

Murgatroyd always felt uneasy around Shakti, even though he knew he was her star employee. He always felt like a mouse being pawed about by a playful cat. He took a deep breath and uttered the most plausible thing that came to mind. "She's eating her dinner?"

In return for his stupid reply, the talons grabbed his shoulder again and gave him a short shake. "No, idiot. She's GONE!"

"Hah?"

"She didn't even order anything! Drank our water, ate our bread, swallowed our amuse-bouche and vanished without a trace! Bloody vagabonds, I tell you! Didn't think there were any in Singapore! Thought economic prosperity had gotten rid of them all."

"Gone?"

"Yes, gone! What, your ears aren't working or something?" Abruptly, Shakti's expression softened. She seemed to sense that she had been a little too rough on him, a little too cruel. She tried to make it all into a joke, and putting on a heavy Singaporean accent, she playfully wagged a scolding finger at him. "Oi, next time you want to flirt with customer, must flirt with paying one, okay? You remember, Shwet Foo: boss knows all!" Using the palm of her hand, she gave him a maternal pat on the cheek, and shoved him lightly in the direction of the kitchen.

Shakti could still remember the day she hired this strange *ang moh* boy as a waiter for the Colonial Table. Blonde as a Swede, but his speech was peppered with the Singaporean slang and accent of a local. He had puzzled her exceedingly. Shakti admitted that she had hired him purely for his looks. Well, not exactly his looks—he was rather pasty and sickly-looking, and had terrible posture besides. She had hired him purely for his race. A white waiter painted brown serving brown and yellow guests powdered white—it was all too absolutely bloody brilliant to be true. Other than that, he'd had no outstanding qualifications whatsoever. He seemed to have somehow gotten through the education system without learning very much at all. He was, frankly, rather dim-witted and uninteresting. When asked about his most memorable dining experience, he'd replied that the Tutti-Frutti Ice Cream Shop had served very good ice cream before they closed down. He also said that he liked the little paper parasols they gave him with his sundaes because they were very "high class." He had never been a waiter before, and had been retrenched from his previous job as a shoe store clerk. He unconsciously picked his ears when he wasn't talking. Despite all that, as Shakti's red pen hovered over his application, waiting to mark it with a large red *X*, she could only think to herself: a white waiter painted brown, serving brown and yellow guests painted white. It was absolutely too bloody brilliant to be true.

"And your first name really is Murgatroyd?" she had asked.

"Erh," he had replied uneasily, rubbing the nape of his neck. "Easier to call me Shwet Foo, lor. Everybody call me Shwet Foo."

Unfortunately, it turned out that it *was* too brilliant to be true—mostly because the Colonial Table failed miserably, and Murgatroyd's brown-skinned waiting career dressed as a turbanned Indian manservant came to an end. But by that time, Murgatroyd had been exhaustively trained by Shakti Vithani herself. She had urged him to imitate his parents' speech as best he could (although he could never get rid of the Singaporean lilt.) She bought him volumes and volumes of the Jeeves and Wooster books by P. G. Wodehouse, insisting that he make the impeccable and witty butler, Jeeves, his role model. When it was discovered that a blind snail with a primary-two education could probably get through the Braille version of *Anna Karenina* faster than he could read a single page of Wodehouse, she bought him the BBC TV serialization of the stories on DVD.

She told him the various ways escargots were prepared; the proper spoons to use with caviar (mother of pearl), the correct pronunciation of exotic words like *foie gras* (not "foy-ee-grass"), *entrée* (not "N-Tree"), and "Thai" (not "thigh"). Through it all, he still stubbornly insisted that the small paper parasols were the very pinnacle of "high class."

Shakti's rigorous education left him more than just a better waiter; it left him a fantastic one. And yet, whenever he changed out of his waiters' garb at the end of evening (or depending on how long the patrons lingered, the wee hours of the morning), he was incapable of taking his improvement with him. It remained behind, hanging on a coat peg in the back room, along with his black waiter's jacket. All of the attributes that made him the best waiter at the restaurant faded away—the quiet and collected sophistication, the flawless sensitivity to others' moods and whims, the confidence and poise. Away from the restaurant, he was once again the hapless, witless Murgatroyd Floyd Shwet Foo in the photo on his government-issued identity card, staring stupidly at the camera through half-closed eyes, his mouth slightly agape.

As Murgatroyd sat on the late-night bus, he examined his IC to pass the time. Tonight he sighed, tracing his finger over his signature, and thought how much the photo made him look like an idiot. He remembered the strange woman in green and her question. Was this life where he belonged? He lifted his head and surveyed the pale yellow interior of the bus, as if looking around could somehow answer his question. The only other passenger—a beefy Chinese man who had fallen asleep with his head slumped against the window—gave a loud grunt in response. Murgatroyd sighed again and pressed the buzzer for his stop.

He continued to mull over this question as he disembarked from the bus and walked the length of the quiet, lamp-lit street to his flat, the shrill singing of the cicadas in his ears. He enjoyed walking home in the dark, cool night. And sometimes he pretended that the cicadas were singing just for him. As the waitstaff were never allowed to leave the restaurant before the last guest had departed, he normally returned to find that his parents had already gone to bed, but not before thoughtfully leaving some dinner for him waiting on the table. He entered the flat, turned on the lights, and shambled into the kitchen—quietly—so as not to wake them. Hands in pockets, Murgatroyd stared glumly at the plate of raw green beans smothered in peanut butter and strawberry jam, and thought of how odd his parents' tastes had become since his job had prevented him from eating dinner with them. One night, it had been sausage slices floating in apple juice. The night before, it had been boiled garlic cloves and what looked and tasted suspiciously like shoe rubber. Still, he thought. It was nice of them to set aside some for him every night. It had been busy at the restaurant, and even though he was hungry, he felt queasy just looking at the beans. He sighed, stored them away in a Tupperware container to eat the next day, and made himself a comforting mug of hot Milo. Stirring in two heaping teaspoons of salt, he remembered the green card in his trouser pocket and placed it on the table in front of him. In stylish jet-black script, it read:

Ann.
THE QUEST
mobile: +65-97277055

Ann? Just Ann? What a funny name, thought Murgatroyd, pouring more salt into his Milo. And what exactly was the Quest? Maybe a software or computing company? What could he do for them? He didn't know anything about technological stuff. He hadn't even made it to junior college. Maybe they were a magazine? What did they do? And what did getting a job with them have to do with making him happy? What a strange thing this all was! Nothing like this had ever happened to him before! It was probably nothing. But maybe it *was* something. Maybe she worked for a talent agency. Maybe she thought he had what it took to be an actor! Or a model! But wouldn't a talent scout have been friendlier? Less abrupt? Less insulting? And how did she know his name? Except for his parents, nobody called him Murgatroyd anymore.

He wasn't used to this much thinking. He felt dizzy. He gulped down the rest of his Milo, and the warm, salty chocolate sensation in the pit of his stomach stopped the world from spinning and reassured him. Anyway, it was too late to call her, especially for a Thursday night. Yes, it was far too late. Perhaps he would wait until tomorrow, when he could ask his best friend Kay Huat for his opinion on the matter. Kay Huat was smart. He always knew what to do. Yes, he would wait until tomorrow. He felt calmer now. Much calmer. As he washed his mug and placed it on the dish rack to dry, his mind wandered off into the stars.

CHAPTER 6

Because L'Abattoir opened only for dinner, not lunch, Murgatroyd had to report for work at four p.m. Every Friday, he and Kay Huat would meet during Kay Huat's lunch break. These days, Kay Huat was a jazz connoisseur, and they would spend most of the hour in CD stores, looking for new albums to add to his collection. Kay Huat's jazz craze began about four months ago, when he'd had an amazingly expensive sound system installed in his flat. In addition to listening to CDs, he now had a vintage record player, and on weekends, he scoured trendy vintage record stores for trendy vintage jazz recordings. In his spare time, he surfed the Internet looking for rare albums to buy.

He was also now in the habit of making Murgatroyd listen to certain songs several times in a row, urging him to appreciate the brilliance of a certain phrase.

"Do you hear it? Genius, man. Pure genius." Kay Huat would close his eyes, melting into a puddle of finger-snapping, toe-tapping delight. Murgatroyd would furrow his brow and try to figure out which part of what he was listening to was the genius part.

Of course, this hobby was far less physically taxing than one of last year's hobbies. Last year, Kay Huat was a self-proclaimed yoga fanatic, and their noontime meetings involved rigorous Iyengar, Sivananda, and Bikram yoga sessions at a fitness studio near his office, followed by a lunch of nutrition bars and fruit juice.

Kay Huat picked up and dropped hobbies as easily and quickly as someone browsing through items in a store. Golf, polo, aikido, hang gliding, bungee jumping, scuba diving, knitting, the flute, the trombone, the violin, the pan pipes, swing dancing, tap dancing, line dancing, sculpting, painting, cake decorating, quilt making, taxidermy: the list went on and on. It wasn't that he was bad at any of them—in fact, he was *very* good at *all* of them. Rather, none of them could hold his interest. It was as if he was searching for something that, in the end, no hobby could offer. His longest-running activity so far was his attempt to write the Great Singaporean Novel—a project that was still ongoing and that already numbered 1,300 single-spaced pages. Kay Huat worked on his novel in the late evenings and early hours of the morning. And nowadays, he did so while cultivating his newfound appreciation for good jazz.

Today, Kay Huat and Murgatroyd met at the Raffles Place MRT station—only a five-minute walk from Kay Huat's office—and together, along with the hundreds of other office workers who were taking their lunch breaks, they braved the underground corridors connecting the subway stop with the surrounding buildings. Upon his return from university in America, Kay Huat found that the most difficult readjustment he had to make to life in Singapore was getting used to the crowds: people packed together like sardines in the trains during rush hour; people jostling and elbowing each other for space to enjoy a leisurely weekend at the shopping mall; people queuing up for half an hour to an hour outside popular restaurants; people hovering over you impatiently in the food courts, waiting to take your table. At certain times and in certain areas of Singapore, it felt as if people were water. They didn't walk, they flowed. They poured out of buses and trains, they gushed through corridors, they rushed up and down stairways and escalators, they flooded open areas and plazas. But over the past few years, Kay Huat had gotten the hang of it again, and he and Murgatroyd skilfully navigated the current of humanity that rushed through the narrow, brightly lit corridors, hemmed in on either side by snack kiosks and cheap fashion boutiques, mobile-phone accessory stores and vendors selling CDs, DVDs, and VCDs.

Kay Huat took the lead, his tall, muscular body cutting a path through the crowd until they arrived at WyWy Music House. It was surprisingly spacious for a store in an underground complex: twelve aisles of music CDs arranged alphabetically and according to genre, and six listening stations where an attendant, armed with a razor blade, would slice open the plastic packaging of any album you desired to sample before making your final purchasing decisions and pop it into a CD player for your listening pleasure. The owner of WyWy was a skinny, pink-haired twenty-year-old named Cassandra Lim who wore black horn-rimmed glasses and pinstriped vests. *The Straits Times* had recently done an article on her and her store, calling it "a must-visit for jazz lovers." Business had skyrocketed since.

A man on a mission, Kay Huat set to work collecting CDs to sample, only half listening to Murgatroyd recounting the strange events of last night.

"Her name is Ann, is it? What did she look like?" Kay Huat handed Murgatroyd another CD to carry.

Murgatroyd added it to the stack of ten he was cradling in both hands. "Erh. Don't know."

"Eh, what do you mean, 'don't know'? Figure? Face? Doth she teach the torches to burn bright?" Kay Huat chuckled at his great literary wit. "That's from Shakespeare," he explained to Murgatroyd, who could only remember that Shakespeare was someone important mentioned in school at some point. "Here are some more CDs."

Murgatroyd tried to remember in greater detail what Ann looked like before concluding that he couldn't. "She was sitting down. How to tell figure, meh?" Then Murgatroyd told him about the missing left eye and the green right eye.

Kay Huat gave a mock shudder. "Sounds like a fright to me. Ooh. I've heard good things about this one." He handed Murgatroyd a Taiwanese bossa nova album.

Murgatroyd shifted uncomfortably under the weight of his musical burden. He peered out from the side of the stack at his friend who had just finished with the F section and was now eagerly thumbing his way through the Gs. "So do you think I should I call her? What is this Quest? Do you think it's safe?"

Kay Huat frowned. "Let me see it again."

Carefully shifting the stack of CDs to one arm, Murgatroyd fumbled about in his right pocket for the green card and handed it to Kay Huat.

Kay Huat examined it closely. He held it up to the neon light overhead. He turned it over several times in his hands and ran his finger lightly around the corners. Then he began sniffing it, first caressing the edges with his nostrils, then pressing the card flat to his nose and inhaling deeply. The other patrons turned to stare at Kay Huat. The owner, Cassandra Lim, had been gazing dreamily at him since he walked into the store, but now she gazed with even more intensity. He looked like some eccentric business-card connoisseur, savouring the scent of the card's ink, the card's texture, its rectangularity.

Abruptly, he flicked the card in Murgatroyd's direction. It hit him in the nose and fluttered to the floor.

"No need to call," Kay Huat said, turning his attention back to the CDs. "It's a scam."

Murgatroyd's face fell. He'd dreamed big things last night because of this card. He had dreamed of modelling Bata-brand shoes and of being an astronaut going to the moon.

Meekly, he couldn't help but ask, "Are you sure?"

Kay Huat stopped what he was doing and put his arm around his childhood friend. "Eh, Shwet Foo. I'm your best friend, right?"

Murgatroyd nodded vigorously.

"You trust me, right?"

Murgatroyd nodded even more vigorously, sending a destabilizing shiver through the stack of CDs in his arms.

"Then trust me, lah! It's a scam! I'm going to listen to these. Be right back."

Clapping his friend on the shoulder, Kay Huat liberated him of the unwieldy stack and went off to the store's listening station to sample a few of the tracks. He left a forlorn Murgatroyd in the middle of the aisle. Even though Murgatroyd had known that the strange woman and the strange card probably didn't mean anything, he couldn't help but feel as if a heavy man in football cleats had placed a foot on his heart and given it a good, firm press. Nevertheless, Murgatroyd squatted down to retrieve the green card from the floor and carefully slid it into his back pocket. Perhaps Kay Huat was wrong, he hoped to himself. But he knew Kay Huat was right. Kay Huat was always right.

Murgatroyd wasn't the only one who knew this; the rarefied universe of private wealth management was beginning to catch on as well. After a mere two years into his career, Seng Kay Huat had acquired a reputation in the Asian banking world as a fast-rising young investment advisor with a track record nothing short of flawless. He possessed a natural, God-given talent for finding out when and where money was to be made, and for shifting around his clients' funds appropriately. He had an instinct for determining which investments would profit and which would lose, which companies would suddenly turn belly up and which would unexpectedly skyrocket to success. He seemed to know when markets would turn bullish or bearish, when a stock would peak or plummet, when a country was on the verge of economic boom or collapse, and when to ride out a storm and when to cash in one's chips.

It was this talent that was causing the denizens of the exclusive world of regional private banking to nod in admiration at the mention of Seng Kay Huat's name. It was this talent that had compelled dozens of other banks to offer him gainful employment among their ranks, and that had forced his own employer to raise his position, salary, and benefits to levels positively absurd for such a relatively new employee.

Of course, it was apparent to all, even from the moment of his birth, that Seng Kay Huat was destined for success. By age five, Kay Huat was reading better than his father. His primary and secondary education record had been a long list of various awards and achievements, leadership positions, high marks, and so on and so forth. Even beyond his talents and achievements, there was something else about him. There are some beings in this life who possess an aura of greatness about them, who—when they move and speak—emanate a golden haze of brilliance, as if they were gods and goddesses deigning to live in the world of men. Seng Kay Huat was one such being.

Which is why his deep and abiding friendship with the hapless Murgatroyd (or as Kay Huat knew him, Shwet Foo) was such an unlikely one. The teachers at Da Qiao Primary had never ceased to marvel in disbelief at the oddity of the pair walking together down the school corridors. Even now as adults, they managed to turn heads wherever they went—the handsome, well-built, confident Chinese man and the gangly, hunched-over *ang moh* at his side, absentmindedly picking his ears. The impression was that of a magnificent superhero who had somehow gotten stuck with a defective and shabby sidekick. It seemed too impossible to be real, and yet, their friendship was genuine. Admittedly, his treatment of his friend wasn't always the most considerate, but Kay Huat had been truly fond of his hapless friend—inexplicably so—ever since the day he first rescued Shwet Foo and put an end to the torment the latter endured every day at the hands of the other children.

Three weeks after Murgatroyd's disastrous debut at Da Qiao, the boys still had not tired of hurling his shoes into the Angsana tree in the schoolyard during recess. By then, Murgatroyd had learned how climb up the tree and retrieve them, but he could only do so at the end of the school day, otherwise they would be promptly hurled into the branches again. After three weeks of this, however, Murgatroyd had decided to take preventive measures instead, and was desperately scuffling with the boy who had just stolen his shoes. Or rather, Murgatroyd was doing all the scuffling, while the larger boy simply stood there, grinning as Murgatroyd lightly pummelled him about the waist, and dangling the white canvas sneakers out of Murgatroyd's reach before swinging them lightly into the leaves overhead. It was when the young Murgatroyd crumpled into a sobbing heap on the ground that the young Kay Huat, who had been looking on from the sidelines all the while, suddenly felt unspeakably moved. The boy obviously needed protection. Kay Huat decided that the right thing to do, the heroic thing to do, was to take action.

"Oi! Leave the *ang moh* alone!" he bellowed, pushing his way past the now silent knot of boys who had surrounded the weeping Murgatroyd and were peppering his little body with light kicks. (They'd learned their lesson the first time and nowadays kicked softly, but with great rapidity.) They stopped and stared in astonishment as Kay Huat climbed the tree and retrieved the shoes.

"Hey, *ang moh*!" Kay Huat shouted at the blubbering boy on the ground below him. "Don't cry! Don't cry, okay! See? I got your shoes!" Tossing the stolen footwear to Murgatroyd from on high, Kay Huat must have seemed to Murgatroyd an angel sent from above.

Gaining a firm foothold in the crook of the tree, Kay Huat issued a command to the crowd of boys gathering below him in the yard. "From now on, nobody tease the *ang moh*!"

The boys who had been bullying Murgatroyd slinked away, silent and embarrassed. Kay Huat nimbly clambered down to help Murgatroyd to his feet.

"Eh, what's your name? I'm Kay Huat. Primary Five." He extended his hand.

Wiping away the tears from his eyes, the other boy had at first mumbled a funny-sounding name in a British accent. Something like "Muhka Toi."

"Hah? Say again?"

Then the boy seemed to remember something. "Shwet Foo. My name is Shwet Foo. Primary One."

Kay Huat had laughed heartily at the name before giving his new friend a clap on the back that almost sent him tumbling onto the ground once again. But then he frowned. "Only Primary One? You don't look like Primary One. How old are you?"

"Nine."

Kay Huat mulled silently over this for some time before deciding that it might be acceptable for him to continue associating with the younger boy, despite this rather large two-year age difference.

That incident had been the start of an enduring friendship—perhaps, if Kay Huat were truly honest with himself, the only true friendship he had ever really experienced. Certainly, Kay Huat had *many* friends, accumulated over the course of a lifetime—the contingent of other old school chums from Da Qiao and Raffles Institution; the buddies he'd acquired during National Service; his fellow Stanford alumni; a select handful of work colleagues—but none of them could hold a candle to Shwet Foo, who seemed to understand him and care about him more deeply than anyone he had ever known. And in turn, no one else could elicit in him, Kay Huat, the same brotherly concern and affection he felt for his best friend.

Scenes from the past he and Shwet Foo had shared together ran through his mind like a slideshow. Playing card games, Mastermind, and marbles with Shwet Foo on the floor of his parents' old flat (and letting Shwet Foo win about a third of the time); playing "cops and robbers" in alleyways and market corridors; catching frogs in the park at night with a torch; Shwet Foo helping him collect stamps for his stamp collection; him scaring Shwet Foo with ghost stories of blood-sucking *pontianak*; Shwet Foo attending his school track meet and greeting him after his race with a clean hand towel and an icy-cold can of 100Plus; Shwet Foo ironing his uniform for him the night before the national debate championship while he practiced his speeches; him tutoring Shwet Foo in English; him tutoring Shwet Foo in science; him tutoring Shwet Foo in all subjects and secretly doing parts of his homework for him; Shwet Foo listening to him strategize about how to get Melinda Fong—his first crush—to talk to him; him giving Shwet Foo advice on how to ask a girl for a date (and Shwet Foo getting slapped by a girl in consequence); telling Shwet Foo about his basic-training experiences while on weekend leave over grilled chicken wings and coconut water at the shore; opening his student mailbox in California to find postcards and letters from Shwet Foo; and last but not least, Shwet Foo coming to the airport to welcome him home after his four years abroad.

That act of homecoming had been a particularly emotional time for Kay Huat. He remembered sitting on the plane, only half watching the movie playing on the personal television screen in front of him, engulfed in simultaneous regret and happiness. Unlike the majority of his peers who had come to the US on scholarships from the Singapore government, Kay Huat's funding had come from Stanford itself, and as such, had no strings attached. He didn't need to return to Singapore to fulfil a mandatory term of employment, and his friends envied him for it. "Eh, Kay Huat, what for you go back?" his friends had asked him at his goodbye party the night before.

"My father needs me," he had answered, managing a halfhearted smile. His father really did. Kay Huat's mother had passed away only weeks before he had departed for the US, and his father had spent the past four years wifeless and, effectively, childless. As an only son, Kay Huat had an obligation to return. And he wanted to. He missed home dearly, but he couldn't help thinking about the opportunities that awaited him if he stayed abroad . . .

Such thoughts had kept him awake all through the flight. But when, pushing his baggage trolley past customs through the automatic sliding glass doors, he saw them—his father and Shwet Foo standing side by side among the crowd, waving at him to get his attention—his doubt vanished and joy and relief washed over him like a gentle ocean wave.

"Ah-Boy, welcome home," his father said, somewhat awkwardly.

Shwet Foo shyly handed him an oil-stained brown paper bag. "I got you curry puff. I thought maybe they don't have in America."

Wordlessly, Kay Huat had embraced his father, then his best friend.

With the unexpected wail of a tenor saxophone, Kay Huat drifted back into the present and looked over at his friend standing in the country western section staring dejectedly at the floor. And suddenly a pang of pity, a small one, skewered him neatly through the heart. Taking off the headphones and deciding to sample CDs some other day, he decided that his good friend Shwet Foo should be treated to some lunch.

Sneaking up on him from behind, Kay Huat put his arm around his friend and ruffled his hair. "I buy CDs some other time. Come, we go *makan*. My treat." With that, they exited the store, Kay Huat firmly but gently steering Murgatroyd by his shoulders.

CHAPTER 7

Peculiarly enough, the pang of pity Kay Huat had felt for Murgatroyd remained with him, even after he and his best friend had finished lunch and parted ways. The pang seemed to have lodged itself in the region of his chest, making itself at home around his lungs and lower throat. Despite the frequent sips of warm tea Kay Huat took as he sat at his office desk, it would not go away. In fact, it was hanging around too long to be considered a mere pang. It was really more of a prolonged irritant. Whatever it was, it lingered on throughout the rest of his workday and persisted into the evening, when he left the office, got into his car, and drove to the Golden Serenity Hawker Centre in Ang Mo Kio to meet his father.

Deep down, he knew why the feeling was there. And he knew also that what he felt wasn't just pity pure and simple—there was some guilt mixed in with it as well. Although he had told his friend otherwise, mingled with the odour of high-quality carbon and ink that had wafted up his nostrils as he had held that card to his face was also the unmistakable odour of truth. The card, its one-eyed bearer, and whatever mystery and adventure it hinted at—it was all genuine. The real deal. Kay Huat knew this instinctively, and Kay Huat was almost always right.

But really, he thought to himself as he waited for a stoplight to turn green, by hiding the truth he was doing his friend a favour. Whatever this "Quest" was, it was far too big and far too much for little Shwet Foo to handle. He had only lied to his friend to protect him from harm. Handling whatever this was would require someone far more capable and far more qualified. *Someone like . . .*

Catching a glimpse of himself in the rearview mirror, he swept back a few stray hairs with his fingers and gave himself a roguish wink.

As was typical of a Friday night, Golden Serenity Hawker Centre was packed with hungry people in search of a good dinner and a chance to unwind after a long week of hard work. Golden Serenity was especially famous for two reasons: choice and cheapness. Choice: two whole stories of the open-air building were devoted to hawker stalls selling every possible local dish imaginable, and several of the stalls had won rave reviews from local publications and food lovers for their wares. Cheapness: the shoddiness and age of the building, not to mention the lack of air conditioning, kept most of the tourists away and the prices low. It was so crowded that Kay Huat had to circle around the car park a few times before a space finally opened up. He sighed and felt a bit annoyed at the fact that he had to do this every night. His father, Seng Hong Low, had owned and operated a char kway teow stall in this hawker centre for more than thirty years, and although Kay Huat had told him that he had more than enough money to support him in his old age, Seng the elder refused to retire.

"Ba, I make plenty of money now! Can support you in style, what! Can take you to restaurants. Can send you on nice vacation. No need to fry noodle all day. Time to enjoy your old age, lah."

Seng Hong Low had frowned and waved away his upstart son with a dark, sinewy arm. "If I don't work, got nothing to do. What for I sit around all day and grow fat? Live like that, might as well die! Anyway," he said, tapping the side of his head with a bony index finger, "keeps my mind sharp!"

Only after months of pleading and persuasion did Seng Hong Low agree to leave his small HDB flat and move into his son's luxurious two-bedroom condominium. But it was understood that, with his moving in, his son would never mention the possibility of his retirement from noodle frying ever again. And so, every weekday morning, Kay Huat dropped his father off at the hawker centre on his way to work; every weekday evening, Kay Huat gave his father a ride back home; and every Saturday and Sunday, at his own insistence, Seng Hong Low drove himself there and back in his own battered little white van.

Kay Huat believed that his father refused to retire out of pride. What Seng Hong Low didn't tell his son was that his work also kept his mind off his wife, Kay Huat's mother. She was dead, but the memory of her still brought on the dull, throbbing sensation of grief whenever he was idle. For all of his married life, he had worked hard and tended assiduously to his own health to ensure that his wife, the mother of his only son, would be well cared for during the remainder of his life, and well provided for after his death. What had never occurred to him was the unlikely possibility that he might outlive his wife, who suddenly and inexplicably died of a heart attack six years ago while she was brushing her teeth.

Hong Low dealt with the loss of his wife in the same way he had always dealt with any tragedy when it intruded upon his life—he worked harder. Saving up his wages from an assortment of jobs—janitor, night-shift security guard, electronics store clerk—Hong Low picked a space in Golden Serenity Hawker Centre to call his own, between Golden Treasure Pig Organ Soup (stall #01-52) and Melodee Fish-Head Curry (stall #01-54), and he pursued his true passion in life—making char kway teow. Even though he rarely indulged in the pan-fried noodles himself, preferring to subsist on a simple diet of watercress pork-rib soup and steamed rice, during the married years of his life, he had taken great joy in whipping up a plate of his wife's favourite dish whenever he could and beaming with delight as she—skinny as a bird—gobbled up every last bit. At the age of thirty-seven, she died, small and avian-like as ever. And Hong Low never suspected the invisible toll that his lovingly prepared lard-coated noodles had taken on her arteries. Kay Huat had learned this from the doctor, but had successfully kept it secret from his father all these years: it would have destroyed Hong Low to know that he had contributed to his wife's death. Now that she was dead, what could Seng Hong Low do but set up a char kway teow business—a poor man's Taj Mahal in memory of a beloved wife?

Kay Huat emerged from his silver Porsche and sighed as he approached the crowded hawker centre. People. Always people. And sweaty people, no less. The heat from hundreds of individual stovetops and ovens and toasters and grills at each hawker stall, combined with the heat given off by hundreds of individual bodies compressed into a single space, combined with the fact plain and simple that Singapore was located on the equator, made the interior of Golden Serenity feel like the interior of a giant steamer. The ancient electric fans bolted to pillars overhead didn't do much good on a night like this, although they made up for their lack of effectuality by sounding more like helicopters than temperature control units. As Kay Huat rolled up his shirtsleeves in preparation for forging his way to his father's stall, he couldn't help thinking of what the French existentialist philosopher Jean-Paul Sartre had once written: *hell is other people.*

For dramatic effect, he stood on the threshold of the hawker centre and took a deep breath. He placed one foot, then the other, onto the white-tiled floor, which always looked grimy, even when it had been hosed down and scrubbed. And then, he plunged himself into the thick of it. Elbowing and shimmying his way between the customers queuing at the more popular hawker stalls and the customers seated at the densely packed green plastic tables, he arrived finally at stall #01-53: True Love Char Kway Teow.

But before approaching the stall, Kay Huat did what he always did. Standing behind a pillar about five metres away, he surreptitiously watched his father at work. The sheen of sweat on his father's bald head, the face brown and flushed from the great flames of the gas stove, the wiry, muscular arm circling briskly over the massive wok, keeping its contents in perpetual agitation—Kay Huat took all of this in and was filled with admiration for the old man; all the labour and love he had put into caring for and providing for his family, which now only consisted of the two of them. And it occurred to him that he wanted to make the old man proud. Yes, Seng Kay Huat decided. His father was the reason for which he would undertake . . . well, what he was about to undertake, which, in another light, might have seemed downright dastardly. It was for Seng Hong Low and all that he as his son owed him that Kay Huat would seize this opportunity of a lifetime, even if it meant gently shifting it away from under his best friend's nose. Interestingly enough, the sensations of pity and guilt that had been irritating him all afternoon subsided instantly. He felt much better. Perhaps it had just been indigestion.

Finally making his presence known, he walked up to the stall and nudged aside a skinny bespectacled teenager who had been waiting for his order.

"Hi, Ba."

"Ah-Boy," his father grunted. "How was your day?"

"Not bad, not bad." Kay Huat entered the stall and stood beside Seng Hong Low. "Here, you go rest. I help you for a while."

"No need, lah."

"Never mind! Go rest, go rest."

Pressing a dollar coin into his father's hand and gently shooing him in the direction of the beverage stall, Kay Huat took over the wok. Illuminated by the glow of the bursts of flame that came shooting up from the stove, Kay Huat's natural aura shone all the more brightly. Even the sweat that rolled down his face looked like drops of liquid gold, and passing patrons stopped briefly in front of the stall to gape in admiration.

By the time Kay Huat and Hong Low had finished with the day's closing, it was a little after eleven. As the car sped home, they sat together, quiet and exhausted. Hong Low was struggling to keep from nodding off.

"Ba, if you're too tired, I can drive you tomorrow morning."

"No need, Ah-Boy. Saturdays and Sundays, I drive myself."

Kay Huat let a minute pass, and then tried again. "Ba, I not doing anything tomorrow. Let me drive, lah."

Hong Low lost his temper. "Already said no need! So difficult for you to understand, is it?"

"Okay, okay." Kay Huat tried to soothe him. "Sorry, Ba. Just trying to help."

Hong Low immediately felt sorry for his outburst and tried to lighten the mood. "Eh, Ah-Boy. If you want to help, why don't you find a nice girl to marry and give me grandchildren?"

He was only half joking, and Kay Huat sensed this. Hong Low saw his son frown and hunch forward, as if he were concentrating on the road. "Maybe someday, Ba. No time for girls now."

"If not now, when?" Seng Hong Low had always been curious about the conspicuous absence of romance in his son's life. He was always working. Always working on work. Always working on activities. Always working on something. He was beginning to suspect that his son was gay.

"Later, lah. I'm still young."

"*Aiyah*. You don't want to get married, is it?

"I do, but not now."

"Then what are you waiting for?"

Kay Huat wondered if he should tell his father the truth. What he was waiting for the world to discover was that he—Seng Kay Huat—was a great man. That he was waiting to become the Great Singaporean Novelist. That he was waiting to rise up through the ranks of the private bank and become one of its top executives. No, it went beyond even that. He was waiting to invent something, to do something, to *be* something. Waiting until he was on the cover of *TIME* or *Asiaweek*. Waiting to win the Nobel

Prize. He was waiting for something even bigger and better than all of these things. He wasn't sure what he was waiting for; he only knew that at times the world seemed too small, too petty, to accommodate his ambitions. He was waiting to *achieve greatness*, and he wasn't going to let any pretty girl sidetrack him or tie him down in the meantime.

"Did you hear me, Ah-Boy? What are you waiting for?"

I'm waiting for something that could be just around the corner! Something that I'll find out the moment we get home and I pick up the telephone!

Seng Hong Low threw up his hands at Kay Huat's stubborn silence, and the last five minutes of the drive passed without another word.

Once they arrived home, Hong Low went to take a shower before collapsing into bed. Kay Huat retreated to his room. Sitting down on the edge of the bed, he picked up the telephone on his nightstand. His fingers trembled as he dialled the number he had taken the trouble to memorize earlier that day.

We're sorry. The number that you have dialled is incorrect.

He tried thirteen more times, but to no avail. "Damn it," he muttered as he slammed the handset down in frustration. How could this be? He was never wrong. He waited ten minutes and then tried again. *We're sorry. The number that you have dialled is incorrect.*

"I am *not* incorrect!" he snarled. Sitting heavily on the edge of his bed, he gripped at his hair in frustration and took several deep breaths to calm himself down. *I am never incorrect*, he thought. It was all very strange.

Seng Kay Huat had no idea just *how* strange it all was. He scoured the Internet until two in the morning, searching for any hint of information about the Quest and about Ann, but he found nothing. And yet, even as Kay Huat had been dialling the number for the sixth time, another phone call to that very same number had gone out from Murgatroyd's home. And, without any trouble at all, Murgatroyd had gotten through.

CHAPTER 8

Against the advice of his best and only friend, against his own better judgement, against his own belief that calling people any time after ten p.m. (much less eleven thirty p.m.) was very inconsiderate, and inconsistent entirely with the timidity that came so naturally to him, Murgatroyd's trembling fingers had dialled the number on the card. He had been so nervous that he'd kept getting the last digit wrong and dialled the wrong number twice. Finally, he had gotten it right, and a recorded message instructed him to meet with Quest Representative Ann at twelve thirty sharp on Sunday in the open grassy area behind the Orchard MRT subway station.

So that was how Murgatroyd found himself standing in a field of Filipinos at twelve noon on a Sunday. (He had arrived half an hour early, just in case.) Singapore, like most wealthy Asian countries, employed most of its menial labour from its poorer neighbours, and many of the domestic workers came from the Philippines. Although there were a few men here and there, the crowd was composed mostly of women—maids escaping from their demanding and miserly employers on their weekly day off. There were several reasons why this large patch of green was a favourite escape destination: it was easily accessible by public transportation and one street over from the lively Orchard Road shopping district; it was within walking distance of the money remittance offices and Filipino convenience stores of Lucky Plaza; it was a "natural" setting in its own way (though those who preferred nature with fewer of the comforts of civilization could head to the Botanical Gardens); and, importantly, it was free.

The women sat in groups of two or more upon sheets of newspaper, towels, or plastic mats spread beneath them to keep their clothing clean. Most of them were eating lunch—takeaway food they had bought nearby or dishes they had made at home or in their employers' kitchens, with snacks and cakes laid out for all to partake in. Some were busy comparing newly purchased items with their friends—high heels and purses, blouses and jeans, nail polish and hair accessories. To Murgatroyd's left, a group of six were busy concluding a Bible-study session with group prayer. To his right, three women sat together ignoring each other, chatting away on their mobile phones. Being obviously alone and not Filipino, Murgatroyd was already beginning to draw attention from the people surrounding him, who would glance at him from time to time, wondering who he was and what he was doing here. Maybe he was meeting his Filipina girlfriend? Maybe he was a white sleazebag looking to pick up a Filipina girlfriend? Maybe he was a foreign journalist here to do research?

"Who's that white guy over there?" a nearby woman asked her friend in Tagalog as they reclined on the grass, waiting for their newly applied toenail polish to dry.

"How should I know? He looks harmless, though. Scrawny."

"At least he's not fat. Sometimes white people can be really fat. It's the food they eat. Mostly burgers. It's disgusting."

"Hah. The Chinese ones are just as bad. My boss, she's huge even though she goes to the gym all the time. She eats lots of cakes and watches TV all day and wonders why she can't lose weight."

"Hey, this guy's kind of weird. Look at him picking his ears!"

All this was in earshot of Murgatroyd, but although he had the feeling that his presence was generating some conversation, he couldn't tell what kind of conversation he was generating since he didn't understand Tagalog. With each passing minute, he felt himself reddening with embarrassment and overexposure to the sun. Beads of sweat were already running down his temples and accumulating on his nose. He wished that he hadn't run out of deodorant that very morning because large, smelly wet patches were appearing on the armpits of his T-shirt. He also wished he had applied some sunscreen. All in all, he thought, this was not going to make a very good second impression. He scanned the field for the umpteenth time, wondering if he'd gotten the time or the place wrong.

"So. You've arrived early."

Murgatroyd turned around to find Ann staring intimidatingly down her nose at him with her one good eye. She was still wearing the black patch over her eye and she was again dressed all in green; this time, in an ankle-length, fern-coloured cotton sundress and a floppy straw hat trimmed with a green polka-dotted ribbon. He didn't remember her being so tall, but come to think of it, she had been sitting down when they met.

Then he looked down at her feet. Green shoes. With very high heels.

Ann looked down at her feet. "Yes. I don't usually wear heels, but these were so comfortable, I thought I'd make an exception."

"Erh. I see."

Silence ensued. Murgatroyd attempted to make some small talk. "How come so dressed up?"

"I'm not."

"Oh."

More silence ensued. Murgatroyd was trying to figure out if he should wait for her to bring up the Quest, or whether he should broach the subject. Suddenly, Ann gestured across the Filipino-festooned field with a sweeping motion of her hand, nearly smacking him in the forehead.

"Behold!" she declared. "These are the hands which keep Singapore clean, fed, and pampered! The people who keep her windows gleaming, her children cared for, and her dogs walked! Who must leave their own families behind to care for other families! Who bear the brunt of their employers' anger! Who keep this great nation sleek and content in exchange for pitiable wages!"

At the conclusion of this speech, which Ann delivered in stentorian fashion, everyone surrounding them stared silently in astonishment, except for one small group, who broke into a flurry of cheering and applause.

Murgatroyd felt himself redden even more. "Should we . . . should we sit down?"

"No. I prefer to stand."

"Oh."

They stood there for a little while, Ann persisting in staring down imperiously at him before breaking the silence.

"Well?" she asked in an expectant manner.

"Hah?"

"Well, Murgatroyd, why are we here?"

"Oh. Erh. Erh," he felt flustered, embarrassed. "You know, what."

"I know nothing. Why?"

"What?"

"What are we here for, Murgatroyd?"

Murgatroyd was bewildered. She was the one who started this whole thing! Was she joking? He decided, after studying the expression on her face, that she most certainly wasn't joking. Where should he start?

"I th-thought," he stammered. "I thought about—about what you said about me belonging here."

"What about it?"

"I . . . I think maybe—I think maybe I don't belong. At—at least sometimes I don't feel like it."

Ann arched one eyebrow. Or at least, that's what Murgatroyd thought she did. With the sun shining in his eyes, and from his lesser height, it was difficult to see her eyebrows. "Let me get this straight. You *think . . . maybe* you *feel* you don't belong *some*times?"

Murgatroyd was getting quite frustrated. "I don't belong here," he declared. "I DON'T belong."

"Oh-ho! Now we're getting somewhere!"

"Where?"

"Where what?"

"Where are we getting to?"

Ann sighed. "I was speaking metaphorically."

Murgatroyd could only reply, "Oh," and once again, they lapsed into silence. After a few seconds, Murgatroyd mustered up the courage to ask a question.

"Erh. I wanted to ask you something."

"What?"

"Hah?"

"What did you want to ask me?"

"Oh. About the Quest."

"What about the Quest?"

"What is it?"

"What, the Quest?"

"Yes, the Quest."

"Ah yes. The Quest." Her one green eye flashed and glistened with suppressed enthusiasm. "Murgatroyd," she announced. "Let us sit down."

"Can we go someplace more shaded? Like under a tree?" Murgatroyd examined his arms, which were looking ferociously pink.

"No. I prefer the sun."

Promptly sitting down cross-legged on the ground, Ann immediately began uprooting blades of grass with her fingers and tearing them into tiny bits. Murgatroyd felt obliged to join her (in sitting, not in tearing).

Ann began with a question. Questions always made Murgatroyd rather nervous because most of the time when he answered questions, he answered them wrongly.

"Tell me, Murgatroyd," asked Ann. "Would you say this field is crowded?"

Murgatroyd looked around. It certainly looked very crowded to him. So he nodded.

"What if I were to tell you it wasn't?" Ann looked at him expectantly, waiting for a response.

"Erh. I guess some more could fit. But then it would be very cramped."

"What if I were to tell you that this field was practically empty?"

Murgatroyd laughed uneasily.

Ann gave him a stern look. "It's not a joke."

He stopped laughing. Ann continued.

"There are currently four hundred people, perhaps a little more, occupying this field right now. What if I told you that four *million* people and their full-grown pet elephants could occupy this field comfortably with room to spare? What if I told you that it was the same way with all the space in all the world we know, or we *think* we know today?"

Murgatroyd shook his head. "Cannot be."

"Ah, but it can!"

"Cannot!" He shook his head again. Murgatroyd rarely expressed open disagreement. He stared down at the ground and he lapsed into heavy Singlish, as he always did when he was nervous. "I know I not so smart one, but how to fit so many?"

Ann didn't respond. He looked up to find her perfectly still and silent. With her legs crossed and her back so straight, she looked as if she were deep in meditation, except for the fact that her eyes weren't closed. Or at least her visible eye wasn't. It was wide open. And it seemed to Murgatroyd as if it were growing more blazingly brilliant and intensely green with each uneasy second that passed.

Then she began to speak. Her voice had changed in quality. It seemed almost as if a low growl was issuing forth from her lips, but it wasn't husky or scratchy. On the contrary, her voice was devastatingly clear and her words perfectly articulated. And the words she spoke were a sharp knife slicing directly into his heart.

"Murgatroyd, do you remember your first day of school?"

She didn't pause for an answer, but he found himself nodding anyway.

"You remember the day you went to Uncle Yusuf's ice cream shop and found it empty?"

He started in amazement. "How did you—" he began, but she still didn't pause. And her voice grew deeper and darker.

"Remember how you felt when you were running. Running to escape the pain and the humiliation. Running towards the one thing—the only thing—in the world that you knew to be good and true and safe and at home. Do you remember that moment? That moment when your legs felt sore and red and you felt as if you couldn't breathe anymore and you finally spied Uncle Yusuf's in the distance? It felt as if you were running home, didn't it? And as you ran towards it, all the pain—the pain in your bleeding nose, in your aching chest, in the entirety of your puny little body—began to dissolve as it grew closer. All the taunts of those strange boys who hated you for no reason you knew, the sharp sting of your nose being bashed in, the smell of shoe leather and dirt, the metallic taste of your own blood running into your mouth, and more: the fear, the terror of being despised and alone. Utterly alone. All of that began to melt away as you got closer. Closer to Uncle Yusuf. Because in the back of your mind, you knew that he cared for you, and you loved him and you knew he loved you. And so you made your mad dash for the ice cream shop, crazed with pain and grief and misery. And you felt relief already—the foretaste of relief and rest and love washing over you. Sweet relief. And then it hit you. There was something wrong, wasn't there? You could sense it even several metres away, before you peered into the darkened interior to find it empty. No Uncle Yusuf. No ice cream in the display case. No light. No music drifting from the radio, no glass bowls lined up on the shelves behind the counter, twinkling with cleanliness. Nothing except the unfamiliar packing cartons strewn around the empty floor, a stool in the corner overturned, piles of crumpled newspaper here and there, tools sitting ominously atop the ice cream display case, waiting to dismantle it forever. But most importantly of all, no Uncle Yusuf. He was gone. And you knew somehow, even then, that he was never coming back. Even though you would return periodically for years afterwards, harbouring the hollow hope that all would be restored, that Uncle Yusuf would be there behind the counter to greet you with a wide smile on his face, you knew that he was never coming back. And you felt pain, didn't you? Pain and sorrow in your stomach, clawing at you from the inside out. You screamed and cried, but it wouldn't go away. And when all the sound and motion you were capable of left you drained, you curled up into a ball, the shameful taste of tears and blood still under your tongue and in the crevices between your teeth. You knew how alone you were. How alone. You knew how alone . . ."

In the time Ann had been speaking, Murgatroyd had quietly clenched his teeth and closed his eyes, held powerless by his bewilderment at this insight into his innermost childhood thoughts and the soft, almost hypnotic voice in which it was delivered. His eyes flew open and he opened his mouth with the vague notion of pleading with her to stop. But they weren't sitting in the field anymore, and Ann wasn't sitting beside him.

Where was he? Gradually, his mind reoriented himself. They were still in the field, but someone had exploded it. No, not exploded . . .

unfolded it. There was no other way to describe it. It was as if someone had unfolded an origami crane, but instead of smoothing it out flat, had simply let it lie undone with all its intricate folds and creases bared. Great multifaceted structures of dirt and grass, almost crystalline in their angularity, protruded from the ground below. They seemed, inexplicably, to jut unmoored from the sides of the sky and from above. And on this massive three-dimensional structure, he himself was seated. There was nobody in sight. Most every facet of grassy field was bare, but every now and then he could make out a small speck on one of the facets. To his amazement, he realized that these specks were the Filipinas who had been sitting in the field all around him. Some were seated upside down or sideways, but if they were, they didn't seem to notice. All the sound—the animated chatter and laughter surrounding them—hadn't changed a bit. And if he concentrated hard enough, he could match the snatches and snippets of conversations to different individuals who were chatting to others over great distances as if only a few centimetres separated them from each other. On one facet, very far away, on the underside of a grassy trapezoidal arch, he could make out the miniscule figure of Ann. And from this miniscule figure came a surprisingly audible voice.

"There's more than enough room after all. Don't you think?"

Murgatroyd found himself again in the crowded flat field. Gravity had resumed. The Filipinas were once again seated together in small clusters, and seated next to him, staring at him solemnly but with a faint smile in her eye, was Ann.

Murgatroyd opened his mouth, and when he did, his voice came out in a very croaky whisper. "Who are you?"

Ann corrected him. "Who are *we*, Murgatroyd. Who are *we*?"

CHAPTER 9

Ann took something out of her bag and handed it to Murgatroyd. It was a ball of tightly crumpled aluminium foil, about the size of a small lime.

"I always carry this around with me. It's a very useful way of explaining a potentially complicated concept. Now, Murgatroyd: think of that ball of foil as the world. Feel the surface."

Murgatroyd rolled the ball between his palms and fingers. It was slightly rough and jagged.

"The surface of the ball—the part exposed and visible to us, is what we call the Known World. But you'll notice too that there's more to this ball than meets the eye."

Ann took the ball from Murgatroyd and uncreased it ever so slightly so that instead of a compact, round ball, it was more of a loosely crumpled wad.

"See?" Ann said, pointing to the crannies and crevices that had been hidden in the ball's interior, but were now exposed to the outside. "And if you undo all of the ball,"—Ann proceeded to do just that—"you can see that most of the ball consists not of what is on the surface, but what is crumpled and packed together to form the interior."

Ann smoothed out all of the creases and lay the sheet of foil flat on the grass between them for Murgatroyd to behold. Even flattened out, the foil had a rugged texture to it, its surface crisscrossed in wrinkles and lines from where it had been crumpled.

Ann continued: "Remember how the surface of the ball represented the Known World? The rest of this foil—the parts you weren't able to see when it was rolled up into a ball—all this represents the More Known World. Murgatroyd, look around you."

Murgatroyd looked around.

"All of what you see around you now, and in fact, all that you've ever seen almost all your entire life, is the Known World—the surface of the ball. Now, tell me what you saw just a few minutes ago. You didn't see this field the way it is now, did you?"

Murgatroyd shook his head. "It was like this, but . . ." he couldn't think of any other word for it, "but unfolded." He put two and two together. "Like the ball!"

Ann smiled. "Exactly. You caught a glimpse of the More Known World. Most people go through their entire lives perceiving only the Known World. That's all they ever experience, all they ever know. But beyond the limits of their perception—or at least what they *think* are the limits of their perception—lies . . ." Ann gestured towards the flattened sheet of foil, "the More Known World."

Murgatroyd's eyes widened. "So that was the More Known World?"

"Just a small part of it. The More Known World is vast—unimaginably vast and intricate beyond conception. The name is a bit of a misnomer, actually, because there's still a lot of it we *don't* know about at all; we're not even sure that it *is* possible to ever explore all of it, even if our numbers were tripled and we were given millions and millions of years. Just look!" Ann pointed to the sheet of foil. "It's covered with creases. Make note of each crease where it was folded. Make note of every kink in each crease, every irregularity. Look even closer. The foil isn't even completely flat: there are still tiny folds, tiny ridges, tiny valleys that can't be smoothed out entirely. Now imagine that each one of these creases, kinks, irregularities, folds, ridges, valleys is a new portion of the More Known World—we call them Territories. They're innumerable: in reality, more innumerable than what you see represented in this imperfect model before you.

"What you saw just now was a tiny—an infinitesimal—part of the More Known World. In fact, what you most likely saw just now was a fusion of the Known World and a Territory of the More Known World. You saw this portion of the Known World—this field—slightly uncrumpled; you saw the unseen facets of this world that most people never see and will never be aware of."

It was clear that Ann had explained this many times before. Yet, as she explained, it seemed that even she herself couldn't resist being awed anew by the amazing facts that she was uttering for perhaps the umpteenth time. Her face never altered, maintaining its steady expression of calm intensity and nonchalant seriousness, but the words spilled out of her mouth with increasing rapidity; her eye positively glowed with excitement and joy. "If they only knew that this field could unfold to produce a thousand different surfaces. If they only knew they could stroll through any of the wide, open spaces separating every blade of grass, and that each of those spaces possessed its own unique geological and climactic features—glacial plains, lush forests, swamplands, star canyons, gossamer stalactites, shimmering fields of terrafluffs; if only they knew they could perch on any one of the millions of layers in the sky, or eat their picnic lunches on any groove of any leaf in that single tree over there," (Ann pointed to a small frangipani tree about twenty metres to her right), "and experience countries consisting entirely of waterfalls, or mountain ranges formed entirely out of yellow straw and sky.

"If they *only knew* how *much* of the world there is! If only they knew!" Abruptly, Ann re-crumpled the sheet into a compact ball. "But most people don't know. And many don't want to know. So many will always be perfectly content to experience only the surface of this tiny little ball." She sighed, and as if repeating to herself something that had been told to her time and time again, said resignedly, "And if they're content, then that's fine. After all, the Known World itself is remarkable and holds many wondrous things." She sighed again. "But there's so *much* more."

There was a brief pause as Ann seemed to contemplate this. Murgatroyd took the opportunity to venture a question.

"You keep saying most people can't see the More Known World. How come I can?"

"Because," she answered, placing the ball back inside her bag, "it just so happens that you don't fall into the category of 'most people.' You, Murgatroyd, are what we call an Oddfit."

"Come again?"

"An Oddfit. I'm one too. Most Questians are. About four-fifths of them, to be precise."

"What are Questians?"

"One thing at a time and first things first. Ask me what an Oddfit is."

As both the terms "Oddfit" and "Questian" puzzled him equally, Murgatroyd was happy to oblige.

"Erh. What's an Oddfit?"

"Excellent question." With no ball of foil to keep her hands busy, Ann's fingers turned back to shredding the blades of grass around her, this time methodically splitting them lengthwise and arranging the halves in a little heap. "All people in the Worlds fall into three different categories: Sumfits, Oddfits, and Stucks. All of them," and here she paused briefly before continuing, "*all* of them have the ability to experience the Known World to its fullest, and with few exceptions, none of them will ever suspect that there is any more to the physical world besides the Known.

"Most people are Sumfits. In fact, about 99.5 percent of the world's population are Sumfits. With proper training and willingness on their part, a Sumfit can learn to perceive, experience, and inhabit a certain number—a certain *sum,* if you will—of Territories in the More Known World *in addition* to the all of the Known World. But transferring between Worlds and Territories is an extremely draining process for a Sumfit. As a result, many Sumfits who are able to access the More Known World settle permanently there in a Territory of their choosing, or make transfers only once in a while."

"People live in the More Known World?"

Ann nodded. "The number isn't huge, but there are about four thousand Sumfits who've chosen to make some part of the More Known World their home. To continue, Sumfits make up most of the worlds' population. However, every now and then, for reasons that still remain a mystery to us, someone ends up being born an Oddfit. Oddfits have no difficulty transferring between the Known World and the More Known World, or even among the different Territories of the More Known World. But even beyond that, Oddfits are blessed with a unique ability. A unique ability indeed.

"Only Oddfits have the ability to discover *new* Territories. Only Oddfits can sense, discover, and explore portions of the More Known World that have never been visited before. Only Oddfits," Ann leaned forward and dropped her voice to a conspiratorial whisper, "have the capability to make the More Known World *more known.* And *you,* Murgatroyd—or should I say *we,* Murgatroyd—happen to be Oddfits. Now what do you have to say to that?"

Murgatroyd did have something to say. "Wow."

Ann nodded. "Wow, indeed."

"But how . . . how did I become an Oddfit? Are my parents Oddfits?" Murgatroyd asked.

"No, your parents are Sumfits. Interestingly enough, oddfittingness doesn't seem to be hereditary at all. The likelihood of an Oddfit, or even two Oddfits together, producing Oddfit offspring is about the same as that of Sumfit parents producing Oddfit ones. Oddfittingness just happens. We have no idea why. Similarly, we have no idea why some people are born Stucks."

"Stucks?"

"Stucks are even rarer than Oddfits. They are people who are unable, however willing and however much training they undergo, to access any part of the More Known World. They are confined to the Known World for the entirety of their existence. Like oddfittingness, stuckness just happens. About five years ago, two Oddfits who were part of the Quest gave birth to a Stuck baby girl. They were immensely sad—all the Territories they could go to, all the parts of the More Known World they themselves had made known! But their own daughter would never be able to see any of it, not even a small portion. And worse still . . ." Ann trailed off.

"What?" Murgatroyd asked. "What was worse still?"

"We'll get to that later," Ann said, shaking off the barely perceptible tone of melancholy that had crept into her last few sentences. "They ended up producing a lovely series of illustrated picture books dedicated to her—each one documenting to the fullest extent possible every Territory they had ever visited, just so that she could learn about the More Known World without ever going there."

Murgatroyd was too overwhelmed with new information to sympathize with the Oddfit parents the way that Ann seemed to. But his ears did perk up when she mentioned that they had been part of "the Quest."

"What is the Quest? Is it related to Questians?"

"Good. You're quite sharp when you need to be. The Quest is an international Tupperware manufacturer specializing in the production of unconventionally shaped Tupperware containers."

It took a while for Murgatroyd to process this underwhelming answer. "What?"

"I'm joking, Murgatroyd. Look at my face," Ann said, her face as calm and unruffled as it had ever been. "But seriously, the Quest is precisely what its name implies: a quest to explore and expand our knowledge of the More Known World. Think about it, Murgatroyd. Each small area of the Known World contains hundreds, even thousands, of different Territories. It is the purpose of the Questians—those who have chosen to embark on the Quest—to discover and to open our eyes and our minds to the vastness and greatness of the universe as we know it."

"But why? So people can live there? You said just now that some . . . 'Sumfits'? Is that right?"

Ann nodded, even though the term still felt strange on Murgatroyd's tongue.

"You said that some Sumfits live in the More Known World. Wouldn't it help with the overpopulation problem in this world—I mean the Known World?"

Ann frowned and shook her head. "You mean, like resettlement? Colonization? No. That's not the point of the Quest at all. Think of it this way, Murgatroyd: we are tiny ants. Tiny ants who have confined ourselves to our tiny anthill on our tiny patch of the earth, completely unaware of the meadows and jungles and deserts and rivers and oceans and caves and mountains and islands and continents and moons and stars and planets and even the great sun shining overhead. It's not a matter of figuring out what parts of the great universe we can utilize for our own selfish, petty means. It's a matter of putting aside our own ridiculous self-importance in order to attempt to understand it in all its magnificence and splendour. This, if you will, is the 'point' of the Quest, and if you choose, Murgatroyd, you too can be a part of it."

"Me?"

"Yes, you. The Quest depends on the ability of Oddfits to explore unknown parts of the More Known World. Without Oddfits, the Quest would consist only of theoretical postulation."

Murgatroyd still couldn't believe his ears. "Me? Join the Quest?"

"Well, if you choose."

"But . . . but I don't understand. If I'm really an Oddfit, why haven't I ever been able to see the More Known World before this?"

"For one thing, you're rather old to be discovering your Oddfit abilities. Most Oddfits are identified and trained at a much younger age. You're twenty-five, if I'm not mistaken?"

Murgatroyd nodded.

Ann nodded in return, but more contemplatively. "Yes. That's old. *Exceptionally* old. The younger an Oddfit, the easier it is for him or her to perceive the More Known World. The fact that you were able to see it at all just now is actually quite remarkable, considering your age and the fact that it was only your second time."

"My *second* time?"

"Yes. Surely you remember the first time. You visited Yusuf's ice cream freezer, didn't you?"

Murgatroyd's jaw dropped. "That was real? I thought that was something I imagined . . ."

"Murgatroyd, that was probably the most real experience you've had so far in your life. Yusuf, by the way, was one of the three Beginners."

"Beginners?"

"The three Oddfits who originally began the Quest sixty-five years ago: Francesca, whom we call the One; Hector, whom we call the Other; and Yusuf, whose official title was the Another, but who always preferred for us to just call him Yusuf. At first, they sought only other Oddfits, but after a while, they began to find Sumfits who were eager to join as well. I was ten years old when the One found me. And Yusuf was the one who found you. Unfortunately, he passed away before he could send us more of your details, which is why you've gone undetected until now."

Murgatroyd's memories of those days began to resurface. "Uncle Yusuf said that things were underway . . ." he murmured.

"Yes, they would have been if he hadn't died so suddenly. He'd actually already retired from the Quest when he found you. You were the last one he found."

The pain from remembering Yusuf, combined with this confirmation of his death, caused Murgatroyd to breathe in sharply and suddenly. Though it seemed silly to cry over something that had happened so long ago, he felt his eyes getting watery. Wiping his face with the back of his hand, Murgatroyd asked, "How did he die?"

Ann's voice took on a slightly softer tone as she handed him a fistful of grass to wipe his eyes. "Old age."

"So the ice cream freezer wasn't a dream? Uncle Yusuf really did take me there?"

Ann nodded.

"And . . . and I could see the More Known World when I was younger?"

"Well, more easily than now, assumedly. What really activates the ability to perceive and transfer to the More Known World is the longing to go home. That's why I brought up those painful memories. You had to access that terrible lonely feeling of not belonging, of yearning for love and true happiness—for home."

"But my home is here."

"Is that what you feel, Murgatroyd? Or is that what you believe?"

Murgatroyd thought for a bit. "I . . . I don't know. Aren't they both the same?"

"You're an Oddfit, Murgatroyd. You don't belong in the Known World. Or at least, you didn't start out belonging to it. An Oddfit child knows intuitively that he or she doesn't fit in this world and yearns for home. It's an acute case of homesickness, if you will. As Oddfits stay longer in the Known World, they become more comfortable with it."

"So Oddfits can grow to belong to the Known World?"

"Yes. Over time, an Oddfit will lose his or her oddfittingness. It may take four years. It may take fifteen. It varies from person to person.

By seventeen, the adaptation process is usually complete. But in the process, they cease to be Oddfits and become Sumfits."

Murgatroyd thought for a while. "So if Sumfits and Stucks belong here in the Known World, where do Oddfits belong? In the More Known World? If this isn't my home, then where is?"

Ann hadn't expected him to ask so many questions; she hadn't really thought Murgatroyd bright enough to do so. She chose her words carefully: something she rarely bothered to do. "We Oddfits don't really have a single place where we belong. We don't belong in any of the Worlds. Our home is our constant motion—our constant quest to discover uncharted Territories. It is only in moving and exploring that we have our being, and our constant motion is driven by the perpetual homesickness we feel whenever we stay in one spot for too long. Or rather, perpetual homesickness is what an Oddfit feels on an instinctual level."

"You mean, we'll never belong anywhere?" Murgatroyd said, aghast. "We'll never have a home?"

"Not as long as we remain Oddfits, we won't. At least not in the conventional sense. We'll never have a permanent location we can call home. But restlessness and curiosity—those are what we consider home."

The initial sense of wonder that Murgatroyd experienced upon learning these truths about the Worlds was beginning to fade into worry as he attempted to think about the consequences of joining the Quest. He thought of his life here in Singapore: his parents, his best friend, his job.

"Will I ever be able to come back?" he asked.

Ann shook her head. "Not at all for the first few years. After that, you'll be able to come back for a few hours at a time, but you'll be able to spend progressively less and less time here on each visit. And finally, you won't be able to come back at all. Remember the Oddfit parents I mentioned earlier? The ones who had a Stuck child?"

"Yes?"

"At first, they could come back to visit every now and then, but after a while . . ." Ann looked grave. "She's being raised by an aunt and uncle."

"But when will the Quest be over?"

"Not for at least several centuries and potentially never."

"Never? What if we finish exploring all of the More Known World?"

"That's certainly possible, but very unlikely, given what we believe to be the sheer vastness of the More Known World. We've already ventured into over two hundred thousand new Territories, and I'd say we've barely scratched the surface."

"What will I tell my parents?"

Ann arched an eyebrow. "How on earth should I know what you should tell your parents? Tell them you're going on the Quest. Or tell them whatever you wish. It's not as if the More Known World is a secret."

Murgatroyd's eyes widened. "Really? How come I've never heard of it?"

"Interesting question," Ann sighed. "And it has an interesting answer—one we've never quite been able to explain ourselves. It would appear that most people—mainly Sumfits and Stucks, but also the very, very occasional Oddfit—actually do not retain any information about the More Known World, even when they're told about it.

"As you may imagine, this makes disseminating information a little difficult. Word never spreads, general interest is never aroused; we even attempted a modest publicity campaign of sorts in the late 1980s using funds from a generous donor sympathetic to our cause. The money went into print advertisements, television time . . . not Internet; Internet wasn't big yet."

Ann shook her head. "As far as we could tell, most people—not all, mind you—would forget about the More Known World within minutes of reading or watching or hearing about it. And the money didn't go far; it was all gone within a month. Stranger still, a surprisingly large percentage of those who did hear about the More Known World appeared to experience negative physical and psychic symptoms: headaches, nausea, bloating, and an aversion to the means by which information about the More Known World was communicated to them. Many of the newspapers, magazines, and television stations reported higher rates of subscription cancellations, lower sales, and drops in viewer ratings, and refused to do business with us anymore."

Murgatroyd scratched his right ear thoughtfully. "So these people *can't* know about the More Known World?"

"Well, from the very rudimentary investigations we've conducted so far, it seems that it's not so much a matter of inability—of 'can't'—so much as a matter of unconscious but voluntary rejection—of 'won't.'"

"Come again?"

"We think that on some deeper, instinctual level, they might not *want* to know about the More Known World, or the Quest, or Oddfits, Sumfits, and Stucks, or any of the rest of it; and that the symptoms they experience are somehow related to this."

Murgatroyd was stunned. "'Not want to know'? How can they not want to know?"

Ann shrugged. "Honestly, *we* don't know." She looked away over Murgatroyd's shoulder into the distance, and very briefly, a troubled, faraway look came into her eye. Almost as if she were talking to herself, she murmured, "Honestly, there's almost too much that we don't know."

Another question popped into Murgatroyd's mind. "What if I say no? What if choose not to go on the Quest?"

Ann gazed coolly at him. "You will eventually adapt completely to the Known World and you'll cease to be an Oddfit."

As Murgatroyd pondered this, Ann spoke firmly. "Murgatroyd, it appears that you are beginning to have second thoughts. Which is fine. The decision is entirely yours to make and it's important that you think it through carefully.

"Make no mistake about it, the Quest will last all your life, and almost certainly will outlast your life, your generation, and many generations to come. I will also tell you now, for the sake of full disclosure, that the Quest can be a hazardous undertaking, especially if you're involved in the exploration side of it, which almost all Oddfit Questians are at one point or another. Embarking on the Quest is serious business, and it means that you'll be leaving your life for good. Even if you could come back to it, it would never be the same. But whatever may come of it, and whatever may become of you, there is one guarantee."

"What's that?"

Ann stopped shredding the grass.

"You will never regret it."

At that moment, the whole world went quiet. The only sounds Murgatroyd could hear were his own breathing, and the earth hurtling through the universe, and his own heart racing towards this wonderful and (dare he think it?) stupendous destiny.

Then he heard Ann's voice, and all the noise came back again. "I hope I have answered all your questions to your satisfaction."

"Yes," Murgatroyd replied in a daze. "Yes, I think so."

"Now I have a question to ask you. Murgatroyd, do you choose to set out on the Quest?"

Murgatroyd had the sensation of being in a very precarious position, as if he were floating very high above the ground and getting very airsick. Without a word, he lay down on his back in the grass to relieve the lightheadedness that had seized him. He attempted to digest the great mass of astonishing information that had just been set before him. So much to digest, and yet so little! Ann had disclosed so much, but there appeared to be so much more beyond the so much that she had disclosed that it seemed as if the past half hour's exchange had only made a tiny dent in it all. He didn't know what to think.

He continued to lie in the grass, hands over his eyes to shield them from the merciless sun, and could do nothing but feel overwhelmed and queasy.

"Murgatroyd."

At the sound of his name, he opened one eye and squinted through a crack in his fingers at the emerald eye that looked unflinchingly back at him.

Ann repeated her question. "Murgatroyd. Do you choose to set out on the Quest?"

Something extraordinarily stupendous is waiting for me.

Murgatroyd sat up. "Yes, I do."

For the first time since Murgatroyd had met her, Ann's face broke into a wide but short-lived grin.

"Excellent." Her features once again assumed their customary cucumberish coolness. "You will need to pack some things for the Quest. Bring a toothbrush and a clean change of underwear."

Murgatroyd waited. "That's it?"

"Yes."

"Erh. Can I borrow pen and paper?"

Ann fished around in her bag for the requested items and handed them to Murgatroyd, who wrote down carefully, "Bring one toothbrush and one underwear." When he had written this reminder, he carefully folded it in half and inserted it into his wallet.

"Are you done?" Ann asked.

"Yes," Murgatroyd answered.

"Then we'll meet back here this evening at seven o'clock."

"Okay, meet back here at seven o—" Murgatroyd realized what he was repeating. "Hah? For what?"

Ann frowned. "For what else? You did say you wanted to go on the Quest, didn't you?"

"But—but—" Murgatroyd stammered. "So soon?"

"Why not?"

"Erh. Erh." His mind raced through the things he had to do. "I—I have to report for work at four. And I have to give my boss notice. I have to tell my parents. I have to say goodbye to Kay Huat. I have . . . things to wrap up."

"'Things to wrap up'? You mean, you need more time?"

He nodded.

"Hmm. Interesting."

"Interesting?"

Ann frowned. "Yes. Very."

"Oh," Murgatroyd replied. Timidly, he asked, "So, is it . . . possible?"

"To have more time?"

"Erh. Yes?"

Ann pursed her lips and turned the matter over in her head. "It *should* be. How many days do you need?"

"Erh. I don't know." He tried to think frantically of a length of time that didn't seem unreasonably long, but long enough for him to figure out the logistics of leaving his entire life behind. "Five days?"

"Five days? You're certain?"

"Yes," he confirmed. He wasn't quite sure why he had chosen five, but there it was.

To his relief, Ann nodded. "All right then. You have five days to set your affairs in order. This Friday at seven p.m. sharp, I will meet you at the farthest end of Bedok Jetty in East Coast Park. Is that understood?"

Murgatroyd nodded. "Yes. Yes. Thank you. Thank you very much."

"Don't thank me, Murgatroyd." Ann stood up abruptly and brushed the shreds of grass off her dress. "I'm only the messenger. Goodbye."

"Wait, wait!" Murgatroyd cried, pulling out the paper and pen Ann had given him and hurriedly jotting down the details. "Okay. Friday, seven p.m., Bedok Jetty, East Coast Park. Is that correct?"

"It is," Ann said. She turned and began to walk away.

"Oh, you forgot your pen!" Murgatroyd called after her.

"Keep it," Ann yelled over her shoulder. "I saw you using it to pick your ears."

Murgatroyd was too astounded by what had just occurred to be embarrassed by this parting observation. He spent the rest of the afternoon in a state of complete shock, wandering about the Orchard Road area, bumping into shoppers and being apologetic. Despite his condition, he somehow managed to catch a bus and find his way to L'Abattoir, albeit one hour late, and proceeded about his work in an uncharacteristically incompetent manner. To thc amazement of his fellow waitstaff, the usually savvy, butler-esque Shwet Foo appeared to be doing an extended impression of a lumbering, brain-damaged water buffalo. Out of exasperation, they finally shut him up in the pantry with a glass of warm water, where he could do no more harm. (Or so they thought, until they found the floor strewn with loose potatoes and white sugar at the end of the night.) Occasionally, during the evening, the kitchen staff would hear an insistent little rapping on the pantry door accompanied by an equally insistent little voice saying that he had something very important to tell Shakti. But as the boss wasn't at the restaurant that night, they simply shrugged to each other and carried on with their work. When the last guest had left the restaurant, they changed Murgatroyd out of his waiter's uniform into his regular clothes, checked the restaurant records to find out his home address, made sure he had enough money for cab fare, and sent him home in a taxi.

CHAPTER 10

Murgatroyd's meeting with Ann had left him completely disoriented and dazed. Ann, on the other hand, had left the scene knowing exactly where she wanted to go. And she didn't have much time to get there.

Immediately after bidding Murgatroyd farewell, she headed to the nearby MRT subway station, caught a train, alighted two stops down the line at Dhoby Ghaut, and strode expertly through a series of winding underground passageways, following signs directing her to the Singapore History Museum. Her hurry was certainly strange—a visit to the museum is rarely accompanied by such a sense of urgency. But stranger still was the series of almost unnoticeable but unusual occurrences that accompanied her brisk progress through the corridors. Out of a leaky pipe in the wall trickled a small stream of water—water that congealed into a pool right where Ann was about to take her next step. She didn't even slow down as she stepped over the puddle and continued on her way. A man passing her in the opposite direction finished eating his banana and carelessly tossed the peel over his shoulder, right into Ann's path. Without batting an eyelid, Ann stepped over that too.

And she began to walk faster. It was a very good thing she'd chosen to wear comfortable shoes.

The lights illuminating the corridor suddenly went out, leaving everyone passing through it in pitch-black darkness . . . except for Ann, who whisked a small flashlight out of her bag and broke into a sprint for the stairwell leading upwards.

She made it to the surface and kept running. A crack of thunder sounded and it began to pour heavy rain. A powerful gust of wind struck an overhanging tree branch and sent it hurtling to the ground. It missed her only by a hair's breadth as she dodged nimbly out of the way. She glanced quickly to her left and right before dashing across the street, but somehow managed to overlook the red and white double-decker bus that was now speeding towards her. Reflexively, she sprang into the air and executed a double somersault, landing herself out of harm's way on the other side of the road.

She stopped running. Panting and soaked to the bone, she doubled over, clutching her knees for support. She looked up. From where she was standing, she could see the museum—its majestic colonial architecture, its gleaming whiteness, its solid rotunda capped with a stately tiled dome. At least that was what she imagined was concealed by the complex network of bamboo-pole scaffolding and netting surrounding the whole structure. It was closed for renovation.

Shit. (Ann rarely swore, but this seemed an appropriate occasion.)

Well, there's no time anyway, she sighed inwardly. *But oh, how I do miss a good museum.* That was her last thought in the Known World. On this visit, at least.

About a minute before Ann thought this thought, up in the stormy skies above, a cargo plane pilot had accidentally pressed a button opening the ramp to the cargo hold. Luckily enough, only one item slipped out before he managed to close the door: a large wooden crate. From the heavens it descended, accelerating towards the earth's surface, and crashed to the ground on the very spot where Ann had been standing right before she had vanished.

***

One of the worst feelings in the Worlds, Ann thought to herself, *is waking up in a new Territory with a splitting headache*—which always happened to her when she transferred too quickly.

Of course, it also didn't help when the first thing you heard was someone shouting at you.

"Are you mad?! What do you think you're doing?"

Ann kept her eye closed and adjusted the patch over her right eye-socket. It was damp from the rain. Her head hurt. A lot.

"Past tense. 'What *did* I think I *was* doing,'" she corrected the voice before opening her eye and promptly shutting it again in pain. The sun was shining a little too brightly in the Spain-Adroit Territory for her taste. "I was going to the museum. It was a stupid thing to do, I know. But I do miss them. That's the one problem with the More Known World: you can't have *really* good cultural history museums when the cultural history being documented is less than one generation old."

"And that's your measure of the More Known World's worth?" the One said admonishingly. "Museums?"

"Of course not," Ann sighed. "I just think it would be *nice*."

Transferring accurately and with precision was already difficult enough, but transferring quickly was extremely difficult, even for an experienced Questian like Ann. She felt grumpy, sore inside and out, and soggy from the downpour that had caught her by surprise in the Known World; though the sun here was already doing a pretty good job of drying her out. As the effects of her haste wore off, she began to get a better sense of herself in relation to her surroundings. Even with her eye shut, she knew that she was sprawled flat on her back in the middle of the One's laboratory. She'd been here many times before.

This Territory was one of the longer-established ones, and the One had chosen it for her abode; that is, if one could call it an abode. The clouds in the sky served as her ceiling, the desert horizon her walls, and the windswept sapphire sand her floor. Ann saw all too clearly in her mind's eye the scene of which she was now a part: the sun overhead, radiating a halogenish, ghostly light, unwavering in its constancy but gentle in its warmth; the undulating blue dunes stretching every which way as far as the eye could see; the ten enormous flat blocks of black granite surrounding her that served as laboratory counter space; and from the sound and direction of the One's voice, the One standing directly above her.

Ann opened her eye again, blinking fast to accustom herself to the light. Sure enough, there was the One hovering over her, but looking not as angry as Ann had envisioned her being from the sound of her voice. Her big brown eyes—far too large for such a small, wizened body—expressed nothing but concern. She held a conical beaker of pale pink goo in one hand, and the other she extended to her younger colleague. It was brown and gaunt, but strong, much like the rest of its owner. Ann lifted herself onto her elbows and grasped it, letting the One pull her to her feet. She had indeed landed smack dab amidst the counters, though happily enough, not on top of any of them. Most of them were covered with complicated glass apparatuses containing different coloured liquids at various stages of simmering, dripping, flowing, and evaporating, except for the one to their left, on which sat a bunch of bananas and a half-eaten bowl of brown rice—most likely, the One's lunch, or breakfast, or dinner.

From the deep pockets of the orange Bermuda shorts she was wearing, the One produced a small flashlight and began examining Ann's eye for signs of concussion. Ann immediately felt sorry for being so snappish.

In response to Ann softening, the One resumed her admonishments. "Quite frankly, Ann, that was stupid. It's been decades since

I've stepped foot in a museum myself, but that was cutting it awfully close. You were almost killed. An Oddfit of your experience can't stay in the Known World for more than, what? Four hours? What's your maximum limit now?"

"Four and a half hours," said Ann, wincing a bit as the One grabbed her eyelid, yanked it upwards, and examined the upper recesses of her eyeball. "Could you be more careful? It's the only one I have left."

The One switched off her flashlight, folded her arms, and raised a sceptical eyebrow. "Four and a half hours?" she repeated.

"Well," Ann admitted, "without triggering any reaction from the Known World *at all*, two hours and fifty-six minutes. But if one is alert and quick, four and a half hours is eminently do-able."

"And how long were you there this time?"

Ann mumbled something under her breath.

"I can't hear you when you mumble."

"Three hours. A little more."

"'Eminently doable,' eh?"

"It's all the exploring of new Territories I've been doing lately," Ann sighed. "How was I to know it would shorten my time by so much?"

The One spoke gently, but sternly. "Because that's the way it works, and you know it. The longer an Oddfit spends in the More Known World, the more severe the allergic reaction she induces in the Known World."

Since Ann had joined the Quest, the One was the closest thing to a parental figure she had. As a result, Ann felt freer to emote when around her. She pulled a sour face.

"Don't sulk, Ann. It's not consciously trying to punish you for exploring; it's merely reacting as any of our own bodies would to a bacteria or virus or any other foreign intruder in our systems. It sees you as a disease, so to speak. The Known World is merely protecting itself when it tries to exterminate you."

Ann didn't answer. In her logical fashion, the One concluded that she probably needed comforting words or something along those lines, but the One also knew that she wasn't very good at that sort of thing. Instead, she offered Ann the beaker of pink goo. "Yogurt?"

"What flavour?"

"Chocolate."

"No, thanks."

"Well, it's not very good anyway. It was an experiment," the One said. Pulling a lid from the pocket of her oversized lab coat, she covered the beaker and let it go, allowing gravity to embed it in the sand. In the absence of cupboards or drawers, she had devised this means of putting things away. "Don't be so glum. Would you rather not explore? Would you rather have it any other way?"

"No," Ann replied. "I wouldn't. And I know it's impossible and impossibly spoiled of me to want it, but sometimes, I wish I could have the best of both worlds. Literally. Like Yusuf did." She gave a great huff.

The One's spine seemed to stiffen a bit in response to Ann's words. "You know as well as I do that Yusuf was an anomaly," she replied coldly. "Why and how he was able to live in both Worlds without losing any of his Oddfit abilities or provoking any adverse reaction from the Known World remains a thorough mystery to us all." Turning her back, she began fiddling with the knobs on a machine that appeared to be made entirely out of small copper cogs.

Sensing the tension her remark had initiated, Ann changed the subject and brought up the actual reason for her visit: "I just came from my meeting with Murgatroyd Floyd."

"And how did it go?"

"Very well. He's agreed to join the Quest."

The One nodded approvingly. "Excellent. He'll come in tonight, then? Does he need a place to stay? He can sleep here on the sofa." She motioned to a slightly raised mound of blue sand to her right.

"Actually, he's requested five days to 'wrap things up.'"

"Five days?" the One asked.

Ann nodded. "Yes, I thought it rather strange as well. I would have thought his oddfittingness levels too high for that kind of hesitation, but he seemed very anxious about how to tell his parents, what he needed to take care before he left, that kind of thing. Is there something wrong?"

"No, no, not at all," the One said, looking as if she were worrying about something that had gone terribly wrong. Divergences from expectations tended to make her feel terribly intrigued and terribly fretful all at once. "It's just . . . strange, as you say. Individuals as oddfitting as he is don't hesitate once they find out who they are; they choose to leave immediately." As she mulled over Murgatroyd's situation further, she began to pace back and forth, ploughing a shallow trough in the sand as she did.

"Why *is* he still so oddfitting?" Ann asked. She'd been wondering about that since she'd been assigned to talk to Murgatroyd a week ago, but she hadn't had the chance to ask. "Shouldn't he have become a Sumfit some time ago?"

The One, still half lost in her own thoughts, nodded abstractedly. "To tell you the truth, when we found him mentioned in," she paused infinitesimally before bringing herself to say his name, "Yusuf's personal documents, I didn't have much hope at finding any oddfittingness left in him at all." She stopped pacing and began tapping her left foot contemplatively, sending up clouds of blue dust. "And when one imagines how oddfitting he must have been when he was born, before the adaptation process began . . . it's not just strange, it's extraordinary."

"Perhaps his attachment has something to do with how long the adaptation process has been going on?" Ann suggested. "We do usually find them when they're much younger. Twenty-five years really is a long time to spend in the Known World. It might have affected his sentiments anyway, however oddfitting he may still be."

"Well," the One reflected, "whatever the explanation, if he's still an Oddfit after twenty-five years, then five more days certainly won't do him any harm."

At these words, Ann started a bit. "But he *has* already spent more time in the More Known World than usual for an undiscovered Oddfit. Will the Known World . . ."

". . . try to exterminate him?" the One said, finishing Ann's thought. "No. It takes months of exposure to the More Known World for one to come anywhere close to being an irritant."

However, being the thorough person that she was, the One folded her arms and concentrated, performing an intensive analysis of Murgatroyd's situation in her head, just to make sure. Two minutes later she came to a conclusion: "He'll be just fine."

"Are you positive?" Ann asked, though she knew the answer. Once the One had made an informed decision, her thoughts were always final.

"Yes," the One responded. "It's a bit unusual, asking for more time, but his situation as a whole is a bit unusual." She chuckled to herself. "Odd even for an Oddfit! I'm looking forward to meeting him."

On that note, the One turned back to her experimental activities. Retrieving the beaker of pink goo from the floor, she uncapped it and poured the contents into a funnel sticking out of the copper-cog machine. Then she immersed the whole apparatus in what appeared to be a giant tank full of frozen fish heads. Ann knew from experience that her former mentor was a very focused being. When she turned her mind to her projects, it meant the end of all conversation. Nothing personal. Ann was feeling a little drained anyway, and lay down on the sofa to rest.

As she nestled herself into the warm sand, she began to feel drowsy. She found three matters drifting through her consciousness. The first had to do with the One's aversion to hearing or discussing anything to do with Yusuf. Ann had always known that the real reasons for Yusuf's retirement were far more complicated than the reasons Yusuf had publicly given at the time: that there had been deep differences in opinion between the One and Yusuf about the guiding ideals and principles of the Quest. The Other had stayed out of it all; he was in general so good-natured and indifferent about such things that he was genuinely puzzled by their arguments and even more puzzled by Yusuf's decision to return to the Known World. In his opinion, the best thing about the Quest *was* getting to explore new Territories.

The second matter was related to the first, if only tangentially: where the One had insisted that the discovery and documentation of the More Known World should be based purely on logic and reason, Yusuf had always argued that there was an inexplicable element to it all that simply could not be ignored. The One found Yusuf's "mysticism" horrifying. There was nothing, she maintained, that did not work according to set rules and laws; one just had to figure out what they were. Being closer to the One and being of a practical, logical, and unspiritual bent herself, Ann had always taken the One's approach to life. But in the past two years or so, Ann had begun to have her own doubts. There were so many things—features of the Known World and More Known World and of the individuals inhabiting both—that seemed to defy rules. Of course, it was probably due to the fact that they didn't know all the rules yet—that was part of what the Quest was about, after all. But increasingly, she couldn't help thinking that perhaps there was something ultimately inexplicable about all of this; that even when explanations were found, there would always be more to decipher, to unravel, to undo . . . like a knot. But not exactly. When one undid a knot, it didn't explain the knot; it just made the knot cease to exist.

Left to its own devices, Ann's mind had begun meandering more and more in these nonsensical mazes. Ann hadn't told the One about these thoughts. She knew the One would be furious, and perhaps devastated, for she looked upon Ann almost as her own child (though she would never admit it). Ann also had thought it prudent to keep to herself the fact that, before meeting Murgatroyd, she had wandered into a church partway through a sermon and sat there for a little while; not to listen, just to contemplate. She'd done it enough lately that one might even have called it a habit—popping into old church buildings for a few minutes whenever she had to make a visit to the Known World. It was the stained glass that drew her, she was sure.

The third matter drifting through Ann's mind had to do with the exceptional nature of Murgatroyd's oddfittingness—how much of it he must have possessed at birth and how it had managed to endure for so long. Then she thought back to the many strange things about Murgatroyd's life she had learned from reading his file. *Odd even for an Oddfit.* Before she dozed off, Ann made a mental note to check up on Murgatroyd sometime in the next few days.

CHAPTER 11

At seven on Monday morning, when Murgatroyd's eyes flew open at the sound of his alarm clock, he felt an unusual sensation. He wasn't quite sure how to describe it. It was a little fluttering sensation against the walls of his stomach, like when he was nervous. But it wasn't nervousness at all. It was much more pleasant. As he stretched out one arm to shut off the alarm clock and tucked the other arm behind his head, he tried to pinpoint exactly what it felt like.

It felt . . . it felt like whenever he had gone to the Tutti-Frutti Ice Cream Shop and Uncle Yusuf had stuck an extra paper parasol in his ice cream. From his recumbent position, he gazed with satisfaction at the long, colourful string of paper parasols that hung like Christmas tree trimming from his walls. He had kept every one of them. He felt another little flutter inside him. *What else did it feel like?* It felt like whenever he took the first bite of something his mother had made and found that it didn't taste funny. He could still remember how much he enjoyed the vanilla sponge cake she had made him for his thirteenth birthday, and how surprised he was that it had turned out delicious, even though he had accidentally mislabelled the salt and sugar containers when helping her reorganize the kitchen the day before.

It felt like all that, but magnified twenty times. In fact, he even felt like doing a little dance. And so he did: jumping up from his customary sleeping place on the wooden floor, he indulged himself in a short little jig.

After he had folded his blanket, which functioned also as a sleeping pad and pillow, depending on which one he felt like having on any given night, he put his hands on his hips and surveyed his bedroom. His mother had done the décor, and in keeping with the minimalist design she thought would best become the room, it was bare of furniture. And in keeping with the functionality she also wanted for the room, it doubled as storage space for four lightly used suitcases, a heap of empty mango crates, twelve cans of expired baked beans that his father was, for reasons unexplained, "saving for later," and three rusty umbrellas.

It was true that entire effect was somewhat marred by the many personal items belonging to Murgatroyd, which gave the space a cluttered feel: Murgatroyd's "bed," alarm clock, and blanket (aforementioned) took up two square metres of space in one corner; a stack of neatly folded clothes next to a little cardboard carton storing his socks and underwear took up another corner; and the paper parasol decorations (also aforementioned) took up space on the wall facing the window. It was also true that some features of the room could, perhaps, have used some improvement—the walls were a garish yellow-green hue, which Kay Huat, the one time he had visited, had termed "vomit," and the glass of the window, which otherwise would have looked out onto the picturesque trees of the nearby nature reserve, was always covered with a petroleum-jelly-like goop that reappeared each time Murgatroyd cleaned it off. But Murgatroyd was too accustomed to the colour of his walls to find them anything but charming, and his father said that the goop was most likely floating tree sap from the park, and that there was nothing to be done about it (though, mysteriously, his parents' bedroom windowpanes remained unsullied).

How many mornings had he surveyed his bedroom in exactly the same way he was doing now? And yet, how exceedingly happy he felt on this particular morning, more than any other morning he could remember! He felt again the irresistible urge to dance. He stooped down to glance at the clock again. It would have to be a short one; he had to make breakfast for his parents before they left for work.

Preparing breakfast was Murgatroyd's daily gift to his parents—his small way of saying, "Thank you" and "I love you" for all that they had done for him. The many, many, many loving and kind things they had done for him—so many of them that sometimes it was hard to remember any of them. But he was sure that there *were* many of them, and did his utmost to never forget their numerousness. Making breakfast was the very least he could do in return. Usually, it was nothing very elaborate. Some days it was only toast, butter, and jam; some days it was fried egg and sausage; and on days when he got up earlier than usual, he might take the bus to a nearby hawker centre and purchase a local-style breakfast for them from there—steamed buns, fried dough sticks, or perhaps chicken congee. But today was a special day. In five days, he was going to set off on an important adventure to explore parts unknown! This called for a celebration! He would make his parents banana crepes with powdered sugar. From scratch.

Murgatroyd trotted happily through the living room, past the dining area, and into the kitchen, humming as he went. After he had sliced the bananas and prepared the batter, he set them aside and sat down at the kitchen table to write a to-do list for the week:

Things To Do Before Friday 7 p.m.

1. *Tell Mum and Dad about Quest.*
2. *Tell Kay Huat about Quest.*
3. *Report for work. Quit job for Quest.*
4. *Buy new toothbrush for Quest.*

He tried very hard to think of any other things he needed to do. There wasn't anyone else that he needed to notify. He didn't need to close his bank account—his parents kept his earnings safe on his behalf. There was nothing else he needed to buy. That would have to do for now, he thought to himself as he heard the shower running in his parents' bathroom. Folding the list and putting it away in his pocket, Murgatroyd turned on the stove and began cooking.

Olivia Floyd stood in front of the closet mirror in her bedroom, assessing her appearance. She was wearing a red silk blouse she had bought a few days ago.

"James," she called to her husband, who was shaving in the bathroom.

"I can't hear you," he yelled back. "The electric razor's too loud."

"JAMES!" she repeated again.

"I CAN'T HEAR YOU," he yelled again.

"TURN THE BLOODY ELECTRIC RAZOR OFF!"

The razor stopped buzzing, and a half-shaven James stuck his head out from the bathroom door, looking peeved. "What *is* it?"

"Do you think this blouse looks good on me?"

James glared at her.

"What?" Olivia asked innocently.

"It makes you look your age." He disappeared back into the bathroom and the razor began buzzing again.

Olivia smiled. He had told a lie. Even though both of them were now in their early fifties, except for a little greyness in the hair and an extra wrinkle or two, they looked very much as they had when they were in their twenties. But then again, she had deserved the slight, since she had asked the question for the sole purpose of irritating him. And she had succeeded. There had been a time, of course, when it would have never occurred to her to intentionally irritate him at all—a time when they had adored each other without question or irony. A time when . . . oh, but it was so long ago now. Smoothing out the blouse, she put it out of her mind, and was adjusting her earrings when she caught a whiff of something unfamiliar in the air.

"James," she called to her husband.

"WHAT?!" he roared.

"Do you smell that?"

James and Olivia Floyd emerged from their room and entered the kitchen, dressed for work, but with a little sleepiness still lingering about their eyes. They were greeted by the warm, sweet smell of fresh crepes and the sight of their son slouching over the stove, cheerfully swivelling the skillet with his right hand and picking his ear with his left.

"Good morning!" he chirruped.

James and Olivia were confounded at their son's excessive and evident happiness.

"Oh! Well now," his father said, slowly regaining his composure. "Good morning, my boy! Smells good! What is it?"

"Banana crepes!" With a flourish worthy of any great chef, Murgatroyd dusted the crepes with powdered sugar and skipped past his parents to set them in the centre of the dining table.

He regarded them with satisfaction. "Eh! Not bad, what? Look like restaurant quality one!" Suddenly remembering how irritating his parents found the occasional heavy Singlish he used and tried to tone down whenever he was around them, he quickly shut his mouth. Casting his eyes downwards, he pulled his cup of Milo close to his chest and sat down.

James joined his son immediately and without a word began helping himself to three at once. Olivia, however, eyed her son with suspicion as she lowered herself into her chair. "Banana crepes! My, how *special*! What's the occasion?"

This was the moment that Murgatroyd had been waiting for. With every flip of every crepe, he had thought of exactly how he would tell them of his imminent departure. Would he be playfully evasive about it? Would he tell them outright, point-blank? How do you inform someone that on Friday you will be setting off on the most wonderful adventure of your entire life?

The moment had come! And yet, Murgatroyd found himself hesitant to let loose the announcement that was incubating in his consciousness, on the verge of being hatched into the great, wide world: *On Friday, I will be setting off on the most wonderful adventure of my entire life!*

Instead, he said, "Oh. Erh. Nothing. Nothing special. Just, erh, felt like it. Something different, lah."

He saw them grimace at the inadvertent "lah" and winced.

James and Olivia shook out the newspaper and divided the sections between them. Picking up their forks and knives, they began eating the crepes in silence. Silently was the manner in which his parents usually ate their breakfast. Murgatroyd thought about this as he reached for the saltshaker. His parents were not really "morning people," nor were they lively conversationalists. The love they displayed towards him and each other, he continued reflecting, was not a chatty sort of love. It was a quieter, deeper sort of love. A love that manifested itself in other ways, like the dinners they left out for him at night. And their concern about his posture, which prevented them from buying him a mattress, no matter how much he had pleaded with them as a child. And the way they were always trying to fix the broken water heater in his bathroom. ("I'm terribly sorry, my boy," his father would say whenever Murgatroyd brought the subject up. "We're really trying to get it fixed, we are. You'll have hot water someday!")

Murgatroyd was quite accustomed to the silence in which the three of them often passed the time. Yet today, for some reason, he felt uncomfortable with it. It felt unnatural. It felt strange. It even felt slightly hostile. He tried to make conversation.

"Erh. How do you like it?"

"Like what?" Olivia answered, dully.

"The crepes?"

"Oh. Oh yes. Very good," she mumbled, turning her attention once again to the business section of *The Straits Times*.

"Yes, very good," James echoed, brushing some sugar off an article he was trying to read about the health benefits of gingko nuts.

Murgatroyd basked in the warmth of this high praise and commenced tucking into his own portion with renewed energy, all the while thinking furiously about how best to break the news to them. Perhaps slowly and gently would be a better approach.

"Mum? Dad? May I ask you a question?"

His parents looked at each other with an unreadable expression on their faces. Then they looked at him.

"Yes?" Olivia asked.

"You don't mind, do you?" he said quickly, feeling foolish. "Erh. Am I bothering you?"

"What's the question?" James asked.

Murgatroyd felt nervous. "It's not that important. Only a little one."

"What's the question?" Olivia asked.

"Erh. Erh. Erh . . ."

"Murgatroyd!" James roared suddenly, slamming down his fork. "What in bloody hell is the bloody question?!"

In the silence that followed, they could hear the faint sound of Mandarin pop music wafting in through the wall from their neighbours' flat.

James burst into a loud, boisterous laugh. "Ha ha! Just joking, son! Just pulling your leg a little!"

Olivia joined in with a high-pitched giggle. "Oh, James! Ha ha! What a good joke! I really did think you were angry for a minute."

"Ha ha! Imagine me angry at Murgatroyd! Our one and only beloved son!"

"Who could imagine?"

"Our dear, sweet Murgatroyd!"

Feeling a little uneasy, Murgatroyd too joined in the laughter, which bordered almost on the hysterical. As it died down, Olivia leaned back in her chair and fanned herself with her napkin.

"Oh my. Oh my," she panted, catching her breath and dabbing the merry tears from the corners of her eyes. "Now, Murgatroyd. What was it that you wanted to ask?"

"Nothing. I mean, well . . . I was just wondering . . . what would you and Dad do if I left?"

At this, Olivia's back straightened, and James's fork stopped in midair en route to his mouth.

"Left?" James asked. "Where on earth for?"

"Erh. Nowhere. Just asking what if."

Olivia's eyes narrowed. "*Why* would you leave at all?"

"Erh. Erh. No reason. Just asking, lor. I mean, erh, just asking."

Olivia leaned forward. "So you're asking what your father and I would do if, one day, hypothetically, you were to decide to leave us for no reason?" She looked deep into her son's eyes. "Is *that* what you're asking, Murgatroyd?"

Murgatroyd rubbed the nape of his neck and looked down at his plate. He'd never noticed before how loudly the neighbours played their music.

"Erh. Yes?"

"Oh." Olivia suddenly and calmly resumed eating. "Is *that* all? Well, dear boy, let me tell you what we'd do." She wiped the corners of her mouth with her napkin. "We wouldn't."

Murgatroyd tried to understand. "Hah?"

"We simply wouldn't do—*couldn't* do—without you, dear boy."

"*Couldn't* do without you," James echoed, finishing the last of his breakfast.

"Not our own dear boy."

"Our own Murgatroyd."

"We'd be devastated if you left."

"Simply heartbroken."

"Couldn't go on."

"No, indeed."

"But," Olivia looked anxiously at Murgatroyd and placed her hand upon his. "You *wouldn't* ever leave us, would you now?"

Murgatroyd couldn't bring himself to lie. He remained silent. Luckily, the question was apparently a rhetorical one, for Olivia gave her son's hand a light but surprisingly painful squeeze.

"There's a good boy. Oh my! Look at the time! We'd better be getting to work." She wiped her hand with her napkin, rose from her chair, and quickly downed the remainder of her tea.

"Thanks again for the superb breakfast, dear boy," his father said, patting him on the cheek so vigorously, it almost felt like a series of small slaps. "Dear, *dear* boy."

The next thing Murgatroyd knew, the front door had slammed shut, and he was alone in the flat, still trying to take in everything that had just happened. He never suspected that his departure would upset them that much. How awfully inconsiderate of him. How could he not have thought of his parents, he wondered, racked with guilt. Maybe he would tell them tomorrow. He began clearing the dishes away. At least they would have one more day of blissful ignorance, until their thoughtless son broke their hearts. *Simply heartbroken*, they had said!

Then a new thought wriggled its way into his head. It went like this: *What if you didn't go on the Quest?*

Not go on the Quest? Wasn't it everything he'd ever hoped and dreamed for? *Not necessarily. What if Kay Huat was right? You know he always is. What if it is a scam? What if you've just been carried away by excitement?*

Applying the sponge to the dishes, Murgatroyd contemplated this horrible possibility for a while. All of it a lie? Everything that Ann said about the Quest, the Known and More Known Worlds, meeting at Bedok Jetty on Friday, even herself? And yet . . .

And yet he knew, somehow, in the very marrow of his soul, that it was all true. Try as he may to let his characteristic apprehensive and uncertain nature take over, he simply couldn't. He had to go on the Quest, he thought in desperation. He *had* to go. He would tell his parents tomorrow morning, he resolved. Tomorrow.

Murgatroyd tried to put the matter of his parents' grief and distress out of his head, at least for the meantime, and continued washing up. He was blissfully ignorant of the exchange his mother and father were having in the lift as they descended from the heights of the eleventh floor of their apartment building to the underground car park.

Facing forward and keeping his eyes fixed on the lighted numbers displayed above the lift doors, James addressed his wife. "Olivia."

"James," Olivia replied, watching the numbers as well.

"Our son was awfully cheerful this morning, don't you think?"

"Yes. Yes, he was, James."

"The crepes were delicious."

"And his cooking is usually only passable at best."

"He had a spring in his step."

"A twinkle in his eye."

"He was *happy*."

"Frightfully happy."

"I wonder why."

"And he spoke of leaving. *Leaving* us."

"Not a good sign."

"Perhaps he's fallen in love with someone. A girl."

"Fallen in love? But with who?"

"'But with 'whom,' Olivia."

"That's what I said, James."

"No, you said, 'But with who?' The grammatically correct version of that question would be, 'But with whom?'"

"Fine," Olivia snapped. "But with whom?"

"How the devil should I know?"

"Well, we can scare her off like we did with the others."

"Do you think it's a girl, though?" James mused. "In the past he's just been plain pathetic when he's been in love—listless and moony-eyed and pining away and all that."

Olivia frowned. "We'll just have to watch him carefully and find out, won't we?"

The lift, having reached its destination of car park level three, opened its doors, and husband and wife proceeded towards their blue Toyota sedan in silence. They slid into their car in silence. James adjusted the red fuzzy dice hanging from the rearview mirror in silence. Then he started the engine and backed out of their parking space in silence. They were driving to Olivia's office building to drop her off in silence. This was what they did every morning, excluding weekends and holidays. On weekends and holidays, they did other things together in silence.

As they merged onto the Pan-Island Expressway, Olivia yawned and watched the world speed past her window—the cars against the blurry backdrop of concrete expressway railing, green trees, and bright blue sky. It was so vivid that it seemed unreal—a toy world populated with play cars and plastic foliage against a watercolour background. Her fingers reached for the radio knob.

. . . Senior Minister Lee Kuan Yew hailed the youths' efforts at ecological conservation as 'admirable' and 'a shining example which he hoped other young Singaporeans would emulate.'

"In other news, in a speech given yesterday, Prime Minister Goh Chok Tong urged Singaporeans to be more innovative and imaginative in their respective sectors, stressing that it would take a combination of hard work and creativity for Singapore to achieve recognition and success on a global scale. PM Goh also said that he hoped the newly opened Imagination Centre in Bukit Batok would play an integral part in the 'Think For Yourself, Singapore!' campaign. SM Lee also expressed high hopes for the future imaginative spirit of Singapore.

"Traffic report: traffic on the PIE towards Tuas is rather slow this morn—"

James switched off the radio.

"Why did you do that?" Olivia asked, rousing herself.

"Because radio news is bloody irritating, that's why."

"Hmm. I find it soothing," she replied distantly, returning to her state of torpor, slumped against the headrest, gazing out the window.

But for one brief moment, before she recommenced thinking about nothing in particular, she asked herself the question that all dissatisfied married persons inevitably ask themselves, however frequently or infrequently: *How did it come to this? Didn't we once,* she thought as they exited the expressway and the scenery transformed into high-rise buildings, *enjoy each other's company*?

A moment is all the time the mind requires to bring the past floating up like the bloated corpses of goldfish. She recalled how she and James first met. It had been her first year in Singapore, her twenty-fourth year of life. Her law firm in London had offered her the opportunity to move and she had hungrily snatched it up. She had wanted something different. She had wanted to live abroad. She had wanted adventure and romance and a fresh green world with the dew still on it. And after only nine months, she was already bitterly disappointed. Her youthful and energetic imagination had not prepared her for interminable evenings and weekends spent with the same unvarying expat crowd in the same unvarying bars, restaurants, and clubs; for the insular and petty agendas of the expat associations and groups to which she felt pressured to belong; for acting in Christmas pantomimes and making sticky date puddings for Queen's Birthday parties; for perpetually wearing balloony white linens and leather sandals to cope with the "dreadful" heat. She didn't want to go "local," exactly—that world was still unfamiliar enough to her for her to recoil ever so slightly from it as all the others did, but she knew that she didn't want whatever *this* world was.

Olivia had been drowning her sorrows in chardonnay one Saturday evening with her "friends" at the bar in the Tanglin Club. And suddenly, across the room, she saw him. Young. Attractive. And different somehow.

He had seen her too. He walked up to her, and introduced himself. "I'm James Floyd. And you are . . ."

"Olivia Bentley," she had said faintly.

And then he had put his mouth close to her ear and whispered. "I've been watching you for the past half an hour, and I see that you detest them all." He drew back and gazed coolly into her eyes. "I do too."

"Yes, it's true," she had murmured. Was this all a dream? "I find them all repulsive."

"Let's get out of here," he had replied. They left and never looked back. They got engaged, then married. They became each other's lives, they became each other's worlds. Oh, what they might have been, if it weren't for . . .

Olivia let herself sink once again into a restful state of apathy and thought no more on the subject, letting herself be distracted instead by the droves of people on the pavement and at the intersections, hurrying to their respective places of work. The car glided, slowly, past Raffles Place MRT station just as its entrance belched up another swell of office workers, surging over the escalators and out into the light of day.

James and Olivia never discussed the state of their relationship, although they were each aware of it in the same way that one accustomed to the state of hunger is dimly conscious of a perpetual muted ache in one's belly—an ache which, over time, simply becomes an integral part of daily existence. They had certainly never dreamed that it would happen, that they would gradually disintegrate into this—this thorough indifference, and even mild revulsion, towards each other. It was as if some poison had seeped, slowly and steadily, into the marriage, corroding it from within, until there was nothing left but a hollow exterior, which itself was beginning to show faint signs of decomposition.

Yet mingled with this contemptuous apathy was precisely that feeling that Olivia felt even now—a stubborn devotion, sickly, but still clutching and clinging to the memory of a golden past when gaiety and love had blossomed so effortlessly between them. And there were moments yet when James and Olivia found it possible to regain a semblance of that past, as distorted as it was. This semblance was to be found in the mutual pleasure they derived from ruining their son's life.

What they had told Murgatroyd that morning, unfortunately, was the honest-to-God truth. James and Olivia couldn't do without their son. The deep satisfaction they felt whenever they peered into his bedroom on weekend mornings and saw him curled up on the hard wooden floor, bearing an uncanny resemblance to a mongrel dog. The low, evil laughter they shared as they concocted new, unappetizing dinners for him after finishing their own delicious meals of fettuccine Alfredo or lamb chops with mint sauce. The pride that swelled in their hearts whenever they had the opportunity to survey him from head to toe and take in their handiwork—the wretched and pathetic specimen of human that stood hunched humbly before them, eyes upraised to them in unquestioning love. These were the shared moments that offered them the likeness of younger, happier days. In a remarkably cruel twist of fate, their happiness together had become dependent upon the presence of the very thing (for they regarded their son as more of a thing than a person) they had first found irksome, then grew to despise. His departure would mean their destruction.

The car pulled up outside Olivia's office building. Olivia looked over at her husband and tried to muster up the energy to say goodbye. She even got as far as parting her lips, a farewell on the very tip of her tongue. But then again, she really couldn't be bothered. She left the car without a word and James drove away to his own place of work.

CHAPTER 12

To be fair, James and Olivia Floyd had never intended for things to turn out the way they did. They weren't what you would call truly "bad people," although they did have their flaws. Olivia couldn't be bothered to cover her mouth when she coughed in public. On principle, James showed up for all appointments at least ten minutes late. Both of them had great quantities of personal charm and often used it to take advantage of others, from getting tables at crowded restaurants without making reservations to getting coworkers to take on some of the extra work they didn't feel like doing. Both of them were very adept at lying, and took perverse pleasure in telling the most outrageous tales with the straightest of faces. Like many well-to-do expatriates working in Singapore, they often complained about the hot and humid weather and tended to think themselves entitled to a standard of living above that of the local populace. When visiting other people's houses, both took a perverse pleasure in using the last of the toilet paper and deliberately neglecting to replace it with a fresh roll. But they weren't *really* "bad people," and they most certainly had never dreamed that one day they would actively seek to make their one and only offspring utterly miserable.

In fact, the day that they found out they were to have a baby—that day so long ago in 1978—was perhaps one of the happiest days of their life together. That evening, as starry-eyed husband and wife, they sat together on the sofa and speculated what the baby would look like, what the baby's room would look like, what the baby's first words might be, what kind of food they should feed the baby, how to get the baby to be fluent in English, French, and Italian (no, English, French, and German) and so on and so forth. They babbled excitedly into the early hours of the dawn until, worn out like two children after some fantastical imaginary adventure, they fell asleep in each other's arms as the first sunbeams of the new day trickled in through the window, flooding the whole living room in fresh, clean light.

The following months found them in a perpetual state of euphoric anxiety. For the sake of the baby's health, Olivia gave up her afternoon cup of tea, her evening cup of coffee, and her morning martini. Fearing that Olivia might contract toxoplasmosis, James abandoned their pet cat by the side of the Singapore River. They spent several weekends in shopping centres searching for the best baby clothing and accessories that two expatriate executive salaries could buy: the softest blankies, the most luxurious cot, the most absorbent disposable nappies, the plushest plush toys, the loudest rattles—all imported, of course. The remainder of their free time they devoted to hunting for books about children and for children. They systematically visited all the Times and MPH bookstores on the island, and even paid a visit to the secondhand booksellers in Bras Basah Complex. And when they didn't find what they wanted, which was often, they demanded catalogues and placed orders from overseas.

From one of the first books they bought—*The Encyclopaedia of Baby Names*—they lovingly picked out names for their growing child. Peter, if it was a boy, Lauren, if it was a girl. Another book they bought—*Cultivating Genius: Secrets to Raising a Gifted Child*—advised them to read opera librettos to the baby during meals and, once the baby was born, to frequently mock the stupidity of others.

By the time Olivia's pregnancy had reached full term, they owned thirty-three books about babies, all housed on the top shelf of the three-tiered powder-blue bookcase they had bought for the baby's room. The bottom two shelves were stocked with children's books: an exquisite anthology of Hans Christian Andersen stories, two volumes of tales from the Brothers Grimm, the entire set of Beatrix Potter books, several Enid Blyton story collections, the complete works of Roald Dahl, and at least five dozen miscellaneous breathtakingly illustrated, award-winning picture books.

The colour of the bookcase matched everything else in the room. "To hell with things gender neutral," Olivia had proclaimed when they found out the baby was to be a boy. She decided on a nautical theme for Peter's room, replete with sailcloth curtains, a mural of a sunny seascape adorning the walls, colourful semaphore flags bedecking the crib, and a hanging mobile with plush toy pirates that played the song "What Shall We Do with the Drunken Sailor?"

"Perhaps he'll become a naval officer. Peter's a fine name for an admiral, don't you think?" James said jokingly, putting away a newly acquired pair of booties in little Peter's dresser.

"Ahoy there, matey. What do you think of that?" Olivia asked her proudly swelling stomach, playfully cocking her head to one side to hear little Peter's answer.

To their disappointment, Peter didn't even answer with a timely kick against the wall of his mother's uterus.

Olivia's water broke during a business lunch with one of her clients, and she was rushed to Mount Elizabeth Hospital in a taxi. She gave birth six hours later to a healthy, screaming baby boy. "It's Peter," James whispered into his wife's ear, enthralled by the infant nestled in her arms, "A wonderful name for an absolutely wonderful boy."

"Yes, it is. Wonderful." Olivia whispered back. She felt utterly exhausted and completely at peace.

Just then, Peter began to cry and wouldn't stop for twenty minutes.

Two young female nurses, loitering in the hallway, raised their eyebrows at each other.

"He can really cry one, hor?"

"So young, already acting like *ang moh*: complaining all the time," the other one giggled.

"Oi. We're *ang moh*, not deaf," James's irritated voice sounded from the room.

Bursting into even more laughter, the nurses scurried away down the corridor.

For the rest of the day, James found himself in a peevish mood.

"Oh, James, don't mind them. You're becoming a cantankerous old fuddy-duddy before your time," Olivia said in a gently teasing manner. James smiled and attempted to forget the whole thing, and yet his irritation still lingered on. And most irritating of all was the faint awareness that he wasn't irritated at the nurses so much as at his very own newborn son.

Of course that's perfectly ridiculous, he thought, waving away the idea as one waves away plumes of cigarette smoke. How in heaven's name could I be irritated at my own son?

Yet he was. And in the ensuing weeks and months, he continued to be irritated at his son. James cringed inwardly at whatever sound the baby made, whether it was a cry of distress or a gurgle of happiness. As James watched the baby sleeping serenely in the cot, he felt inexplicably annoyed. And even as James held the baby close to his chest and watched the tiny, delicate fingers pluck at his shirt buttons, the fascinated blue eyes twinkle in delight, the toothless mouth gape open in a gummy, drooling smile, James felt nothing but profound disgust. And he didn't know why. The baby was as cute as a baby could be. And James had been more than prepared for all the "dirty" aspects of parenting—the soiled nappies; the vomiting and spit-up; the runny noses; the disgusting, scabby cradle cap; and so on. He briefly wondered whether it was all an unconscious manifestation of doubt as to whether he was indeed the child's father, but after five minutes, he decided that such suspicions were absurd.

Unable to come up with any reasonable cause for disliking his own son, James found himself plagued with a constant and gnawing guilt. He'd heard theories of fathers who resented newborn babies for taking up all of their mothers' time and attention—time and attention that would once have been lavished upon their beloved husbands. *That might be the reason*, he thought, inwardly congratulating himself for such an accurate self-diagnosis of his psychological state. He was unconsciously jealous of little Peter for taking Olivia's attention away from himself. Of course, he didn't really *feel* like that was the case. But ah! That was the problem with the unconscious: you weren't really conscious of such things. But now that he had discovered the problem, wasn't he conscious of it already? And didn't he feel consciously that he didn't feel jealous of Peter? Well obviously then, he wasn't truly conscious of his jealousy—he was still in denial, and his pettiness still remained, lurking in the deep dark interior of his mind. How would he go about dealing with this? Perhaps he should go for therapy? No, that was silly, he thought proudly. He didn't need therapy. He would deal with this himself. And there was poor Olivia to think of. The last thing she needed to deal with in addition to caring for her newborn child was the worry that her husband felt (albeit unconsciously) neglected and resentful.

So the guilt gnawed on. It nipped at the toes of his conscience when he came back from work and kissed his radiant wife and gurgling baby boy a good evening. He felt it nibbling at his stomach, which turned every time he picked up his baby boy and tossed him high into the air. And he felt it chewing away at the edges of his heart on nights when he stood in the doorway of the baby's room, gazing at his Olivia under the soft glow of lamplight as she sat in a rocking chair, nursing the baby at her breast and softly humming lullabies.

"Oh, James, aren't you ever so happy?" Olivia would ask—rhetorically, of course—shifting her adoring maternal gaze from the suckling baby to her husband who stood in the doorway, hands in pockets, to all appearances, the very picture of paternal ease. James would smile—a smile that answered, "Of course I'm happy," and amble away to another part of the flat to contemplate his shame.

But most people can't hide their feelings forever, no matter how heroically they may try. Like a small air bubble escaping the lips of a drowning man or woman, the sentiment rises to the surface and, silently and unostentatiously, explodes.

For some, it takes years. James couldn't wait years. It was only a matter of months before he revealed his true sentiments about their child.

"Oh, James, aren't you ever so happy?" Olivia asked him one night (rhetorically, of course) as he stood casually slouched in the doorway, reading spectacles tucked into the front pocket of his button-down shirt, hands deep in the pockets of his khaki trousers. But as she looked up from the nursing infant she held in her arms, she saw a change come over his entire demeanour. He looked haggard and weary. He withdrew his hands from his pockets and clenched them in frustration before burying his face in his palms with a loud sigh. Thrusting them again into his pockets, he began to pace in small circles, his eyes fixed on the floor. Olivia watched her husband's movements with the intensity of concentration one applies to watching every movement, every gesture of a lone actor onstage about to deliver his soliloquy. Abruptly, he turned towards her and the baby, and stood looming over them, blocking the light overhead, enshrouding them in his shadow. In his face, Olivia couldn't help but detect a faint trace of something dangerous, something menacing. She shrank down in her chair, uncertain of what to expect.

"James?" Olivia asked in a small, frightened voice. She lowered the baby from her breast.

Her husband sank to his knees, gripping the edge of her rocking chair, wild anxiety in his eyes. He answered her rhetorical question.

"I'm not happy, Olivia," he whispered hoarsely. "I'm not happy."

Those words of desperation and confusion echoed in the stillness of the room as Olivia silently absorbed the significance of these words.

She gazed sadly into her husband's eyes. "Oh, James. Why didn't you tell me?"

James stood up and began pacing around in an agitated manner. "Well, I—I didn't want to worry you. I'm being silly. I don't know why. I'm sorry, Olivia. I'm sorry. I—"

Olivia interrupted him, "But James. I'm not happy either."

James stopped midpace and stared at his wife. "What?"

Olivia looked around cautiously, as if she feared someone might overhear her. She gestured for James to come close, and then whispered in his ear something he had never suspected for a moment. "To tell you the truth, I find our son rather a nuisance."

And with its usual impeccable sense of timing, the infant in her arms began to cry.

After Olivia finished nursing the baby and put him to sleep in the crib, James fixed them both some hot chocolate and biscuits, and they adjourned to the living room sofa to have their most heartfelt and truthful discussion since the birth of Peter. And in the course of that discussion, they discovered that both of them felt little Peter to be inexplicably irritating in almost every respect.

"Even his cute little baby button nose. I can't stand it," Olivia confessed.

James nodded vigorously, "And his little baby gurgles. They disgust me. Darling, he's adorable . . . I suppose. But he disgusts me."

"James, why do we feel this way? What's wrong with us? Even the worst parents love their children. Don't they?"

It did indeed seem that, for the Floyd family, something had gone deeply, terribly, and horribly awry. It has been conjectured that babies appear cute to their parents in order to ensure their survival. Ordinarily distasteful chores—the changing of soiled nappies, the wiping of bottoms and runny noses, the waking up every other hour in the middle of the night to the sound of someone screaming at the top of his or her lungs—are all dutifully and doggedly endured by new mothers and fathers enamoured with their miniature human beings. Thus, small children manage to procure for themselves comfortable living conditions replete with doting and servile relatives, succeeding where the physically repellent elderly often fail.

Under normal circumstances, little Peter Floyd, a baby certainly not lacking in cuteness, would have been the unrivalled object of his parents' affections, the centre of their universe, the apple of their eyes, the light of their lives, the plum in their pudding, and so on and so forth. Yet, Peter Floyd had been unlucky enough to have been the fruit of two pairs of loins that remained inalterably immune to his infantile charms. In fact, James and Olivia were worse than indifferent. They were downright annoyed.

"We can't help it, can we?" James asked, biting into a gingersnap.

Olivia nodded. "I don't think we can."

"Is it really our fault?"

"We've tried our best."

"We really have."

Olivia sighed. "He's just so—"

"—irritating," James finished. Hearing the rumblings of thunder in the distance, he moved towards the balcony window and peered outside at the rain, which had just started to fall.

"If it were only the nappy changing or the crying. Then a nanny would solve all our problems."

"But it's not all that. It's *him.*" James sighed. "He's just so—"

"—irritating," Olivia finished. She rose from the sofa and took her husband's hand. "Oh, James. What are we to do? I'm so unhappy."

He squeezed her hand sadly, in return. "So am I, dear. So am I."

They stood like that for a few moments, the both of them, clinging to each other, frightened at what they had gotten themselves into. The lights inside their apartment turned the sliding glass doors leading out to their balcony into a mirror; in it they saw themselves dimly reflected against the backdrop of the rainy night sky outside. They saw a pair of sleepless, hopeless human beings facing a lifetime of unhappiness and lovelessness, of going through the motions of happy family life, all the while knowing it to be nothing but a farce. Under the constant strain of dislike for the third member of their family, their own relationship would inevitably suffer. But getting rid of their son was simply out of the question. After all, they weren't monsters.

"A child simply isn't a cat. You can't just leave it by the river," James thought out loud.

Olivia agreed. "No, we have to face up to this. It's our own bloody fault. He's our responsibility. He may be irritating, but he can't help it."

A loud crack of thunder shook the windowpanes, and a shrill wail could be heard from Peter's room. James raised an eyebrow. "Are we sure about that now?"

She sighed. "I'll be right back."

James grabbed her wrist. "Wait."

"Peter's crying."

"I know." He looked her straight in the eye and for the first time in a long time, his mouth widened in a diabolically roguish grin.

"James?"

"Oh, we have to take care of him, all right. We *are* his parents, after all." And here, James leaned conspiratorially towards his wife. "But who says that we can't have some fun while doing it?"

Olivia frowned. "What are you saying?"

"It'll be like a game. How much can we get away with without him suspecting? Without *anyone* suspecting?"

She began to understand, and a sinister smile spread across her own face. "We'll be the very model of perfect parenthood."

"He'll never know we hate him."

"*No one* will ever know."

"Do you honestly think we can get away with it?"

"Why not?" Flushed with excitement, James pressed his wife's two hands fervently in his own. "To all appearances, our conduct will be without fault."

Olivia giggled. "Of course! He's our pride and joy! Can we help it if . . ." she thought for a moment before inspiration struck. "If we accidentally dress him in girls' clothes?"

"Or . . . forget to pick him up from school from time to time?"

"Or misinform him about the location of Peru?"

"Or shrink all his trousers in the wash?"

"And . . ." Olivia turned her eyes towards the room from which little Peter's insistent bawling could still be heard. "And can we help it if we can't hear the baby crying?"

"The rain is awfully loud, don't you think?"

"I can't hear anything, can you?"

"Hear what?"

"Pardon?"

Laughing uncontrollably, they collapsed in each other's arms. It was the first time they had really, truly laughed together since the baby had been born, and the tears of mirth that ran down their cheeks were the expression of their tremendous relief that the magic in their relationship had been restored, albeit at the cost of a human sacrifice: the price of their own happiness was to be the happiness of their unwitting son. But then again, they never really liked him very much to begin with, however appealing they had found the *idea* of him prior to his actual arrival on the scene. It was a sad situation, but it couldn't be helped. Their imaginations running wild with ingenious schemes and tragicomic scenarios, husband and wife confabulated together about how to turn their son's life into a living hell. And what better way to usher in this turning point in their relationship with little Peter than a bestowal of a new name?

They brought out *The Encyclopaedia of Baby Names*—the very first baby book they had bought after finding out the happy news—and as the storm howled and bellowed outside, and as their child howled and bellowed inside, they searched through page after page for a suitably awful name.

"What about a girl's name?" Olivia suggested. "How about Bertha?"

"A girl's name is too obvious. Remember, *no one* must know."

They considered Alf and Archibald, Billy-Bob and Bingham.

"How about Cuthbert?" James asked. "That ought to get him at least two beatings a week at school."

"What's wrong with Cuthbert? I rather like it," Olivia answered.

It was promptly dismissed as a possibility.

They paused over Dempster and hemmed and hawed over Habakkuk and Humbert. They lingered for a long time over Lingonburton (by which James was particularly repulsed, making it a very attractive option.) The *Encyclopaedia* was indeed a comprehensive and massive tome, and page after page, entry after entry, they scrutinized and deliberated upon late into the night until they could barely keep their eyes open. They were just about to call it a night and start on the second half of the alphabet the next evening when, all of a sudden, they found it.

"Murgatroyd," Olivia gasped.

A sharp crack of thunder split the night. But the couple was too enraptured by the name before their eyes, mesmerized by its exquisite and complex monstrosity.

"It's perfect," she whispered.

"What does it mean?"

"It says, 'Murgatroyd. From surname. Meaning unknown.'"

James looked up from the book into his wife's eyes and smiled. "And he shall be called Murgatroyd."

"So let it be done," Olivia murmured back.

On that terrible night, at that terrible moment, their lips met in a long, passionate kiss. And on that terrible night, the fate of little Murgatroyd Floyd was sealed.

CHAPTER 13

Murgatroyd sat on the bus, heading to work. He was picking his ear with his left pinkie, and in his right hand he held a tattered old photo he always carried around in his wallet. It was of his parents and him, taken on a trip to the Singapore Zoological Gardens when he was four years old. In the photo, his mother and father were dangling him playfully near the hyena enclosure. It really was astonishing how little his parents had aged in the past twenty or so years: they still looked almost as young as they did in the picture. Again, he felt a little guilty about leaving them, but they were more than capable of taking care of themselves. And he was grown up, after all. He couldn't stay with them forever, could he? Putting the photo back into his wallet, he turned to the little plastic bag he had placed on the seat next to him. He smiled. Murgatroyd had originally intended to attend to the items on his to-do list in strict numerical order, leaving the purchase of a beautiful brand-new toothbrush for the Quest for the very end—as a sort of reward for completing the list. But because of his failure to accomplish the first item, Murgatroyd figured that the order of the tasks really didn't matter anymore. After washing the dishes, making the beds, and sweeping the floors, he had caught the bus to the nearest Watson's Pharmacy, where he had spent two hours in the dental hygiene section.

The cashier—a sixty-year-old woman accustomed to spending most of her Mondays leisurely reading magazines—found herself interrupted several times by a young Caucasian man who would place a toothbrush on the counter, take out his wallet to pay, then suddenly change his mind and run back to exchange the toothbrush for another one.

"How come take so long?" she asked with a scowl on her face as he placed a toothbrush on the counter with an air of finality that she hoped meant he wouldn't change his mind yet again. "Never buy toothbrush before, is it?"

"No lah, Auntie," Murgatroyd grinned. "This is very special occasion toothbrush!"

Quickly recovering from her shock at hearing his accent, she replied sarcastically, "Huh! Special occasion toothbrush! You sure you don't need to buy special occasion toothpaste also?"

This thought had never occurred to Murgatroyd. Ann had told him only to bring a toothbrush and a clean change of underwear. But wouldn't he need toothpaste as well? Did Ann forget to mention it, or should he follow her instructions exactly? Would toothpaste be provided in the More Known World? He debated briefly whether he should call Ann to ask about toothpaste, but it seemed a rather silly and inconsequential question.

"Erh. Sorry, Auntie, be right back," he said, snatching up the toothbrush. Much to her horror, he trotted back to the dental hygiene aisle to contemplate whether he should purchase toothpaste or not, and which kind he should purchase if he did.

By the time Murgatroyd emerged from the pharmacy, toothbrush and toothpaste successfully purchased (he would decide whether or not to bring the toothpaste later), he only had fifteen minutes to get to work. And he had to wait ten minutes for the bus to arrive.

"Hey, Shwet Foo," Ahmad, one of his coworkers, greeted him as he opened the door of the restaurant for Murgatroyd. "How come so late, man?"

"Where got 'so late,' meh? Only ten minutes late, what!" Murgatroyd returned sheepishly, using his sleeve to wipe the perspiration from his brow, accumulated during his mad sprint from the bus stop to the restaurant.

"Emergency pharmacy trip?" Ahmad asked, observing the green plastic bag.

"Erh. Needed a toothbrush."

"Your first toothbrush, eh? That explains a lot!" Ahmad pinched his nose, made a face, then roared with laughter. "I just kidding one! Relax, lor. Boss not here yet, or else she slaughter you now and *makan* you for dinner." Ahmad's grin broadened. "Maybe she will *makan* you anyway after she hear about you being so blur last night."

Murgatroyd's eyes widened in horror at what little he remembered of last night. It consisted of a lot of bumping into things and indignant yelps, followed by a long period of time spent in a small pitch-black room.

"Erh . . . erh . . . erh . . ." he stammered nervously, a crimson flush spreading outward from his cheeks to the tips of his ears.

"I just kidding again!" Ahmad patted Murgatroyd on the back. "Don't worry, Shwet Foo. We all won't say anything, okay?"

"Erh. Thanks," muttered Murgatroyd, and slinked off to the back office to change. As he pushed open the heavy metal kitchen door, he was greeted with gales of laughter and good-natured mockery.

Teasing the shy and easily embarrassed Murgatroyd had become part of working life at the restaurant. The waitstaff of L'Abattoir regarded their little Shwet Foo as one might a younger, naive cousin—the kind whose back seems particularly suited for a "kick me" sign, and whose buttocks seem particularly suited for the surreptitiously placed whoopee cushion. But the jokes and teasing would only occur at the times surrounding his arrival and departure from the restaurant, for the very instant Murgatroyd put on his patent leather shoes, knotted his bow tie, slicked down his hair, and donned the black jacket, he underwent a complete metamorphosis into another being entirely—a being endowed with superhuman table-waiting powers; a being whose movements and words bespoke deference and authority, humility and capability, all at the same time; a being whom even the head waiter treated with special care and respect. And of course, there was the fact that he was Shakti's pride and joy. While she treated the other staff in what she believed to be an authoritative, strictly business manner (the staff, on the other hand, believed she treated them as if they were idiot slaves), Murgatroyd brought out the maternal in her. This situation would have undoubtedly resulted in jealousy and resentment on the part of Murgatroyd's coworkers, except for the fact that being the object of Shakti's motherly affection seemed to be far more a curse than a blessing.

Parenthood doesn't suit all men and women, and their children find that childhood suits them not at all. Shakti Vithani and her husband tried their best at the whole business, but one would have had to be extremely generous if not downright delusory to call their parenting skills "satisfactory," much less "good." If interviewed, the Vithani children—a girl aged twenty-five and a boy aged twenty-eight—might have called their father "too laid back" and "a bit inattentive." What they really would have meant was that he was completely indifferent and downright negligent—which he was. He had the terrible habit of forgetting that he had fathered any children at all. Whenever the family had gone to the cinema or taken a trip to the zoo, he would purchase two adult tickets from the ticket booth, only registering the existence of his offspring when he felt his wife tugging at his elbow, patiently informing him that his son and daughter were being denied entry. Whenever the family had gone out for dinner, their father would calmly ask for a table for two. If Mr. Vithani was in charge of booking hotels for a holiday, he would reserve one hotel room with a king-sized bed, romantically strewn with rose petals, and an evening champagne and strawberries service. Still, the Vithani children were inclined to be forgiving towards their father's inability to recognize their existence. Eventually, they gave up being upset about it and moved on.

However, if interviewed about their mother, they might not have been so inclined towards gracious exoneration. In fact, if interviewed, they might have called their mother several things considered quite unpublishable. Which was a shame. Shakti did have the best of intentions.

As if to compensate for her husband's obliviousness with regard to their children, Shakti had almost smothered her son and daughter to death—quite literally one time when they had gone on a ski trip to New Zealand. Piling blanket upon pillow upon blanket upon pillow over them, Shakti wanted to be sure they would be warm enough as they slept. Luckily, the eldest, though weak from lack of oxygen, managed to pull himself and his unconscious sister out from under the suffocating heap of linens and goose down before it was lights out for good. At home, Shakti had gone out of her way to see to every possible need that didn't need seeing to, and demanded, in return for her unwanted efforts, their boundless love, gratitude, amicability, and deference. She would ask them if they felt like having chocolate cake from the famous Death by Chocolate bakery on the other side of the island. They would say, "No." She would promptly get in her car and drive the entire length of the island (about forty minutes) to buy them chocolate cake, return home, and serve them each a thick slice with ice cream on the side. They would refuse it. She would call them ungrateful, and tearfully retire to the adjoining room where she would lament loudly in a voice that carried through the whole house about how she was being punished for simply loving her two children and how she just wanted to make them happy.

When the time had come for each of them to go off to university, she had taken great pains to secure each of them admission at various overseas institutions through months and months of shameless networking, calling in favours, and monetary donations. They each, in turn, declined to go to the universities Shakti had picked for them, and instead attended universities of their own choosing—ones they'd been admitted to on their own merits. Both times, Shakti had spent a month in a prolonged fit of fury and tears at the child's wilful refusal of her "gift" and the child's supposed "hostility" towards her.

Life with their father and mother meant a constant alternation between two extremes. With their father, they were nonexistent. With their mother, they were subjected to an exhausting amount of unnecessary melodrama. Given the schizophrenic environment, it was perhaps inevitable that they would either run amok or run away, which is exactly what they did, respectively. The Vithani son dutifully returned to work in Singapore and live with his parents after attending university in Melbourne. One morning, two and a half months after his return, he calmly entered his office, calmly sat down at his desk, calmly pulled out a stainless-steel letter opener from a drawer, and then calmly flew into a frenzy, stabbing one coworker three times in the belly and his boss four times in the arm before he hurled himself through the window and onto the street four storeys below. Miraculously, he survived, as did his victims, and he was now in a mental institution.

It was in all the papers.

The younger Vithani child, who studied at a university in the United States, chose stealth over attempted murder-suicide. She disappeared immediately after her graduation ceremony, leaving behind a dormitory room full of possessions and a confused mother alone at the graduation reception. (Mr. Vithani had accompanied his wife to the States, supposedly to attend the graduation as well, but by the time they had checked in, he had forgotten all about it. Early the next morning, he had embarked on a sightseeing tour of the area, and by the time his wife called to remind him that first, he had a daughter, and that second, she was graduating at that very moment, where in bloody hell was he, it was too late for him to make it now, never mind.) Shakti never saw or heard from her youngest again. It was rumoured that a friend of a friend of a second cousin of Shakti's husband had thought he had caught a glimpse of an Indian woman who looked a great deal like Shakti's youngest daughter while he was passing through a small town in the Ozark Mountains. She was working at a hunting equipment store.

The maternal affection Shakti lavished on Murgatroyd was not quite the sort she had lavished on her flesh and blood. She was utterly unconcerned about the affairs of Murgatroyd's private life, past, present, and future. Nor did she concern herself with his welfare, as evinced by the fact that, despite his being perhaps the finest waiter at L'Abattoir, she had no qualms about paying him significantly less than the most novice waiters in her employ. Towards him, maternal affection took the form of fierce pride in what he had become—what she had made him—and fierce possessiveness, the kind a spoilt little girl might exhibit for her favourite rhinestone tiara. Shakti was immensely eager to show off her protégé to anyone in the restaurant with whom she had managed to strike up a conversation.

"Shwet Foo! Come here," Shakti would beckon, standing near, say, a table of four boisterous Australians on vacation who, though they had just started on their appetizers, had already had a good deal too much to drink.

Murgatroyd would dutifully comply.

"Shwet Foo, these are the Pursers, and these are the Sedleys. They're all newlyweds! They're on a joint honeymoon!"

Murgatroyd would bow slightly and ask them if they were enjoying their dinner.

"Cawr!" Mr. Purser would say, spewing little crumbs of Roquefort cheese all over the table. "How'd you get him to talk like that? He's got an accent, doesn't he? He talks like one of them!"

"Where's he from, then? He looks like one of us!"

Shakti would beam and tell them of the day when Shwet Foo appeared at her office for an interview: her initial surprise at his whiteness, her greater surprise at his accent, the pitiful way in which he conducted himself, plus a few embellishments of her own, such as how he had been able to take only a few steps at a time because he had been incapable of breathing and walking simultaneously.

"Darlings, you should have *seen* him. Completely hopeless! Unkempt, uncultured, and with a hunch in his back that could rival Quasimodo's." (Shakti would refrain from mentioning how her Shwet Foo remained thoroughly unkempt, uncultured, and hunchbacked when he wasn't at work.) "It took months and *months* of training to get him how you see him now. He's the best damn waiter here! If there were a contest, I'd bet he'd win for being the best damn waiter in Singapore! *Months and months* it took!" Here, she would point at her own person with an immaculately manicured fingernail. "*I* trained him personally!"

At this point, the diners might exchange some harmless banter with him, inquire about his origins and education, ask if he was a football fan, and so on—just to make certain that the local accent combined with the ultradignified mien were "the real thing." Murgatroyd would reply respectfully and concisely. At this point, Shakti's face would be glowing like a newly changed light bulb.

"Brilliant!" the diners would exclaim.

"Now, now. It took a lot of training to whip this one into shape," Shakti would say modestly. "Well, my dear. You'd better get back to work." She would pat him on the head or the shoulder as one might a well-trained dog, but with his bearing, it was as if Shakti had dared to coochie-coo Sir Laurence Olivier on the chin. The company would gasp. There would be a moment of suspense. Then Murgatroyd would smile and they would give a sigh of relief. He would bow again to the company. He would glide away to attend to one of his tables. It was a familiar routine.

Tonight, however, it would be Murgatroyd who would seek Shakti out, albeit with much apprehension. As he did up his bow tie, he realized that he still hadn't quite figured out how he would deliver the news of his resignation and was quite frightened of what her reaction might be. Actually, he knew what her reaction would be. She would be angry—angry at the prospect of losing her best waiter at less than two weeks' notice. Angry at his inadequate explanation—how do you tell someone you're quitting your job to embark on a quest to explore unknown territories at the invitation of a strange one-eyed woman? And, most likely, she would be angry at his ingratitude. Shakti had given him not only a job, but also months of personal training. He would have to be careful, he thought, as he took the black jacket off its coat hanger and brushed the lint off its lapels.

As Murgatroyd slipped on the jacket, he felt the familiar surge of authority and confidence filling his veins. His spine straightened, his shoulders squared, his motions became surer, and he felt certain that he could effectively communicate to Shakti what he wanted to say in a precise yet respectful manner. Airily dismissing the exceptional clumsiness of last night from his mind, he glided into the dining area where they would all be briefed about the special dishes of the evening and the guests who would be dining that night—the regulars who were coming, which tables they would be seated at, food allergies and preferences, and so on. The restaurant officially opened for dinner at five thirty, but the waitstaff and kitchen had to be ready and standing by at five fifteen, just in case a guest showed up early, which rarely happened. However, today was exceptional, and at 5:15 p.m. sharp, they admitted a very nervous young woman who (she told the waitress pouring water into her glass) was meeting someone for a first date, and hadn't wanted to risk being late. She occupied her time by humming, darting her eyes towards the entrance every now and then, and drumming her fingers on the table.

Closer to five thirty, more guests began to trickle in, including a nervous young man who turned out to be the nervous young woman's dinner companion. By six, the dining room was half full, with the area immediately surrounding the arena completely filled by glamorous-looking types who preferred to eat dinner at the fashionably later time of eight or nine, but had made the requisite sacrifice in order to dine in the restaurant at all.

As Murgatroyd seated his first table of the evening, he glimpsed Shakti entering the restaurant out of the corner of his eye. As usual, she seated herself, ordered her glass of Coca-Cola Light, and called the headwaiter over for an update on how matters stood for the evening. *Tonight's the night*, Murgatroyd thought to himself, handing a menu to each of his guests. And yet, for some reason, he felt no inclination to do anything, to change anything. No inclination to break the news to Shakti, to quit his job, to go on the Quest.

"May I inform you of some of the specials the chef has prepared this evening?" That was his own voice he was hearing, addressing the guests seated at the table before him. As he did so, he found his eyes wandering, surveying the world around him—a world created by a team of expensive interior designers and bathed in a soft orange glow that had taken a lighting specialist three weeks to get right. The recitation issuing forth from his own mouth—a cloying monologue of culinary delight—seemed to cast a spell over his own person, and without a single pause, stammer, or slip in his speech, he reflected on the wonder of it all. He, of all people—Murgatroyd Floyd Shwet Foo—was privileged enough to inhabit this magical world of porcelain dishware and silver cutlery and spotless white table linen, of pink peonies blossoming in vases, of long-stemmed glasses filled with wines red and white, of men in beautifully cut suits done up in silk neckties, of women with berry-tinted lips and glittering jewels draped about their earlobes, throats, and wrists.

He knew every intimate detail about this world. Over there, to Mrs. Woo's right, was the salad fork with a prong slightly askew, used by Ahmad to fix one of the dishwashers. That fifth pane of glass walling the execution arena had had to be replaced when an unwieldy young calf, crazed with pain and terror, had slammed into it with surprising force. Here, on this tablecloth, just where he was lightly placing his forefinger, was the faint shadow of a stubborn spot of oyster gravy, barely noticeable, left over from Mr. Harold Wong's twenty-seventh birthday dinner.

His own voice wafted back into his ears. ". . . poached pears infused with brandy, drizzled with a dark chocolate sauce, and served with a dollop of hazelnut ice cream on the side. Now, may I answer any questions about the specialties of the evening?"

As Murgatroyd glided away to submit their orders to the kitchen, he reflected on how leaving the restaurant seemed an option far less attractive than it had been earlier that day. Why *would* he want to leave all this? Here, he was truly in his element—the first time he had ever been so in the entirety of his lonely and awkward life. The evening passed as usual, with Shakti calling him over to a table periodically to parade him in front of various diners. That night, he was marvelled at by a group of ten Japanese tourists, the Hwee family (who was celebrating a sixtieth wedding anniversary), and an attractive middle-aged Lebanese man whom Shakti thoughtfully decided to keep company for the rest of his meal. Murgatroyd and Shakti had their routine down pat—her declarations of his complete transformation from caterpillar into butterfly, his modest but elegant responses to any questions asked of him: their timing, their rapport, was impeccable. It was an act refined over years of practice, and Murgatroyd took a certain pride in performing it. He refrained from bringing up the subject of his resignation, not out of fear (resting his hands confidently on his black silk lapels, he felt no fear); rather, he refrained because he found himself incapable of disturbing a dynamic so exquisite—something that worked as well as the inner machinery of a delicate and finely tuned timepiece.

Here at the restaurant were tranquillity and security and familiarity and even a fair amount of prestige. Here, he thought as he swept a tablecloth clean with his silver table crumber, was where he belonged. He caught himself. No, it wasn't. He was an Oddfit. He remembered Ann.

Tell me something, Murgatroyd. Do you belong here?

He remembered Ann's question and the perturbation it had caused him. True, this world wasn't exactly everything he'd wished for, to be sure. But it came close. And it was comforting.

Just past midnight, the last two guests—the nervous young man and woman, now no longer nervous and a tad tipsy—departed from L'Abattoir in a taxi, and the waitstaff could finally clear the last table and begin closing the restaurant. The evening was over, and at long last, they could go home. In the back room, Murgatroyd changed into his casual clothes, and as he did, he underwent his customary transformation into his own self. Little by little, his chest collapsed inward and his spine curved into a hunch. His jaw went slack, the expression in his eyes clouded over into dullness, his fingers fumbled with his buttons and zippers and shoelaces, and he felt himself once again yearning for true happiness and thinking of the Quest. But now, in place of excitement, was profound confusion. How could he have so easily dismissed the Quest from his mind when now it seemed as if he had never longed for anything more desperately in his entire life? Abruptly, he thought of his parents. *Couldn't do without you, dear boy.* Was it true? He was, after all, their only child. Was he being selfish? Was his personal happiness everything? When he was at work, he may not have been happy, but he was comfortable and at peace. Wasn't that enough? Wasn't that all one should expect from life? To be almost content some of the time?

There was a pounding on the door. "Eh, Shwet Foo! Can hurry up or not? Got other people also need to change!"

Murgatroyd gave up trying to tie his shoes and hurriedly emerged from the room, bumping into a grumpy-looking Ahmad holding a bundle of clothes.

"Sorry, lah. Sorry." Murgatroyd apologized before tripping on his shoelace and landing flat on his face at the expensively shod feet of Shakti Vithani.

"Ah, Shwet Foo! Splendid job this evening. The Hwee family in particular was very impressed."

He squinted up at her from the floor. "Thank you."

"Not at all. Well, then," she said, yawning and turning away. "Goodnight. See you tomorrow."

"No, wait!" Murgatroyd called after her.

Shakti turned around. "Wait? What for?"

"I mean, can I talk to you about something?"

"About what?"

"Erh . . ."

Shakti squatted down and looked Murgatroyd squarely in the face, and her voice dropped to a dangerous whisper. "Is it about a raise? Because you do know I pay you *extraordinarily* well."

"No, no. Not about pay, lah," Murgatroyd said frantically, getting to his knees. "About something else."

"About what?" she repeated, patiently.

"About maybe leaving the restaurant!" Murgatroyd blurted out. He held his breath.

"What, 'leaving' as in going home right now like everyone else is doing or 'leaving' as in quitting?"

"Quitting."

Shakti's brow furrowed, and she looked at the other staff scurrying around the kitchen finishing their final chores. "Perhaps we should talk about this outside."

They entered the deserted dining area and sat down at a table. Shakti folded her hands in front of her, her face fixed in a surprisingly neutral, businesslike expression.

"So, Shwet Foo. When you say, 'leaving the restaurant,' you really do mean to say that you wish to quit your job?"

He felt rather taken aback. He hadn't expected Shakti to react so calmly about the matter. "Erh. Maybe. Yes. Maybe?"

"Which is it? 'Maybe' or 'Yes'?"

Murgatroyd clenched his teeth. "Yes."

"For what reason would you wish to quit? Is it an offer from another restaurant?"

He shook his head vigorously.

"And it's not because you're dissatisfied with your pay?"

He shook his head again.

"Do you not like working here?"

He shook his head.

"Well, then," she said, drumming her fingers on the table. "I'm a bit confused. Why on earth would you want to leave?"

Murgatroyd said nothing. Saying that he needed to go on a Quest seemed ridiculous in the extreme.

"As your employer, don't I at least deserve an explanation?"

Murgatroyd nodded.

"Or . . . perhaps, you're not sure whether you want to leave?"

Unable to make eye contact, Murgatroyd stared at the tablecloth for a while. And then nodded again.

Shakti sighed and massaged the temples of her forehead with her index fingers.

"So, basically, you might want to leave, but you're not sure, and you don't really have a reason."

Once again, he was still for a while, and then nodded glumly. Shakti rose to her feet. "I tell you what, Shwet Foo. Why don't you think about it more and talk to me when you have your thoughts in order, all right?"

Another nod.

"But I will say one thing—you're a good waiter, Shwet Foo. I would hate to lose you."

She patted him on the shoulder, and returned to the back room, leaving Murgatroyd to ponder upon the one-way conversation which had just taken place, and which had been surprisingly cordial. *Now what?* he asked himself. He reached into his wallet and unfolded his to-do list. At least he had a new toothbrush. As his eyes skimmed over the rest of the list, he remembered that he still needed to call Kay Huat. That's what he would do. He would call Kay Huat immediately. He glanced at his wristwatch. It was a little late to call, but Kay Huat would understand. Kay Huat would know what to do.

***

Kay Huat sat cross-legged on the black leather sofa in his living room, typing away furiously on his laptop, old-time jazz music wafting through the amazingly expensive speakers of his amazingly expensive sound system. Inspiration had struck him while he was eating dinner, and chapter forty-five of the Great Singaporean Novel was flying effortlessly from his fingertips onto the screen before him. The remains of a partially consumed bowl of ramen noodles sat on the mahogany coffee table in front of him. Balanced precariously on the sofa armrest was a mug of black coffee. He raised it to his lips and took a swig before triumphantly typing up the last sentence of chapter forty-five and moving on to chapter forty-six. Suddenly, his mobile phone rang.

"Oh hell," he muttered, fishing in his pocket for his phone. He didn't recognize the number.

"Hello?"

"Kay Huat?"

"Yes? Who is this?"

"Shwet Foo."

"Shwet Foo? Where are you calling from?"

"Payphone. Just got out of work."

Kay Huat could feel the inspiration draining out of him with every second of this phone conversation. "Can we talk some other time? A bit busy right now."

"Just very quick, I promise. You remember I told you about that woman?"

Kay Huat's ears perked up. He picked up his mug and took a long sip of coffee. "What woman?"

"The one in green. The one who gave me the card about the Quest."

"Oh yeah," Kay Huat said, feigning absentmindedness. "I *think* I remember now."

"So, erh. I tried to call."

So little Shwet Foo had tried as well. Kay Huat almost laughed out loud with relief. "See man? I told you, right? Scam one!"

"No! Not scam!"

Kay Huat leaped to his feet. "Hah? What do you mean, 'not scam'?" He began pacing agitatedly around his flat.

"Not scam!"

"How can not scam? The number didn't work, right?"

By now, Murgatroyd was grinning to himself like a madman. He *knew* Kay Huat would be pleasantly surprised. "It worked! I'm going!"

"What? Going where?!"

"Erh . . . hold on. Running out of time. Must add money."

Murgatroyd dug excitedly in his pocket for change. Just telling Kay Huat about his decision was bringing back his determination to seize his chance and go. Kay Huat's voice, sounding oddly frantic, came faintly through the receiver, which Murgatroyd held pressed to his chest as he put an additional coin in the pay-phone slot.

"Hello, hello? Going where? Hello? Shwet Foo?"

"Sorry, I had to add money."

"Never mind! Going *where*?"

"On the Quest! This Friday!" Murgatroyd got a thrill just saying it. So he said it again. "This Friday!"

Murgatroyd heard a loud crash in the background. "Eh, Kay Huat? What was that?"

"What was what?"

"I heard a sound."

"Oh. Nothing, nothing. Just spilled a bit of coffee." *Just relax, Kay Huat. Breathe deeply. Stay calm. Sound calm. Try to sound happy and calm.* "That's great, Shwet Foo! Good for you, man!"

"I know! But I need your advice. Can we meet tomorrow for dinner?"

"Don't you have work?"

"Got Tuesdays off, remember?"

"Erh, yeah. Of course. Of course. How about my dad's stall at Golden Serenity?"

"Okay, can. Thanks, Kay Huat! Sorry to call you so late."

"No problem, man. Oh, and Shwet Foo?"

"Yes?

"Don't do anything until we talk, okay? Do *nothing*, okay?"

"Okay!"

"See you tomorrow."

"Yup! Tomorrow! Thanks, Kay Huat! Goodnight!"

Feeling confident that all would turn out right, Murgatroyd hung up. And despite the presence of an amorous young couple making out with each other in the shadows next to the payphone, he felt uninhibited enough to dance a little jig of joy.

CHAPTER 14

There is something disquieting and unnatural about empty restaurants. Restaurants are meant to be full—stuffed with people stuffing their stomachs with food. And once the people have stuffed themselves to their hearts' content, they should pay their bills and leave in order to make room to stuff in other people waiting to stuff themselves. An empty restaurant is a starved, sickly restaurant; the stench of desperation hangs about it and drives people away. The prospective customer takes a tentative peep inside and sees its listless waiters, its dusty plates and cutlery, and its overeager proprietor advancing at an alarmingly brisk trot with welcoming arms spread wide before the prospective customer promptly panics and flees to wait forty-five minutes for a table at the busy establishment next door.

Shakti disliked seeing L'Abattoir empty, even if it was because the restaurant was closed, as it was now. It reminded her too much of her failure period, of night after night spent sitting in the empty dining room of the Colonial Table, gulping down calorie-free Coca-Colas, which turned into Coke and whiskeys, then just whiskeys as the evenings wore on. The memory caused her to wince even now: the flies buzzing lazily and loudly through the empty rooms; the few diners they did have looking uneasily at the empty tables all around them, wondering where everyone else was, what everyone else knew that they didn't; the dirty dishes and silverware and perspiring half-empty water glasses which remained uncleared on deserted tables as the waiters, unaccustomed to labour, chatted idly together in the bar area. *But what's past is past,* Shakti told herself as she sat down in the darkened interior of L'Abattoir. *There's nothing to fear anymore.*

On the nights that she came to the restaurant, her usual practice was to leave before the restaurant closed, either while the last guests were still lingering after their meals, or while the staff was still in the process of shutting down for the evening. Lights out and locking up were left to the manager. However, to the manager's surprise, Shakti had shooed him out the door, telling him that she would lock up for the night. The manager, who was very familiar with Shakti's temper, left promptly without a word.

The dining room was dark, illuminated only by the thin beams of moonlight and streetlamp glow shooting in from the gaps in the curtained windows facing the street. Except for the occasional whoosh of a passing car on the road outside, all was quiet. In the shadows, like an old spider absorbed in contemplating prey past and prey to come, sat Shakti Vithani, at the same table where she had sat earlier with Shwet Foo. She was meditating on what had passed between them. It was simply inconceivable. He—*he* of all people—was thinking of quitting *her* restaurant. Leaving *her!* After she had picked him out of the gutter! Her eyes narrowed as she conjured up for herself in her mind the spineless, wretched figure of Shwet Foo. Her teeth clenched in fury. So this is how she was to be repaid! All her hard work, all her loving care, flushed down the toilet by a pasty-complexioned hunchback!

But then again, she was a reasonable person. Perhaps she was being too hasty. After all, he hadn't turned in his resignation yet, had he? She had to get to the bottom of all this. What had spurred Shwet Foo to even consider such a course of action? And more importantly, was it a real threat?

At the far end of the room, something in the shadows stirred. Shakti looked up. She spoke aloud. "I certainly hope you're not this sloppy when I send you out on jobs."

There was no answer. Shakti sighed.

"For heaven's sake, come out already! I haven't got all night, you know."

Again, there was movement, and out of the darkness emerged a thin figure all in black, striding slowly towards her table. As he came closer, it became apparent that what at first appeared to be nothing but a shadow across the lower portion of his face was, in fact, a strip of black cloth. Not that this should have come as a surprise—it was the same cloth he always wore during performances. But then again, he always used the sword during performances too, and to see him carrying it outside the arena, to have him holding it while standing so close to her in a dark, deserted space where no one could hear her scream—that *was* a teeny, tiny bit unsettling.

Arching one eyebrow, Shakti looked as nonchalantly as she could at the glinting blade in his right hand. "So, do you take that thing with you wherever you go?"

Never taking his eyes from her face, he placed the sword on the table, the handle within easy reach. As he seated himself in the same chair that Shwet Foo had occupied only minutes earlier, Shakti couldn't help but admire, as she always did, the wildness and ferocity in the eyes that remained locked on her, as if he were sizing up an enemy before a great battle. During his performances, she noticed the same look in his eyes whenever he was presented with the animal he was to slaughter. On the face of things, treating a helpless chicken or duck or cow as a formidable opponent would be considered a rather ridiculous thing to do. But somehow, when the Duck Assassin did it, staring intently at his victim before the final blow, he made the act something more than the mere butchering of a dumb animal. It became the slaying of a great and powerful beast, the execution of a necessary purifying sacrifice, the completion of an exquisite work of art.

These same wild eyes continued to fix upon his employer as he unwound the strip of cloth hiding his mouth and chin. And even though Shakti already knew, had already seen, what lay beneath many times before, she could never completely stifle the gasp that would inevitably escape her. His face was not disfigured in any way—not in the technical sense of the word—but the mouth that it revealed! A thin gash, inexplicably cruel in expression, as if Whoever, Whatever had made him had slashed a knife across his face instead of giving him a pair of lips. The gash curved slowly upwards into a sickle. Pleased at finally eliciting from his employer some evidence of fear, the Duck Assassin leaned back in his chair and pressed the bony fingers of his hands together in anticipation.

He had already made a modest name for himself by the time Shakti had happened upon him and hired him for the restaurant. His origins were mysterious, and the rumours widespread. Some said that he came from a wealthy family—one that spoiled him in his youth and cultivated his cruelty by allowing him to torture the household servants in the same way they allowed him to torture the household pets. Some said that he came from a wretchedly poor family, and that his mother and father had abused him with all manner of objects, blunt, sharp, and piping hot. Others who claimed to know him better than anyone else did insisted that he was a demon, the son of the devil himself, formed and begotten in the fires of hell. Shakti told everyone who asked about him that he had been a poultry butcher at a duck rice restaurant in the red-light district, which was undoubtedly true; though beyond that, his past was indeed subject to the wildest of speculations. If he did come from hell, Shakti had often reflected, he certainly made one hell of a butcher.

Many years ago, while she was still in the process of designing her new restaurant (not yet christened "L'Abattoir"), Shakti's old Oxford school chum Nigel Viswanathan had mentioned to her an open-air restaurant in Geylang that was fast acquiring a reputation for serving the best duck rice in town—and that one factor working in their favour was that they now slaughtered their own poultry fresh in the back.

"All fresh, Shakti! Completely fresh!" Nigel had told her. Dear Nigel, as his friends called him, never ceased to be astonished at the world, with all its wonders great and small, no matter how long he continued to live in it.

Dear Nigel had recounted his visit to the restaurant thusly: "I ask the owner, 'Hey, sir! How do you make this duck so tender, so tasty like this?'

"He answers, 'Sir, we slaughter it fresh!'

"I ask, 'Sir! How fresh?'

"He says, 'Sir! Right behind those doors there! Just seconds before we braise it.'

"I say, 'Sir! You're pulling my leg!'

"He says, 'No, sir! I prove it, I prove it!' Then, he disappears and comes back with a dead duck in a plastic bag, feathers still on!

"'Touch it, sir!' he tells me. 'Feel for yourself if warm or not!'

"I touch it! Sure enough, still warm! Amazing, no?"

Not actually that amazing, but Dear Nigel was always more than happy to be impressed. Shakti, on the other hand, was not so much impressed as quietly furious. From what Dear Nigel was telling her, Sin Mee Famous Duck Rice Eating House was a cruder, more primitive version of her own idea. While she initially felt jealous that some low-class, nose-picking *ah beng* had beat her to the idea, she was also relieved that she would, at least, be offering a more refined, elegant, pricier version. But she had to make sure. And so on a Sunday afternoon, she gingerly navigated her BMW sports sedan through the crowded streets of Geylang to reassure herself that Sin Mee posed no competition.

On an island where Modernization and Progress had ushered in an era of contentment, convenience, and safety for its citizens, Geylang had become a sanctuary for those who hungered ungratefully for more—those who yearned to indulge in pleasures ranging anywhere from the mildly unvirtuous to the downright illegal to something hovering in between. The lustful satiated their passions in government-sanctioned brothels with prostitutes imported from Malaysia, Vietnam, Thailand, China, and India, while gambling fiends found relief in the illegal secret dens in apartments and alleyways. Late-night eateries lining the main thoroughfare and the *lorongs* just north of the red-light district soothed the growling bellies of midnight gluttons, and among stalls heaped high with great thorny fruits prowled durian addicts, hunting for the finest in season: the orange-gold creaminess of the Mao Shan Wang, the melting pale canary-grey of the XO, the uncomplicated fleshy yellow of the classic Sultan, the bitter brightness of the Black Pearl. Even those suffering from severe nostalgia for the Singapore of bygone "backward" days sought refuge in Geylang, strolling through street after street, feasting their emaciated memories on the colourful unrenovated shophouses and their eroding concrete spiral staircases. It was this unashamed mingling of sensuality and hunger, decay and vitality, memory and forgetfulness that drew people to Geylang. And it was all this that earned it Shakti's repulsion and disdain.

The afternoon had not gotten off to a good start. Shakti had spent half an hour looking for a parking spot, and when she had finally found one, she had to nudge two grubby bicycles out of the way with her back fender in order to claim it. Disoriented by her search for parking, she ended up wandering embarrassedly and hurriedly through several brothel-lined *lorongs*. And then when she had finally made her way to the restaurant area of the neighbourhood, a crack in the sidewalk caught one of her high heels, snapped it in two, and sent her tumbling to the ground. By the time Shakti finally arrived at the stronghold of her imagined enemy, she looked considerably less awe-inspiring than she had intended to look. Her face was shiny and flushed with heat and mortification, and her hair, so fearsomely full-bodied that morning, was deflated and damp. Her expensive and elaborate turquoise and gold necklace lay across her neck tangled and askew, and her feet were now sporting cheap Hello Kitty flip-flops purchased from a nearby vendor after the untimely death of her Jimmy Choos. She had braved many perils to size up this potential culinary rival, but it had been worth it. Now that she was here, she was relieved to find that Sin Mee Famous Duck Rice Eating House didn't amount to anything after all.

It was the type of establishment you showed up at in shorts and sandals after a day of smashing rocks, or whatever smelly construction workers did all day. There were red plastic stools clustered haphazardly around circular tables, all of which could be easily stacked and folded after closing time; bird carcasses hanging on meat hooks in a smudgy glass window which proudly bore a certificate with a hygiene rating of C; and patrons perusing laminated menus with bad photos of the restaurant specialties, accompanied by descriptions in Chinese and ungrammatical English ("famous briase duck rice"). Adjusting her necklace and fluffing her hair, she breathed a sigh of relief.

After sampling a plate of their duck (which, she had to admit, was rich, flavourful, and tender), she struck up a conversation with the owner—a bald, simple, potbellied Chinese man dressed in a dirty off-white singlet and striped Bermuda shorts. And when she had showered him and his establishment with enough flattery, she asked if he would mind showing her the slaughtering area. That was where she first saw *him*: in an open-air, white-tiled area enclosed by walls on three sides. The floor sloped ever so gently towards a gutter and drain in the far corner for the simple reason that bits of animal were much easier to clean off when all one had to do was give the whole place a thorough spraying with a hose. In the very centre of the rectangular area stood a squat stump of a wooden chopping block, dark with use, sticky with clots of blood, flesh, and feathers.

"Come, come." The owner stepped into the slaughtering area, and motioned for Shakti to do the same. She saw that there was somebody inside already: a sullen, lanky Chinese youth who couldn't have been more than twenty years of age, squatting by the far wall where several cages of live ducks had been stacked. The young man was wearing a blood-spattered white butcher's apron, a white hat, and a rectangular white mask which hooked over his ears and covered the bottom half of his face.

"This lady wants to see you at work!" the owner said.

The young man raised himself off his haunches, yanked a duck out of one of the cages by its neck, picked up a cleaver lying nearby, and stalked over to the chopping block. Firmly pressing the side of its head against the wooden surface with his left hand, he raised and lowered the cleaver above the bird's neck several times for precision. As he did so, it seemed to Shakti as if he were looking the bird dead in the eye. Finally, he raised the cleaver high to deliver the final blow. There was something about the manner in which this was all carried out that mesmerized not only Shakti, but the owner as well. Their attentions dangled, suspended from the cleaver poised in midair.

Suddenly, from behind them there came a loud crash, and the spell was broken. The young man—cleaver still bloodless in one hand, duck with head still attached in the other—turned to the area where the cages now lay in an untidy heap. Somehow they had overturned, and some of the cage doors had swung open. The lucky ducks, seizing their opportunity, had escaped, and were now running and flapping around for dear life. Shakti screamed, shrieking and waving her hands madly about her face to protect herself from the terrified birds.

"Catch them!" the owner cried, trying to seize the ducks—a course of action that only agitated them further, causing them to fly and honk and flap even more wildly.

The young man remained motionless in the maelstrom of feathery mayhem and panic—the placid eye of a raging hurricane.

"Oi! Do something!" the owner yelled in his direction, attempting to pin a duck to the wall by its beating wings.

So the young man did.

Without further ceremony, he pressed the duck he was already holding against the chopping block and neatly severed its head. Then he secured the cleaver, blade down, in a concealed holster underneath his apron. From the same place, he drew out two very long, very thin, very pointy knives.

He leapt high, skewering two ducks in midair with the tips of his miniature swords. Landing noiselessly and expertly on his feet, he flicked the carcasses off the blades with a convulsive jerk, and stepped towards his employer. The little bald man had managed to grab a duck from behind and was now clasping it to his chest as it attempted to flap itself free. The young man thrust one of the knives into the duck's exposed stomach, stopping just short of splitting open his boss as well. In the blink of an eye, the duck was neatly slit from belly to bottom, and its entrails were spilling out onto the white tiles.

One by one, every loose duck in the area was cut down, hacked, slashed, stabbed, dismembered, or decapitated in a grisly scene worthy of any old-fashioned Chinese martial-arts flick, until finally, there remained only one, quacking with fear in a corner as *he* closed in on it.

Cowering behind the chopping block, Shakti watched as he took a step towards the duck and drew his arm back to run the hapless animal through. Its doom was imminent. But then, the duck made a mad dash between the man's legs and headed straight towards her, honking and beating its monstrous wings. She screamed at the top of her lungs. Shakti Vithani was to meet her end, torn limb from limb by a mad duck. She screamed even louder and shut her eyes.

A loud thunk. Followed by complete silence.

She slowly opened her eyes, but the terrible duck seemed to have disappeared. She looked to her right. Then to her left. Lodged horizontally in the side of the chopping block, just centimetres away from her head, was the cleaver. And sitting on the metal shelf created by the flat of the blade lay the blood-spattered head of her attacker, tongue out, eyes glazed over in the dullness of death. Several metres away crouched her rescuer, his arm bent, still in the same position in which he had hurled the cleaver. But where had the duck's body gone? It was only then that she registered a warm fluttering sensation in her lap and looked down to see the flopping decapitated bundle gushing blood all over her new white capri pants.

"*Aiyah*. So sorry about that," the owner had apologized, helping Shakti to her feet and walking her out of the slaughter area.

"Where did you find him?" she asked shakily.

"Just one of those boys from around here. He say he need work, so I let him work." He leaned in and whispered confidentially to Shakti, "Good butcher, but I think at night he's . . . one of those."

"One of those?"

"You know, lah. Troublemaking type." As he leaned in closer, Shakti politely cupped one hand over her nostrils. "I hear people talk. *Big* troublemaker, it seems. Between you and me, I think I must let him go."

"What's his name?"

The owner suddenly broke into a toothy grin. "Heh heh, madam. You know something? I don't know. On file somewhere, I think. But everyone call him *Ya Sha Shou*. Like a joke. They say he can really butcher duck with style one, like *gong fu* expert. How to translate, eh? Ah. *Ya Sha Shou*—the Duck . . . Assassin."

Five years later, the Duck Assassin, now in the employ of Shakti Vithani, sat before her, awaiting instructions.

She spoke. "You know Shwet Foo?"

He gave a curt nod.

"I want you to follow him. I want to know what he's up to these days."

CHAPTER 15

The rays of the morning sun streamed into the Floyd flat—a hovering golden mist that enveloped the sofa and coffee table and bookshelves, the uncleared plates on the table, and the traces of eggs, sunny-side up, which had congealed into pools of bright orange. Also illuminated by the golden morning was a trembling figure who sat, scrunched knees to chest, in a dining chair, clutching a mug of salty Milo, a dazed expression on his face. He knew that Kay Huat had told him not to do anything—*anything*—until after their meeting later that evening, but it was too late. The deed was done. What had he been thinking that morning when he woke up, determined to conceal the truth from his parents no longer? What had he been thinking as he hurriedly scrawled the news on a sheet of notebook paper and sealed it in an envelope? What had possessed him to go through with it and hand the envelope to his father on his way out of the flat to go to work?

"What's this, then?" his father had asked, puzzled.

"Open it in the car," Murgatroyd had replied with a tremor in his voice. He wondered now whether it had been the wise thing to do.

***

On the Pan-Island Expressway, a blue Toyota sedan with red fuzzy dice hanging from the rear-view mirror swerved suddenly, almost crashing sidelong into a lorry.

***

"You did *what*?" Kay Huat asked just as his father set down two plates of char kway teow in front of Murgatroyd and himself. It was surprisingly uncrowded in Golden Serenity that Tuesday evening, and Seng Hong Low could even leave his stall for a few minutes to bring the boys their food personally.

"Eh? What did Shwet Foo do now?" his father asked, smiling at his son's friend.

"Erh, hi, Uncle," Murgatroyd said embarrassedly, looking down at the steaming noodles in front of them. "Thanks for dinner."

"Hah! Where got free dinner? Must pay, what!" the sinewy Seng Hong Low held out his hand, palm up, as Murgatroyd fumbled for his wallet. Then he laughed.

"Silly boy! Of course you don't need to pay! Kay Huat!" he called to his son, who was looking distractedly into the distance.

"Huh? Yes, Ba?"

"You watch out for your friend here. Too trusting, this one." Wiping his greasy hand on his shorts first, he ruffled Murgatroyd's hair and jogged back to his stall to attend to other orders. Seng Hong Low had a soft spot for his son's friend—a gentle, innocent sort. Very blur, he thought, reflecting on Shwet Foo's cluelessness. Blur like *sotong*, but a good boy, all the same.

"You did what?!" Kay Huat repeated again.

"I gave them a note telling them that I was leaving on Friday to go on the Que—"

"I *know* what you did!" Kay Huat exclaimed, spattering sauce all over the table as he waved his chopsticks in the air. "I just can't believe you did it! Don't tell me you're going to quit your job as well!"

"Erh. Planning to tell my boss tomorrow."

"What?!"

Murgatroyd silently prodded his char kway teow with his chopsticks before extracting a piece of beef and chewing it slowly. He hadn't expected his friend to be so agitated.

Kay Huat rested his elbows on the table and shook his head in disbelief. For a moment, he forgot himself and how his own plans were being disrupted by Shwet Foo's foolhardiness to marvel at . . . well, the very fact of Shwet Foo's foolhardiness itself. "You're really going, huh?" He was saying it, but he couldn't believe that Shwet Foo *was* really going. The little guy had somehow managed to muster up enough gumption to tell his parents. He was making plans to leave his work. Spineless little Shwet Foo. "I can't believe it."

Murgatroyd patted his friend consolingly on the arm. "I'll miss you too."

Kay Huat abruptly drew his arm away and began digging into his food. "Never mind about me. Tell me everything."

"Everything?"

There was a glint of hunger in Kay Huat's eyes as he leaned in closer, a bit of noodle dangling from the corner of his mouth. *"Everything."*

So, Murgatroyd told Kay Huat everything, albeit in a somewhat muddled fashion. He told him about the meeting with Ann on Sunday and everything he had learned: the More Known World and the Quest, Sumfits and Oddfits and Stucks, and how he was an Oddfit. He told Kay Huat that he only had to bring a toothbrush and a clean change of underwear, and that the new toothbrush he had bought yesterday had blue and yellow bristles that would fade with prolonged usage, indicating that the toothbrush needed to be replaced. He told Kay Huat how he had tried to tell his parents and his boss yesterday, but couldn't work up the nerve. He told Kay Huat how he had to meet Ann at Bedok Jetty on Friday and how she had been wearing very high heels. And he ended by telling Kay Huat how he gave his parents the letter that morning.

Kay Huat was used to his best friend's imperfect and confusing way of expressing himself, and managed to put everything together. "So, you're meeting this woman at Bedok Jetty on Friday? What time again?"

"Seven."

"A.m. or p.m.?"

"P.m."

"And you have to bring a toothbrush and underwear?"

"Yes."

Kay Huat mulled over this information. "I see." He took a long sip of sugar cane juice.

At that instant, it dawned on Murgatroyd that he was truly going to miss Kay Huat very much. He too had never forgotten that day when his friend had saved him from the merciless torments of his classmates. Kay Huat had been like an older brother to him, always taking care of him, always giving him advice, always providing a shoulder to lean on. And it also occurred to Murgatroyd that, as unlikely as it seemed, Kay Huat—his handsome, perfect genius of a friend—was really going to miss him as well.

"I really will miss you!" Murgatroyd said, tears beginning to pool in the rims of his eyes.

"Ach!" exclaimed Kay Huat, waving away all sentimentality with a flick of his hand. "Don't worry about it, lah. Eh, you need a ride to Bedok Jetty on Friday?"

Murgatroyd was amazed by his friend's generosity. "Erh. If can. If cannot, never mind, I can find my way."

"Of course, can! Don't be stupid one! Must send my best friend off, what! I'll leave work a little early and pick you up."

Murgatroyd smiled gratefully. "Wah, Kay Huat," he said, choking slightly on his words. "You're really good to me."

"What are friends for, right? No need to get emotional now, lor. Wait until Friday."

"Thanks, Kay Huat!"

"Okay, okay, enough already! No need to thank anymore!"

Kay Huat slurped up the last of the kway teow, and as an afterthought, asked, "So how did your parents take it?"

"Don't know yet. They hadn't come back from work yet when I left to come here."

"Mmm." Kay Huat took a tissue out of his pocket and wiped his mouth pensively. "I think they'll take it very hard."

"You think so?" Murgatroyd asked, hearing with much dread the confirmation of his own suspicions. "They did say they would be upset if I ever left."

"Yeah. You know they . . . like having you around very much."

"Yeah. I didn't realize." Murgatroyd glumly took out his own pack of tissues and rubbed at the new sauce stains on his T-shirt. "I feel a bit selfish for leaving them alone."

"Mmm," uttered Kay Huat, looking off into the distance. Murgatroyd followed his gaze and saw that his friend was watching his father deliver a plate of noodles to another table. "It is hard to be alone. Even though Ba doesn't say, I think without Ma, he gets very lonely." Kay Huat broke out of his reverie. "Still. What must be done, must be done, right?"

"Yeah," Murgatroyd gave his assent in a somewhat hollow tone. "Yeah . . ."

"I'll be right back."

One remarkable thing about Seng Kay Huat—in addition to the other innumerable remarkable things about Kay Huat—was that he not only looked like a hero, he also walked like a hero. Chest out, shoulders back, head held high, he strode purposefully to the toilet as if he were striding off to saddle his warhorse for battle. After relieving himself, he washed his hands at the sink and stood for a while surveying himself in the mirror. He wasn't the vain sort, but with such good looks, who could help but give in to a little well-deserved self-admiration? Even in the unflattering fluorescence of hawker-centre toilet lighting, his handsome features glowed. He gave his arm muscles a little modest flex, taking in with a little modest satisfaction the veins and bulges that appeared and disappeared, quick as a heartbeat.

Continuing this factual assessment of his person, he reflected on how, with a physique, a mind, and a personality like his, he was meant for greater things. The universe had, very simply, designed him for that purpose. Sure, monetary success was a good thing. But such paltry material achievement was the triumph of lesser beings. Not him. He was to make his mark on the world. He was to protect the helpless and fight evil and accomplish great things. And as he now knew, he was to join the Quest in order to do . . . something. Something great. And perhaps it involved exploring some area or some part of the world that he now couldn't quite remember. Funny. He usually had a very good memory. He did remember, however, that there were only certain types of beings called—what were they called, again—who could actually do the . . . thing . . . that this Quest involved people doing. Huh. Even the details about that whatever-it-was appeared to have slipped his mind. In any case, none of that could have been all that important; otherwise, he would be able to remember it.

But wait. It was all coming back to him. The Quest, he was sure he remembered little Shwet Foo telling him, involved doing lots of great deeds—deeds that the one-eyed woman hadn't gone into any specific detail about, but that involved spectacular feats, righting wrongs, high-speed car chases, thrilling swordfights, and all of the things that Kay Huat had always known he was destined to do. He was positive that

Shwet Foo told him that those who ran the Quest were very selective about whom they allowed to join, permitting only the best and the brightest, the smartest and the strongest, and the most exceptional to enter their ranks.

Yes, that was what Shwet Foo had told him. He was certain. More than certain. And (this part, Shwet Foo hadn't told him) they had somehow accidentally chosen Shwet Foo. There could be no other explanation for it. He loved his little friend dearly, but he also knew that Shwet Foo was no match for a feisty Yorkshire terrier, much less for the challenges of going on a Quest. Shwet Foo, he suspected, barely knew how to tie his shoelaces. Shwet Foo had done poorly in every subject he had taken at school and, before this job, which he had miraculously managed to keep, it had taken less than a month for him to get fired each time. Shwet Foo was nice, but as his father had said, blur like *sotong*—completely and utterly clueless. So clueless that he had never so much as suspected what Kay Huat at the age of fifteen had figured out within ten minutes of meeting Shwet Foo's parents for the very first time—Mr. and Mrs. Floyd disliked their son immensely, if they didn't downright hate him.

Poor Shwet Foo. Of course, it wasn't his place to interfere, was it? For all these years, Kay Huat had shielded his friend from that heartbreaking knowledge. After all, Shwet Foo was more than blissful in his ignorance—completely convinced of his parents' love for him, and more than happy to remain their one and only devoted son. And wasn't that what mattered? That Shwet Foo was happy? And what better way to preserve his friend's happiness and benefit mankind than by going on the Quest in Shwet Foo's place? He was Seng Kay Huat. Once these Quest people saw him, once they met him, they would take him. He was sure of it. How, he thought as he surveyed himself again in the mirror, could anyone believe that *this* wasn't capable of tackling any little Quest that needed fulfilling out there?

Feeling that his breath smelled too greasy, Kay Huat bent over the sink and rinsed his mouth out a few times. He was glad that things seemed to be unfolding in a manageable way now. Over the course of the past few days, he had undergone a series of emotions—frustration at his repeated failed attempts to get through to the number on that green business card, doubt about what he had thought to be his infallible instinct, despair at perhaps never achieving his destined greatness, determination to achieve *some* shadow of greatness by becoming a famous novelist, dull self-pity as he tried to drown his sorrows in the process of writing. Last night, after Shwet Foo had called him to tell him the "good news," he had felt bereft of all literary inspiration. He had abandoned working on the novel and lain sleepless in bed all night. He had racked his brain thinking about how this could have possibly come to pass and what course of action to take. But now he knew. He knew all the details. And he felt optimistic that the situation was under control and that he was once again on the path to his destiny.

The only thing that worried him was how his father was going to manage in his absence. Not physically—Ba was still strong, had friends, and with his own savings and income along with the money and investments Kay Huat had secretly set aside for his father, was well taken care of financially. But how would the disappearance of his son affect him? Kay Huat answered his own question: in the end, it would make Ba proud. After all, he was doing it for Ba as much as for himself (and Shwet Foo, of course). What had he said just a few minutes ago to Shwet Foo? What must be done, must be done.

Giving one final rinse and spit, he exited the toilet and strode back to the table where his friend was engrossed in rolling a little ball of earwax back and forth between his right thumb and forefinger. Kay Huat shook his head, much like an indulgent pet owner upon returning home to find his living room floor strewn with rubbish and a stinky dog wagging his tail happily in the midst of it all. Ah, little Shwet Foo. He didn't know any better.

"Ready?" Kay Huat slapped his friend on the back, startling him. "Let's go. I'll drive you home."

"No need. Can take bus, what."

"No trouble, lah. I like driving at night." Also, Kay Huat liked taking care of his friend in little ways. It gave him a nice, big-brotherly feeling.

"Good night, Uncle," Murgatroyd said as they stopped at Seng Hong Low's stall on the way out.

"Good night, Shwet Foo!" Hong Low gave the boy a parting affectionate hair ruffle.

"I'll come right back to pick you up," Kay Huat said, gently pressing his father's shoulder in passing.

"Okay, Ah-Boy," Hong Low replied. As he watched the pair walk out of the hawker centre, he couldn't help thinking how, although he was proud of his son, he wished that he wasn't quite so big-headed.

As they walked towards Kay Huat's car, Kay Huat suddenly felt a slight chill, as if something had rushed by quickly, leaving a gust of wind in its wake. As he whipped his head around, he thought he saw some movement in the shadow of a tall tree on the side of the road.

"Oi, Shwet Foo. Did you see that?"

"See what?"

"Something in that tree."

"Just a bird, lah."

Not quite convinced, Kay Huat went over and examined the tree. He found nothing. *Strange*, he thought, and put it out of his mind.

It turned out that Murgatroyd had been right. It was nothing but a little bird. A little bird who, having obtained the information it needed, had stepped around the corner and made a call on its mobile phone. Around midnight, it winged its way to L'Abattoir where, much to the manager's absolute astonishment, Shakti Vithani had remained behind to close the restaurant for the second night in a row.

The little bird hadn't managed to overhear everything that had passed between Kay Huat and Shwet Foo, but he told Shakti what he *had* heard.

"A Quest?" Shakti said to herself softly. "For the More Known World?" Shakti smiled. "Huh. For some reason, that sounds kind of familiar." Shakti had indeed heard of the More Known World many years ago, during the failed publicity campaign Ann had mentioned to Murgatroyd. Something had aired briefly about it on TV, but Shakti had gotten bored and changed the channel. "A Quest," she repeated again. "So that's what Shwet Foo was on about last night."

Behind his face cloth, the Duck Assassin yawned. He examined the tip of his sword. Hearing Shakti think aloud to herself wasn't very interesting.

"Keep following him," she told the Duck Assassin. "And report whatever you find. I want to know everything he does, everything he says, everything he *thinks*. Tell me all of it."

The Duck Assassin gave a curt nod and, in the blink of an eye, was gone.

CHAPTER 16

Murgatroyd arrived home that night in a nervous sweat, anxious to find out how his mother and father had taken the news he had handed them that morning. He entered to find the flat dark and empty. His parents weren't home. *Maybe they went out for dinner or a movie*, he thought to himself as he groped his way into the kitchen and turned on the light to make himself his bedtime cup of Milo. He wasn't quite sure if he was relieved or disappointed. All throughout the car ride home, he had envisioned a variety of possible reactions his parents might have had to his impulsively written letter.

The most desirable scenario was the one where his loving mother and father, ecstatic over the good news, reprimanded him lightly for not informing them sooner and drove him themselves to the Bedok Jetty on Friday evening to give him a tearful yet joyful send-off. Unlikely, but hopefully not *too* far-fetched. Another scenario involved his parents being exceedingly unhappy about the whole affair until Ann unexpectedly showed up, sat them down, explained everything, and convinced them beyond a shadow of a doubt that the Quest was absolutely the most wonderful thing in the world that could happen to their only son.

The worst scenario involved finding out that his mother and father had secretly hated him since the day of his birth and wished to make his life miserable by preventing him from going on the Quest, thus dooming him to an unremarkable and mediocre existence. Thankfully, that was just downright preposterous.

A fourth scenario involved space aliens with big ray guns.

Surveying the empty kitchen, Murgatroyd decided that he was disappointed rather than relieved. The prospect of waiting until they came back home, or worse, until morning, for their response made him twice as jittery and three times as sick. Even the Milo wasn't helping to calm his nerves. He needed to lie down. He stumbled into his darkened bedroom and lay down on the area of the floor where he usually slept. But something was wrong. It felt different and strange. Sort of spongy and too high up.

Murgatroyd realized that separating his body from his customary sleeping area on the ground was an entire bed.

With a great gasp, he leapt to his feet and turned on the light. There, in the middle of his room—taking up most of the room, in fact—was a queen-sized bed complete with sky-blue sheets and two tremendous, fluffy pillows. He couldn't believe his eyes. Mouth agape, he circled it, prodding at the bedding, running his hands over the brass bed frame. He couldn't believe his fingers. He sat down cautiously on the edge of the mattress and bounced himself a little on the springs. He couldn't believe his buttocks. Finally, he lay down on his back, sinking into a softness that yielded under his weight so satisfyingly that it was almost unendurable. Tears streamed freely down either side of his face and made two salty, wet spots on his new covers right beside each ear. He was in heaven.

But why would his parents buy him a bed, after insisting for all these years that doing without a bed would be better for his spine? To be sure, he had yearned for a bed for as long as he could remember. As a small child, he had even kept a special scrapbook filled with advertisements for beds and mattresses that he had cut out from various magazines. In his spare time, he would flip through its pages, ogling the curvaceous craftsmanship of intricately wrought iron railings, and drooling over the inviting firmness of luxury orthopaedic mattresses with improved back support. And now! Now, he himself possessed a bed! A real bed of his very own! He raced to his bathroom to properly cleanse his body for this inaugural night of bliss.

Five minutes later, Murgatroyd woke to find himself sprawled in the bathtub naked. The showerhead above was turned on full blast and spraying him with water. He must have passed out from shock. For the first time since he could remember, the water was warm.

***

After his gloriously hot shower, Murgatroyd sat in his bed, back propped against the pillows, skin scented with lavender soap, cheeks flushed red, eyelids drooping with contentment. He was determined to stay awake until his parents came home, but he was overcome with drowsiness. Slowly but surely, he slid down further and further underneath the covers until he was sound asleep. That night he dreamed no dreams. And in the morning, when his mind returned to the world of the living, he had the sense of returning from a void in which he had rested unconscious and snug, enveloped in velvety darkness. He was almost afraid to open his eyes, lest he discover it all to be nothing but a dream, lest the pleasant springiness beneath his body give way to cold, unyielding imitation wood. Murgatroyd took a preliminary peek, and was greeted by the golden sheen of the railings at the foot of his bed. *His* bed. His very own bed. What time was it? It was 7:55! Why hadn't his alarm clock rung? He had to make breakfast! He had no time to make breakfast! What could he make in a hurry? What was that sizzling sound coming from the kitchen? What was that delicious smell?

He hurried into the kitchen to find his father transferring slices of bacon from a frying pan onto a plate lined with paper towels. His mother stood near the sink, dicing red capsicum peppers into little cubes. They looked up at him in unison.

"Good morning, Murgatroyd," said his mother.

"Good morning, Murgatroyd," said his father.

Murgatroyd wondered if he was dreaming. "Erh. What are you doing?" he asked.

"We're making breakfast, silly goose. What else?" Olivia replied.

"I hope bacon and omelette sounds all right," James chimed in.

Olivia pointed her knife in his direction. "Since you're leaving the day after tomorrow, we thought we'd spoil you a bit."

"Not to mention celebrate the news, old chap! Going on a great Quest, eh? Doesn't happen every day, does it now?"

"We'll be making breakfast tomorrow and the next day as well. You just sleep in."

"That's right. Let your mum and me take care of everything. You need your rest."

Murgatroyd's vision became blurry. His father tore off a corner of oily paper towel from the bacon plate and handed it to him. Dabbing at his eyes, Murgatroyd sank into a chair. He was quite overcome. How could he begin to express everything he felt at that moment? He began with the obvious.

"You . . . you bought me a bed!"

"You noticed!" Olivia exclaimed.

"You fixed my hot water!"

"You noticed that too!" she exclaimed again. "Our dearest boy. Do you like them?"

"I do! I like them very much!" Murgatroyd affirmed. "Thank you." He repeated his gratitude softly. "Thank you . . . thank you . . . thank you . . ."

Olivia put down the chopping knife and kissed her son's forehead. "Think nothing of it. Special gifts for a special occasion. Our little boy is leaving in two days to go on a Quest to do . . . great things."

Murgatroyd's eyes widened. "That's right! I'm leaving in two days! Isn't it a waste to buy new things now? How much did it all cost? Can return the bed or not?"

"Don't worry," said James reassuringly. He sat down across from his son, and handed the spatula to Olivia so she could finish frying the omelette. "Like we said, it's a special occasion." He made as if to speak some more, but then closed his mouth. After some hesitation, he opened it again. "But there's something else too—"

"James! Not now!" Olivia implored, looking in her husband's direction.

"If not now, then when, Olivia?" James turned back to his son. He took a deep breath. "This isn't easy news, son," he said slowly.

"What is it?" Murgatroyd asked, a sense of dread creeping upon him. The happy expressions on his parents' faces had disappeared. They looked anxious, distraught.

"Well. You remember Dr. Loy? My old racquetball partner at the club?"

Murgatroyd thought for a while, then nodded.

James went on. "I went to see Dr. Loy yesterday morning to ask his opinion about . . ." his voice trailed off. He swallowed hard and went on. "Well, *something*. And as it turns out . . . now you mustn't take it too hard."

"There's still hope," Olivia insisted, nudging at the edges of the uncooked omelette with the spatula. "Dr. Loy said that there's still hope."

Murgatroyd braced himself for the worst.

James heaved a sigh. "Dear boy. I have cancer."

The world, so wonderful only a few seconds ago, fell apart.

"Cancer?" Murgatroyd repeated.

"Breast cancer, to be exact."

"*Breast* cancer?"

"It's very rare, but it does happen. That's not all, though. Dr. Loy said that it's very likely the cancer has spread."

"Your father has to go for more tests," Olivia added.

"After I take them, they'll be able to give me a better estimate of how many weeks I may have left."

"But he did say there was hope, James! Don't forget, there's still a sliver of ho—" Olivia's words dissolved into gentle sobs. Wiping away her tears with her left hand, she hefted the frying pan up with her right and executed a perfect omelette flip.

"There, there, darling," James said. "Stiff upper lip! You're right. There *is* still hope. We'll get through this. You'll see."

Murgatroyd stared dully into the distance. "Cancer . . ."

"You mustn't let it bother you too much, Murgatroyd," his father said. "After all, you have other things to think about. You have to go on that Quest."

"Yes," Olivia seconded. "You have to go on that Quest."

"We'll miss you terribly, though."

"We would have missed you enough as it was."

"But what with this whole ordeal . . ."

"But don't worry about your father."

"Yes. Your mother can take care of me just fine."

"We'll be perfectly all right. After all, you can't let something like your father having cancer keep you from leaving us and doing that Quest thing. We won't have it."

"No, we won't." Despite his best effort to put on a brave front, James's eyes sparkled with unshed tears. "Oh dear. I'm terribly happy about your Quest, but I *do* wish it had come at another time."

"Now, James dear, don't talk that way. That's selfishness and self-pity talking. No more of that!" Motioning for Murgatroyd to go sit down, Olivia set the bacon and omelette on the dining table and began piling food onto her son's plate. "Come now, Murgatroyd, you have to build up your strength in the next two days, don't you?"

James made a great show of helping himself to a large portion of omelette and tucking in, but Murgatroyd noticed that his father was only feigning eating by shuffling the food around his plate with his fork. Murgatroyd didn't feel very hungry either. The three of them sat, pretending to eat for what seemed like an eternity.

"Murgatroyd," his father addressed him, his eyes on the cubes of capsicum he had arranged into a heap on one side of his plate. "Before you leave us to go on this Quest, I have something to ask of you." James raised his eyes to meet his son's. "Do you mind if I ask it?"

"Of course, Dad. What is it?"

"If I don't make it . . . if we never see each other again . . ."

"Dad, don't say such things! Of course we'll see each other again!" Murgatroyd knew he was lying.

"Yes, yes. I'm . . ." James suppressed a quiver in his voice. "I'm sure we will. But if, by the *teeniest, tiniest* chance we *don't*, I want you to remember all the good times we shared. Like that blind man's bluff game I used to play with you when you were little."

Murgatroyd tried to remember. "The one where you would blindfold me and leave me in an unfamiliar place to see if I could find my way home?"

"And you always *did*, you wily little devil, you!" His father smiled and punched him playfully on the arm. Or at least, he had meant it to be playful, for it almost knocked Murgatroyd clean off his chair. "I want you to remember those kinds of things, and remember that I loved—" James corrected himself. "That I *love* you. I love you very much."

Murgatroyd could restrain himself no longer. Quaking and blubbering and wailing as his parents had never seen before, he assaulted his father with a great hug. He buried his head into James's right armpit. The tears and mucus flowed freely from his eyes and nose, making a large wet patch on his father's shirt.

"There, there now!" exclaimed a somewhat-alarmed James as he tried to pry himself loose from his son's embrace. "No need for this! No need for this! Let's try to be calm about things!"

Insensible to his father's struggles to extricate himself, Murgatroyd continued to wail and clutch at his father until, out of sheer fatigue, his hold began to loosen, allowing James to hastily push his grieving son away.

"Look at the time!" James cried. "Your mother and I have to be getting to work!"

Olivia leapt up. "We'd better get going!"

"Son, you finish the rest of breakfast. We'll see you later."

"Goodbye!"

"Congratulations again! We're so proud of you!"

In the blink of an eye, Olivia and James had grabbed their briefcases and slammed the front door behind them, leaving Murgatroyd sniffling to himself at the dining table.

The door suddenly opened again, and his father's voice called out, "And don't even *think* about not going on the Quest and staying behind to help your poor parents get through this terrible crisis, even though it would help us *immensely*."

The door slammed shut again.

There was, of course, no question about it.

***

As the lift descended, James turned to Olivia. He grinned.

"How do you think that went?"

Olivia smiled. "Rather well."

"Funny, isn't it? Can't remember a damned bit about what he explained in his letter."

"Hmm, it is funny, isn't it? Well, we'll never know now. Bit of a shame I flung it out the car window."

James's grin widened. "You're adorable when you're angry."

In response, his wife leaned in and kissed him long and hard.

"I suppose it doesn't matter *what* this 'Quest' thing is, does it?" she whispered once their lips had parted. "The important thing is that the boy must be stopped."

***

Back in the flat, Murgatroyd had made a phone call. And in the Madagascar-Aplomb Territory of the More Known World, Ann had received it. She had been in the kitchen of her abode, indulging in a glass of sparkling wood-scented water. The early hours of her morning had been spent composing detailed reports on the two new Territories she had been helping explore during the past month, and it was time for a break. Luckily, sparkling wood-scented water was her favourite drink, for in the archipelagos of Madagascar-Aplomb, there was little else available. Some of the more populated Territories had settlements of up to a hundred people and were able to facilitate regular imports of food and beverages from the Known World. The Territories that were widely chosen for settlement also tended to have plants that could be eaten or made into drink. Madagascar-Aplomb, on the other hand, had no edible plants—at least, as far as she knew. And it had only one resident: herself. She had chosen the Territory for its tranquillity rather than its practicality. In Madagascar-Aplomb, there was no dry land. Only water stretching out as far as the eye could see. Floating on the eternally calm waters were enormous blocks of pale-coloured wood—islands, one could call them. There was also sky—a cloudless stretch of pale blue that turned lilac with the rising and setting of the sun. That was all there was.

In one of these floating wooden islands, Ann had created her abode. Although waterproof, the wood was soft, and readily yielded under the pressure of any sharp metal object. Ann had used a gardening spade and a spoon. The block of wood she had chosen was so large that she had been able to hollow out for herself a bedroom, two sitting rooms, a kitchen, and a series of filing closets where she kept important documents in meticulously organized stacks, each one up to two metres high. Her bathroom was a small open-air deck fitted with a set of wooden stairs that led into the surrounding seas.

There were never storms in Madagascar-Aplomb, only the light showers that provided Ann with her drinking supply. A catchment area Ann had carved out on the top of her abode collected the fizzy water that fell from the skies, and funnelled it through a long tube Ann had drilled through the wood to a little basin in her kitchen. And it was from this little basin that Ann filled her cup—the only cup she possessed. She lived on this water and a small supply of groceries she would bring back weekly from another Territory. Some would have called the place inconvenient, but Ann didn't really think so. "Simple." That was the word for it.

The dwelling had taken her a little over fourteen months to complete in full, and although her handiwork was simple, crude even, she felt completely satisfied. The feature that gave her the most pleasure was the floors and ceilings, which she had shaved so thin as to be almost transparent. Through the translucent wood above she could see the sky, and through the translucent floor below, the gentle lapping of the waves. And at a certain time of day, the sunlight would stream through the room, through the ceiling and floor, hitting the water beneath and making it shimmer and flash.

Ann had been standing in her kitchen, staring at the sky, sipping water, and thinking of how she should call Murgatroyd to check on his wellbeing. The phone rang.

"Hello?"

"Hello? Can I please speak to Ann?"

"This is she."

"This is Murgatroyd."

Ann was pleasantly surprised by the coincidence and she tried to let it show in her response. "I know. Why are you calling?"

Like her mentor, Ann had never been very good at expressing warmth.

Murgatroyd hesitated. "I . . . I can't go on the Quest."

Ann set her cup down on the floor, instantly on the alert. "That's a shame. Why can't you go?"

"I can't leave my parents."

"*Can't* leave them?" she asked. "Why on earth not?"

Murgatroyd took a deep breath. "My father has cancer."

Ann was silent for a moment. "Oh. That *is* a shame. I'm really sorry to hear that, Murgatroyd. When did you find out?"

"Just now."

"I see." Taking the mobile phone with her, Ann walked briskly to the filing closets.

Murgatroyd continued. "My parents said I should still go, but I think they actually want me to stay."

"Do they now?"

Entering the fifth closet, she cradled the phone between her chin and shoulder. She took down a tall stepladder hanging on the wall to her right and set it next to Stack 6M.

Murgatroyd gave a little cough. "Erh. I'm sorry about all this."

"Sorry?" she repeated. Climbing the stepladder, she examined the colour-coded alphabetized tabs lining one side of the column of files. Lightning quick, she whisked a file out of the stack, leaving the rest of the column undisturbed.

"You know, lah. All the trouble you had to go through. But I should stay. My father is more important than the Quest."

Ann descended the stepladder carefully, Murgatroyd's file tucked underneath her right arm. "Quite."

"I'm sorry," Murgatroyd said, feeling compelled to apologize again.

Ann sighed. It was a sigh of disappointment and frustration. "I'm terribly sorry to hear the bad news about your father. But Murgatroyd, may I ask you something?"

There was no reason for Murgatroyd to say no. "Erh. Yes?"

Ann was now sitting on the floor, spreading out the contents of Murgatroyd's file in front of her. "Do you believe everything your parents tell you?"

Murgatroyd was stunned. "Say again?" he asked, though he had heard her perfectly.

"Just a question. If you do change your mind, I'll be at Bedok Jetty on Friday anyway. Perhaps I'll see you then. Goodbye."

She hung up and surveyed the documents before her. She wasn't quite sure what looking at them again would do. Unable to push the matter from her mind, and unassured by the One's conclusion that all was fine, she had perused the file several times since. Now she looked through its contents for the ninth time since Sunday: copies of school transcripts for Murgatroyd Floyd Shwet Foo, a clipping of a newspaper interview with "promising Singaporean teen" Seng Kay Huat, dental records and medical checkup results, restaurant reviews for the Colonial Table and L'Abattoir, a thick sheaf of research and observation notes, and the like.

She felt now what she had felt each time she had looked over the file since her meeting with the One: puzzled. She couldn't believe that she had somehow missed it all before. Murgatroyd's life simply wasn't unfolding according to the expected pattern. It wasn't just the fact that he possessed such a high level of oddfittingness and that he had somehow managed to retain it for so long—that was only the first peculiarity. The second was his obvious emotional attachment to the people in his life, and his life in the Known World itself—entirely out of keeping with his extreme oddfittingness. The more oddfitting you were, the greater the sense that you didn't belong, the greater the unhappiness, the restlessness, the acute emotional and mental isolation. And the greater the desire to leave it all behind. Oddfits with Murgatroyd's levels of oddfittingness didn't ask for more time once they found out who they were; they left the Known World without a second thought.

Then there was the third peculiarity—perhaps the peculiarest of all: the unhealthy, downright harmful relationships he had with his employer, his best friend, and above all, his parents. At the heights of their oddfittingness, Oddfits inspired feelings of mild disdain and were perceived as awkward and eccentric. But *this* (and here, she reached for the photocopy of the photograph she had scrutinized so many times before—a little terrified Murgatroyd and his gleeful parents by the hyena exhibit at the zoo) she never seen or heard the like of.

Something was terribly wrong.

Murgatroyd had to be removed before it was too late.

She made up her mind. She would contact the One and the Other and arrange an emergency meeting. She would request that an exception to the guidelines be made for Murgatroyd. But first, she had some other calls to make.

***

Stunned by what Ann had said about his parents being liars, an uncharacteristically angry Murgatroyd had redialled Ann's number to give her a piece of his mind. What did she mean? Was she accusing his parents of lying to him? About *cancer*? There had been very few times in his life where Murgatroyd had been provoked to feelings of outrage, and this was one of them. To his surprise, he found himself speaking with someone from the KFC delivery hotline. In his confusion, he ended up ordering a twenty-four piece family meal, all drumsticks and thigh meat, with extra whipped potatoes and coleslaw.

After Murgatroyd hung up, the phone rang again.

"Murgatroyd, it's Ann. Could you do me a favour?"

Murgatroyd sputtered, too caught off guard to remember the exact words he wanted to use to express his indignation. All he could come up with was: "You know, what you said just now about my parents was not very nice."

"Yes. Unfortunately, niceness is not one of my strong points. In any case, tomorrow morning, I want you to go to the 7-Eleven convenience store on Tampines Street 81."

The specificity and unexpectedness of the request surprised Murgatroyd. "Hah? What for?"

"Just to visit a friend. Trust me. He'll be expecting you."

"But—" It was too late. She had hung up again.

Murgatroyd felt very confused. His mind replayed the two conversations he had just had with Ann, but in reverse. Visit a friend at the 7-Eleven? Why did she want him to do that? Did he believe everything his parents told him? Why shouldn't he believe them? Weren't they his parents, after all? Of course the right thing to do was to stay with his cancer-stricken father.

He consoled himself. If he didn't have the Quest, at least he had his job. He counted himself extremely lucky that his attempt to talk to Shakti that night about quitting had been so unsuccessful. At least he was still employed, and he was sure that would help a little with his father's medical bills. But in the meantime, he sat in the kitchen, concentrating hard—as per his father's request—on all the good times that they had shared, and on all of his father's admirable qualities in general. The KFC deliveryman arrived, and not knowing what else to do, Murgatroyd paid him and took the food with a sigh. The faint nausea that had seized him at the sight of his mother's heavy, eggy omelette after he had learned about the cancer, was now intensified ten times over by the greasy smell of deep-fried chicken. He ran to his bathroom to throw up. Feeling somewhat better, he then retired to his new bed and recommenced thinking loving thoughts about his father.

Or at least, that was what he tried, with the utmost discipline, to keep his mind on. Lying in bed, the covers pulled up to his neck, he nestled his head against the soft blue pillow and tried to think of how good his father and mother were to let him indulge in such luxury. But then again, wasn't it normal for everybody to have a bed? Hadn't his parents been sleeping in a bed all this time? And didn't they already have hot water in their bathroom? Kay Huat had always had a bed *and* hot water. Squinching his eyes shut, he tried to remember how happy he had felt that morning of his first day at school when his father had personally given him a haircut for the occasion. He could only remember feeling distressed and disappointed at what he had seen in the mirror. Taking up his father's reminder that morning of the blind man's bluff game they used to play, he tried to recall what fun it had been. His most vivid recollection was of one time where he had scrambled around in the jungle alone and terrified until a tall, dark-skinned, moustachioed stranger wearing big rubber boots and gardening gloves, and wielding enormous pruning shears, had discovered him whimpering in a dark, dank grove of trees. Gently taking up little Murgatroyd in his arms, he had carried him to his lorry and called the police, who had returned him to his parents.

Even worse than these unhappy and ungrateful memories, Murgatroyd found his thoughts straying in the direction of self-pity, frustration, and even anger at not being able to go on the Quest at all; at being forced by this unfortunate turn of events to give it all up and stay with a mother and father who never seemed interested in spending time with him or talking with him, and who seemed, despite all their professions of affection and love for him, distant somehow—cold, and at times, cruel.

There! He had dared to think it! And his eyes and heart grew large with fright at the dreadful things he had just thought. What was wrong with him? He jumped up and hastily began to make the bed, smoothing and stroking the sheets and pillows, meditating deliberately on how soft and beautiful they were. He squatted down to glance at his alarm clock, which was still sitting in its usual place on the floor. It was almost time to leave for work! Nearly six hours had passed and he still had to change out of his pyjamas and clean up the flat! With a feeling akin to relief, he changed his clothes, washed the dishes, and, fleeing the swarm of disquieting thoughts, dashed off to catch his bus.

Once at work, Murgatroyd threw his whole grief-stricken self into his role as waiter extraordinaire. He found an unexpected amount of comfort in the seamlessly placid and elegant demeanour he assumed as a matter of course. It felt as if he were in a protective shell—no, even more than that—a protective, form-fitting bodysuit, for the role fit him so snugly that it muffled the emotional tumult brewing inside him. The anguish and sorrow, the rage and confusion, all felt muted, as if something heavy and soft had been wrapped around them so that they couldn't cause him pain.

It was in this emotionally numb state that he was descended upon by Shakti, who waylaid him as he returned from the dining room to deliver an order from one of his tables.

"So, Shwet Foo. How are you this evening?"

The question—uncharacteristic for Shakti—jolted him unpleasantly out of his muffled consciousness. He wasn't quite sure what to say. So, uncharacteristically, he lied. "Well."

"Still thinking about leaving?"

"Erh." Murgatroyd shook his head and stared down at his shoes. "No, no. Actually, I'm not leaving at all."

This piece of information caught Shakti by surprise, but she did her best to act as if she didn't care. "Really?"

"Erh. Yes?"

"So you're not leaving."

"No."

Shakti was silent for a long time, as if she were carefully weighing his answer. She decided that he needed to be taught a lesson.

"'No'? But you thought you'd waste my valuable time on Monday by telling me that you were thinking of leaving?"

"Yes. I mean, no. Erh. What I—"

"What *you*? Never mind what *you*." Shakti leaned closer. "What *I* want to do is impress upon your soft, soft brain the gravity of your situation. You're walking on the very thin ice of my patience, Shwet Foo. And if I were you . . ." she tried to think of a good way to end her warning. "If I were you, I'd get off the ice."

Murgatroyd lowered his head. "Yes, Mrs. Vithani."

Shakti smiled thinly. She couldn't resist giving a last wounding swipe. "It's always a difficult quest, don't you agree, Shwet Foo?"

He froze in surprise. "Erh. Say again?"

"A difficult *quest*. Finding new employment, that is."

"Oh. Yes. Erh. Yes, it is."

Thoroughly rattled, Murgatroyd ran to the back room to regain his composure. In the meantime, unbeknownst to him, Ann was bringing his plight to the attention of the One and the Other.

CHAPTER 17

The Aminah Caves of the Himalaya-Ablaze Territory were the first caves to be discovered in the More Known World. Yusuf had found them in his third year on the Quest. He loved the Caves. He wasn't sure why, but then again, no Oddfit ever knew the exact reasons why he or she felt more drawn to some Territories than others. There were many things that they didn't know yet, and Yusuf was sure there were many things that they would never truly be able to understand. All Yusuf knew when he happened upon these caves was that they were his. Or perhaps he was theirs. He didn't quite know. What he was certain of, however, was that they were the one place he could remain for long periods of time without feeling, too acutely, the anxious and perpetual homesickness that was the curse and the blessing of the Oddfit.

In the chilly depths of the Aminah Caves, which he had discovered and therefore had the honour of naming, a young Yusuf had set up his abode: a small bedroom well-stocked with heavy blankets and candles, a kitchen chamber more than cool enough to keep food and store drinking water in, and a passageway that no one else knew about until after Yusuf had passed away. At the end of this downward-sloping passageway, the Questians who had come to sort through his possessions found that there was more to Yusuf's abode than he had ever told anyone, even those who had visited him often. There were four rooms, all of them at a natural constant temperature of negative 28.9 degrees Celsius—the perfect temperature for storing ice cream. Two of the rooms appeared to have functioned as experimenting chambers. One of the rooms contained five large ingenious-looking machines for churning ice cream using manpower alone. And the last room was greater and its contents more wonderful than anyone in the history of the Worlds could have ever believed possible.

How Yusuf had managed to produce so much ice cream, the means by which he had managed to distribute it throughout the Territories, and how he had dared to discover a space so large that it defied any attempts to calculate its height and breadth and depth and keep it to himself remained a mystery—a knot yet to be unravelled.

It was in the space that had once been the Great Freezer that Ann had arranged to meet with the One and the Other to discuss the case of Murgatroyd Floyd.

"That's a bit out of the way, don't you think?" the One had asked. "Why can't we just meet at one of *our* abodes?"

Ann had been adamant, arguing that the extra exercise would do them all good and that there was something especially invigorating about the air in the Aminah Caves. She was right, but those weren't really the reasons she had chosen to meet where the Great Freezer had once been. There was a superstitious part of her that wanted to use its associations with Yusuf and the undeniable mystery of the space to strengthen the proposal she was about to put forth to the One and the Other. (How the One shied away from that word: "mystery.") What she was proposing would defy one of the few rules governing the recruitment of new Questians, but she believed that Murgatroyd's wellbeing—nay, his very life—was at stake.

It was possible to transfer to the interior of the Caves themselves, but Ann had felt a bit too worked up about what she was going to say—a combination of anticipatory aggressiveness and, more unusual for her, nervousness. A short trek beforehand would calm her down. She transferred to the topaz fields of wild-growing grain surrounding the Caves and commenced walking briskly towards the meeting place.

From the outside journeying in, the Caves were magnificent: petrified blue-grey clouds billowing forth from the land's surface. The rock they were formed out of was Aminate—similar in every way to obsidian except for its colour. All through this great rock formation snaked a series of tunnels, hollowed out, it was conjectured, by some elemental force at some bygone point in time: streams of liquid perhaps, or wind currents, maybe an ancient rock-eating fungus. Yusuf's abode lay somewhere within them, and getting to it was so complicated that the trail markers he'd planted for the benefit of any visitors approaching his abode from the exterior also served to remind himself of the way back whenever he emerged from the Caves to retrieve drinking water, bathe, or empty his chamber pot. Thankfully, the trail markers were still in place: clusters of spiral-shaped mushrooms. In the sunlight, they were the same blue-grey colour of the Aminate on which they grew, and one had to have a practiced eye to spot them. Ann had taken this way to the Great Freezer several times in the past, and she could pick them out easily. Two clumps of them flanked the entrance to Yusuf's; or rather, the entrance to the vast subterranean passageways in which his abode could be found. In this cold underground world, the mushrooms grew too, but in sunlight's absence, they emitted a steady phosphorescent orange glow. They lined the corridors—not only underfoot, but also on the walls and overhead. Also growing in the tunnels were tufts of softwheat—a variation of its sister species growing on the plains outside. The outdoor variety, if properly detoxified, made a versatile and nutritious stew, excellent with melted cheese or fruit jam. This cave variety made poor eating but excellent wearing. The fluffy white tufts could be spun and woven into a luxuriously soft fabric, and held colour so beautifully that even soft-wheat dyed with the palest of pigments took on a rich hue. Soft-wheat, like the mushrooms, grew everywhere, and whenever Ann passed any, she reached out and ran her fingers through the silky stalks.

The air inside the caves was cold and dry, and grew colder and drier the deeper Ann went. Before too long, Ann had to pull out the sweater and hat she had brought along in her oversized bag. Deeper and deeper she descended, down twisting slopes and around turning bends, one after another, until she finally reached the last long, narrow tunnel, which terminated in a door—a wooden slab on hinges fitted roughly into the surrounding stone. Yusuf's abode. Pushing it open, she entered the rooms within, navigated a few more winding bends, slid down a chute-like tunnel, and emerged into the frozen, wide-open space that had once been the Great Freezer.

The One and the Other were already there. She could make out two tiny silhouettes waiting a considerable distance away, illuminated dimly by the patch of glowing mushrooms they were standing in. It took Ann another twenty minutes to cross the vast, dark plain to where they were. The One was appropriately dressed for a visit to the Aminah Caves: a practical cloak made of soft-wheat-and-wool blend, a heavy shawl swathed around her neck, a giant fur turban, and mittens. The bulky clothing would have overwhelmed anyone else of that slight a frame, but the One's presence far exceeded her size. The Other, who took great pride in his ability to withstand discomfort and inclement weather conditions of all sorts, was not only standing, but standing on one leg while maintaining a painful-looking yoga pose. He was wearing hiking boots, tiny track shorts, and a spandex cycling top. Remarkably spry for a man of sixty-five years, he could cover as much Territory as the fittest of the younger Oddfits—oftentimes more, because of his experience.

Ann took a battery-powered lantern out of her bag, switched it on, and set it at his feet. By the new light, Ann could see that the Other had grown even more tan than when she'd last seen him; almost as brown as the One, but with a ruddy red glow.

"Hi, Ann. Long time no see," he chirruped, breaking out of his pose to stretch his hamstrings.

"Yes, it's been three months, Other," Ann replied, addressing him by his title because reminding the Other that he had a title always made him happy. The Other was so good-natured, easygoing, and predisposed to being content that it was easy to make him happy. Sure enough, like a toddler rediscovering the pleasures of a once-favoured toy, his face broke into an enormous grin.

"I've been exploring," he explained. He was always exploring. That was what made him happiest. "Twelve new territories in just three months. Not bad, eh? One of them has great rock-face for climbing. And great rapids for rafting. And great cloud dirt for skiing."

Ann smiled inwardly. The One and the Other were about as different as any two beings could be.

"Can we get on with things?" the One asked grumpily. Stiffly, she rose to her feet. There was a reason why she'd chosen a warm desert for her abode.

Ann pulled Murgatroyd's file out of her bag. "We need to discuss Murgatroyd Floyd's situation."

"We do?" the Other asked, scratching his head. "Why? You said on the phone that he's decided not to join the Quest after all."

The One folded her arms. "Yes, Ann. Just out of curiosity, what *is* there to discuss?"

At this display of condescension, Ann could feel the anger that she'd spent the last hour trying to dissipate bubbling up within her. Forgetting the well-reasoned argument she'd practiced in her head earlier that day, she went straight to the point.

"We need to change Murgatroyd's mind about the Quest. The Known World is destroying him."

Once the words were out of her mouth, she knew that she had said it all in the worst way possible.

The Other looked quizzically at the One. "We can't change people's minds for them, can we? It's not . . ." he searched for the word he wanted. "Ethical."

"You're right," the One affirmed. "We can't. You know that as well as anyone, Ann. If this is your way of explaining yourself, you need a lot more training." Thinking even more on the two sentences Ann had just uttered, she frowned. "Did you just say he's being *destroyed*?"

Inwardly, Ann slapped her forehead. Outwardly, she tried to look unfazed. "Yes," she stated, straightening her spine. "Yes, I did."

"What in the worlds are you talking about? He's still alive, isn't he?"

"Will you let me explain?"

"By all means, please do," the One said, her voice oozing sarcasm.

"Yes, do! This is quite interesting," the Other chimed in enthusiastically. He plopped himself down on the ground and crossed his legs as if he were waiting for a bedtime story.

Ann struggled to regain her composure—she almost always had it, so on the rare occasion she lost it, she always found it immensely difficult to get it back. After a few calming breaths she did, and she proceeded to point out to her audience of two the perplexing inconsistencies of Murgatroyd's situation: how long he had been in the Known World, but how oddfitting and out of place he still was, almost as if he hadn't been undergoing adaptation at all.

"Ridiculous," the One snapped. "If he wasn't adapting, he'd be dead by now. It's the only way an Oddfit can continue to live in the Known World."

"And yet, he hasn't turned Sumfit, has he? Shouldn't he have by now?"

The One sighed. "Didn't we discuss this already?" She turned to the Other to explain what she and Ann had discussed a few days ago. "He probably started out at an exceptionally high level of oddfittingness, so it's taking him longer to adapt."

"Oh, I see." The Other nodded approvingly. "That sounds like a good explanation."

"What?!" Ann said indignantly. "No, it doesn't! It's no better than mine. And I have other reasons to believe that Murgatroyd isn't adapting."

"Really?" the Other asked, his eyes wide.

"Really," she affirmed. "Tell me: what's it like for a very oddfitting Oddfit to live in the Known World?"

"They don't feel like they belong," the Other promptly answered. "They feel homesick all the time. Depressed. They don't understand things the same way others do. They don't get things right, and they say things wrong. Other people think they're weird." Having revisited his own unhappy childhood experiences of oddfittingness to come up with this answer, the Other looked profoundly sad. He sighed deeply and, with an abstracted look in his eyes, wrapped his arms around his head, almost as if he were giving his brain a consoling hug. "It's terrible, really."

"Yes, it is," Ann said pityingly, almost sorry that she had asked the question at all. "But imagine if other people didn't just think you were weird. Imagine if they wanted to make you miserable."

The Other gasped and, clutching his knees, nimbly rolled himself into a horrified ball.

"Now look what you've done!" The One bent down and patted him comfortingly.

"I'm sorry," Ann said. "But I think that really *is* what's happening. Look!"

Crouching down next to the Other as well, Ann took a piece of paper out of the file and lightly brushed the crown of the Other's head with it. Cautiously, he raised his head, and the three of them looked together. It was a copy of a class photo from Murgatroyd's secondary school days. Murgatroyd, the only white child in the class, was also wearing what appeared to be complicated and needlessly ornate orthodontic headgear.

"According to his official dental records, there has never been anything wrong with the alignment of his teeth," Ann informed them. "And look at this."

It was a page torn out of *Prestige* magazine: "An Interview with Singapore's Restaurant Queen" the title read. It was a picture of Shakti Vithani dressed in a scarlet, puffy-sleeved Versace gown with an oversized gold crown on her head and a black leash in her hand. The leash was attached to the shirt collar of a docile Murgatroyd kneeling on all fours in his waiter's tuxedo. Ann read the caption out loud: "Queen Shakti and her star waiter."

Last but not least came the photo of the Floyd family by the hyena exhibit at the zoo. "He looks like he's having a good time, doesn't he?" Ann remarked dryly.

"No! He doesn't!" exclaimed the Other. Ann sighed. She always forgot that the Other didn't get sarcasm.

The One broke in. "Ann, what's your point?"

"The point is that Murgatroyd hasn't adapted. And worse still, the Known World is obviously doing something to him. Something bad. Something destructive. He can't stay there. We have to tell him."

The One spoke quietly. "Tell him *what* exactly? That we *think* the Known World is 'doing something bad' to him and that he *must* leave it? That goes against all our principles. Choosing to exile one's self permanently from the Known World is a tremendous, life-altering decision. People can't be told to choose it. It's not right. They have to choose it themselves."

"And he *will* choose it himself, once he knows the facts," Ann argued.

The One shook her head. "These aren't facts."

Ann was speechless for a time. "You're joking, right?"

"You're not the only one who's read his file, you know. I have. The Other has. At least two or three other Questians have. From what *I* read, he's as happy as someone that oddfitting can possibly be, apart from the very occasional bouts of homesickness and discontent. He loves his parents, he loves his best friend, he loves his job. If anything, that's a sign that adaptation is indeed underway."

Ann couldn't believe her ears. "Fine. You're right about that," she conceded. "I can't explain why he thinks he's so happy. But he can't possibly be *truly* happy. I mean, *look* at him!"

Ann pulled out a photocopy of Murgatroyd's identity card, blown up to several times its original size. Together, they studied the unflattering but accurate portrait of Murgatroyd—the half-closed eyes, the half-open mouth, the hunch in the neck and shoulders. Even though the photo was in black and white, one got the impression that there was a sickly tinge to his skin.

"That's not very nice," said the Other. "He can't help the way he looks."

The One nodded in agreement. "Really, Ann. I didn't expect you to be so superficial."

Ann let out an exasperated growl, shut the file, and slammed it on the ground. The One and the Other were shocked. This was the most infuriated they had ever seen her. Ann was never infuriated. Abrupt, sometimes. Curt, often. But never angry like this. It was in fact only the second time in her life Ann had ever been so enraged.

"So we can't warn him?"

The One gave her an icy gaze. A gaze that made clear that the answer was "no" and that she was thoroughly embarrassed for Ann and her unprofessional behaviour. "In fact," she added, "From this moment onward, you are forbidden from further contact with Murgatroyd Floyd until your appointed meeting time with him on Friday evening—*if* he chooses at his own free will to come."

"What?!" Ann exclaimed. "This is ridiculous!"

The One's face darkened further. "Ann, the decision is final."

The Other shrugged apologetically in Ann's direction.

Ann could only glower in response. "Fine."

With that, she transferred back to her abode in Madagascar-Aplomb, stomped to the dock and plunged into the sea, clothes, shoes, and all. She needed to cool off. As she began swimming the first of fifteen laps around her floating wooden home, she reflected that it was a good thing she had taken matters into her own hands before the meeting. Murgatroyd, she hoped with all her might, would meet with Ivan. She wasn't going against principles or disobeying the silly prohibition that the One had just put in place. Not at all. She was simply trying to provide Murgatroyd with more information on which to base his ultimate decision.

Still, Ann had conveniently omitted to inform the One and the Other of what she had done. Just in case.

CHAPTER 18

Murgatroyd stood across the street from the 7-Eleven convenience store that Ann had directed him to. Ann hadn't told him what time in the morning he should get there, so he had set off right after his parents had left for work. It was now 9:56 a.m.

He hadn't gotten much sleep the night before. After he'd returned from work last night, he had called Kay Huat to tell him the bad news about his father and about not being able to go on the Quest.

"So you're not going, eh?" Kay Huat had said in response to the news. "That's too bad."

"Yeah," Murgatroyd had said glumly.

"But I think you've made the right decision. After all, your father is more important than the Quest, right?"

Murgatroyd sighed heavily. "Yeah."

"You're doing the right thing, Shwet Foo," Kay Huat reassured him. And ever the loyal and dependable friend, he attempted to cheer Murgatroyd up by listing all the reasons why not going on the Quest was a good thing. There were two.

Despite Kay Huat's best efforts, Murgatroyd still felt dejected when he put down the phone and went to bed. He hadn't slept very well, spending all night lying on his back staring into the dark, kept awake by the emotional tumult he had been feeling the whole day—a combination of the terrible news about his father's breast cancer and his own distress at the new streak of selfishness that he seemed to have developed recently. This new selfishness bothered him a lot. Why did he feel so resentful at not going on the Quest when it meant helping his parents and spending precious time with his ailing father? And why, all of a sudden, did he feel so ungrateful towards his parents? These thoughts and variations of these thoughts churned inside his head until the sun rose and the birds began chirping outside. His father's cheery voice announced that breakfast was ready. His father and mother had made French toast.

Despite his parents' best efforts to draw him into conversation that morning (such efforts alone were far from commonplace and should have surprised him), Murgatroyd had continued to dwell on these matters, even as he had sat with them, mechanically depositing breakfast into his mouth. He, of course, had informed his parents the night before that he had decided to stay with them instead of leaving for the Quest. And they had shown obvious delight, even though they'd initially made some sounds of protest. This morning, however, all protest had subsided into pure gratefulness.

"My *dear* boy, we are so glad," Olivia had said, bestowing a light kiss on her son's forehead. So light, in fact, that Murgatroyd hadn't even felt it, though he heard the smacking sound of her lips. But of course, that was just his imagination. Of course she had kissed him. Of course his parents loved him. Of that he was utterly convinced. How could he doubt it? And yet he did.

But what reasonable cause did he have for these doubts and inklings of mistrust, which seemed to have sprung out of nowhere? He couldn't pinpoint anything exactly. Hadn't they always been good and kind to him? *Hadn't* they?

Bringing his mind back to the present, he walked up to the 7-Eleven. From the outside, it looked just like any other 7-Eleven. Through the floor-to-ceiling glass windows he could see the modestly sized shelves stocked with snacks and amenities, a magazine rack, a soft-drink dispenser and Slurpee machine, an ice cream freezer, and near the cash register, a heated display case of steamed buns and another one of curry puffs. Murgatroyd wasn't sure what else he had expected, but part of him, however miserable he felt, had hoped that since the store was presumably connected to Ann somehow, it would have at least looked a little different.

Murgatroyd entered the store. There was nothing out of the ordinary. Then he noticed something incongruous. Seated behind the counter was a distinguished Chinese man of slim build wearing a navy-blue double-breasted suit, a button-down collared shirt of the richest lavender hue, and a silver necktie. A red carnation adorned his breast pocket, his hair was perfectly parted and impeccably combed, and he appeared to be absorbed in solving a crossword puzzle. So absorbed, in fact, he hadn't registered Murgatroyd's entrance at all. Near his elbow sat a half-empty box of Cadbury's assorted chocolates.

Murgatroyd approached the counter and waited. The man still didn't look up.

"Erh. Excuse me," he ventured, timidly.

The man shifted slightly, reached for a chocolate with his left hand, and popped it into his mouth.

Murgatroyd coughed. Not because he wanted to get the man's attention, but because he was suddenly overcome with a small coughing seizure, which caused the man to leap backwards, wrinkle his nose, and hastily move the chocolates to a ledge behind him where they would be safe from contamination.

"Sorry," Murgatroyd wheezed as the coughing spell began to subside.

The man produced a white handkerchief and, holding it to his nose and mouth, drawled in affected Queen's English, "I suppose you want something?"

It took a few seconds for Murgatroyd to express exactly what he wanted to say. "Erh. Are you Ann's friend?"

"Ann's *friend*?" The man pronounced these words with some incredulity, saying the word "friend" slowly and exaggeratedly. Recoiling in disdain, he looked as if Murgatroyd had dared to request something completely bizarre. Like a gold-encrusted hedgehog or a griffin claw.

"Ann. You know Ann? She told me to come here today to meet a friend of hers."

"To*day*?" the man asked with the same incredulous disdain.

Murgatroyd grew even more flustered. "Erh. Yes. Ann's friend." An idea struck him, and he leaned in closer, only to have the man shrink away, clutching his handkerchief to his face as if Murgatroyd had the plague. "Erh . . ." Murgatroyd began, trying to whisper as loudly as he could to a man who was trying his best to keep his distance. "You know. For the Quest."

The expression on the man's face convinced Murgatroyd that not only did he think him disease-ridden, but also completely mad.

At length, the man decided to respond. "I haven't the faintest idea of what you are speaking. Let me go get my supervised."

Murgatroyd thought he'd misheard. "You mean your supervisor?"

"No," the man snapped. "My *supervised.* You don't expect *me* to deal with these insignificant little things, do you? *He* deals with all of it. *I* supervise *him.*"

Tucking his crossword puzzle book under his arm and picking up the chocolates, he turned and briskly exited through a door behind the counter. A few seconds later, through the same door emerged a surly teenager sporting a bright pink, spiky hairdo and at least five eyebrow rings.

The teenager proceeded to scowl at Murgatroyd for what seemed like an eternity, making the latter feel extremely uncomfortable. That is, until he spoke.

"Good morning, sir. Can I help you with something?"

Much to Murgatroyd's astonishment, the words were not only exceedingly courteous in and of themselves, but they were also delivered in a voice inexplicably rich, creamy, and flavourful. Murgatroyd felt all the tension in his body melt away. He was surprised, certainly, but not ill at ease, or even confused. He could even describe the sensation he was feeling down to the minutest detail, and it took the form of a vivid scene in which he himself was playing a part. It was his nine-year-old self returning home after his first day at school, miserable, humiliated, and soggy. It was unlocking the door and finding a pair of dry, freshly laundered flannel pyjamas on the table by the entrance. It was changing into them and then following, with his nose, the heavenly scent wafting from the kitchen. And inside the kitchen, sitting on a table, waiting for him, was a steaming bowl of tomato soup. Of course, that wasn't what had happened at all.

"Sir?"

"I'm here," Murgatroyd said, his voice surprisingly clear, "to meet Ann's friend."

"Oh, it's you!" The teenager's voice bespoke pleasant surprise, even though the scowl never left his face. "Yes, Ann told me you were coming. Did you have any trouble finding the place?"

"No. Quite easy to find."

"Oh good. I'm Ivan. Ivan Ho." Ivan extended his hand.

They exchanged a handshake. "Murgatroyd. Murgatroyd Floyd Shwet Foo."

"Shwet Foo. That's a strange name."

"My parents thought it would help me fit in better at school."

"Did it help?"

"Erh. No, not really. No."

"Oh. That's a shame," Ivan said. "Must have been terrible. At least that's over and done with." He grinned.

Murgatroyd had never had such a pleasant and effortless conversation before. Usually he dreaded talking with people he didn't really know. He always felt that the other person was bored and he never knew what to say to make himself more interesting. Ivan, on the other hand, seemed as if he actually wanted to be talking to him, which was probably because Ivan did really want to be talking to him.

"So you're going on the Quest, is it?" Ivan asked. "That must be why you spoke to Ann." Ann actually had told Ivan very little about the whole situation. All she had said was that Murgatroyd was an Oddfit whom she had talked to about joining the Quest. Ivan didn't mind the lack of information—he always liked meeting new people.

"Erh, no. Actually, I'm not going on the Quest after all," Murgatroyd said a little sheepishly.

Ivan raised his eyebrows in curiosity. "Really? But why not?"

Murgatroyd shrugged. "Erh. Not a good time. My father has breast cancer."

"Oh. I'm so sorry," Ivan said. He tugged on his eyebrow rings, almost as if to express his condolences. "It's just that it seems like such a great opportunity, you know? If I were an Oddfit, I'd take it. But you're right. That does seem like a good reason not to go."

"Are you a . . . a Questian?" Murgatroyd asked.

"Me? No."

"How do you know Ann?"

"Oh, from a long time ago. A long time," Ivan explained. "But every now and then, I do make a trip to the More Known World. It's where I keep my pets."

"Your pets?"

"Yes. I'm not much of a Sumfit. More like a One-fit. It's tiring having to transfer so much between there and here. But they're worth it, my pets." Ivan's eyes lit up. "Do you want to see them? Oh, even better! Do you want to feed them?"

Before Murgatroyd could respond, Ivan pulled out a short stack of index cards and offered them to him. "These are instructions for how to get there. They're numbered, just in case you drop them and need to put them back in order. You shouldn't have any problems."

Murgatroyd took the cards. "Aren't you coming? I've never transferred by myself before."

"I just transferred there the day before yesterday, and I don't think my body can take another visit so soon. It can be quite dangerous for a Sumfit to overtransfer himself." Ivan reached over and patted his new friend on the back. "You'll be fine. The instructions are quite detailed. How to get there, how to feed them, how to get back. That's all you need to know. They'll be happy to see you. Usually, they only get fed about once every two weeks."

Murgatroyd looked at the first card and read it aloud.

"Step One. Enter the back room behind the counter."

It was the same door that the man in the suit had entered only moments before. Ivan turned the handle, pushed it open, and gestured for Murgatroyd to come round the counter. He ushered Murgatroyd through the door before closing it behind him. "I hope you like them!" Ivan called through the closed door. Even muffled, his tomato-soup voice still felt warm and pleasant in Murgatroyd's ears.

The back room was dimly lit and cramped, filled with piles and piles of cardboard boxes of all shapes and sizes. Room had been made in one corner for a large paisley-print armchair and a stained-glass lamp, in and under which sat the man in the suit. He was polishing off the last of the chocolates, engrossed still in his crossword puzzle. He ignored Murgatroyd.

Murgatroyd placed the first index card at the bottom of the stack and read the second one: "Step Two. Find the crack in the wall."

Murgatroyd looked around. He didn't see any crack. "Hallo, sir?" Murgatroyd called to the man, who looked up slowly and disdainfully.

"Do you know where the crack in the wall is?"

"*Wall*?"

Murgatroyd decided that he would find the crack himself. And he did. It was hidden behind several large cardboard boxes of instant ramen—a hairline crack running from where the wall met the floor to the height of Murgatroyd's knee.

Murgatroyd read the next card: "Step Three. Look straight at it. Feel homesick and alone."

Murgatroyd found out that feeling homesick and lonely on cue was very difficult. He tried for a good eleven minutes to no avail. In his frustration, he slumped down with his back against the wall and hugged his knees to his chest. So much for his supposed Oddfit abilities. What's more, now that he wasn't going on the Quest, this might be the one chance he'd ever have again to see the More Known World. And here he was, trapped in a dark room with an unfriendly stranger. He felt helpless and restless all at the same time.

It was then that he heard a sound like fabric ripping. Looking up, he saw that the crack had opened to reveal a flight of stairs bathed in a dim violet light.

He read the fourth card. "Step Four. Go all the way up the stairs." He began his ascent.

The ascent took a very long time. Murgatroyd felt as if he'd been climbing continuously for a good fifteen minutes at least. It seemed as if he were heading towards some sort of light source, for the higher he climbed, the less dark it got. The strange thing about the light was that it had started out as a deep violet hue, but was slowly transforming into red, then orange, then yellow, and now, a pale white—as if he were climbing up a sunrise. Ten minutes later, he was quite overcome with fatigue, and was about to sit down on the steps to take a short break, when the stairs ended.

He found himself in the middle of a very open, empty, and brightly lit space, blue and speckled like a robin's egg, with no walls or floor or ceiling, but no horizon or scenery or sun either. He couldn't tell whether he was outside or indoors.

He read the fifth card. "Step Five. Walk to the glass tank."

He looked around: nothing but speckled blueness as far as the eye could see. A very tiny wisp of activity caught his eye. There! Far in front of him, slightly to his left, was a cluster of hovering tiny black dots. Gradually, his eyes began to make out the faint outlines of a rectangular glass tank.

This all should have struck Murgatroyd as very peculiar indeed. Yet, it didn't. Just as when he first heard Ivan's tomato-soup voice, he had that unfamiliar and pleasant sense of coming home. He approached the tank, and as he drew near, he saw that the tank was filled with little flying insects buzzing about. They looked suspiciously like mosquitoes.

He read the sixth card. This was the longest set of instructions so far.

"Step Six." Murgatroyd read slowly. "Locate the circular panel in the glass on the side of the tank. Unlatch the panel. Open it quickly and stick your arm in."

For the first time in this whole endeavour, Murgatroyd felt a twinge of fear. Were the instructions serious? He turned quickly to the seventh card to see what it said.

"Step Seven. Hold your arm steady inside the tank and count backwards from sixty. Admire and bond with the mosquitoes as you feed them."

So they *were* mosquitoes. Still hoping that the cards weren't really telling him to stick his arm into a tank full of blood-sucking creatures, Murgatroyd skipped ahead to the eighth card.

"Step Eight. Don't feed them too long, or they'll get too fat! Withdraw your arm, making sure to shake the mosquitoes off first, and close and latch the panel."

Maybe the ninth card would read, "Just kidding." Murgatroyd read the ninth card. "Thank you for feeding my pets! Aren't they sweet?"

Murgatroyd sighed, flipped back to card six, and began carrying out the feeding instructions. Once Murgatroyd's arm was inside the tank, the mosquitoes flocked to it, covering it in a seething, humming mass of ravenous insect hunger. At first, he felt nauseated, but as he continued to watch how lustily they suckled at his pale, thin arm, the disgust and fear began to melt away. Each mosquito, he noted, was completely ignorant of the fact that this arm was attached to a larger sentient being staring at them in wonder from outside their glass enclosure. He was so mesmerized by the spectacle that he'd forgotten to start counting backwards from sixty, so he began counting backwards from forty.

"Thirty-nine, thirty-eight, thirty-seven . . ." The longer he looked at them, the less they appeared a giant, indistinguishable mass. He could pick out individuals now, the delineations of the veins on each wing, the contours of their abdomens swelling slowly with his blood.

"Fifteen, fourteen, thirteen . . ."

Strangely enough, he felt as if he really was bonding with them. He felt an affection for each of them.

"Three, two, one, zero." He shook them off his arm before withdrawing from the tank and latching the panel. His arm felt prickly all over, and already, red welts were beginning to appear.

He looked at the tenth card. "Step Ten. Don't scratch. It will make it worse. Much worse."

All of a sudden, his arm was inflamed in itchiness. He groaned and tried blowing on the bites to relieve the pain.

"Step Eleven. Go back down the stairs. I have some lotion that will help with the itching. See you soon!"

By the time he had finished reading the card, his arm had become a swollen, throbbing, burning, misshapen lump of flesh. Murgatroyd raced to the stairs and began a hurried climb downwards. Unfortunately, he had indeed climbed a long way to the top, and even though he made his way down as fast as he could, it still seemed to take an eternity. Finally, he arrived at the bottom. There was only one small problem. There were no more stairs, but there was also nowhere else to go. Panting from the itching and the pain, he hurriedly flipped through the cards to see if there was another step. In the dim purple light, he could hardly make out the words.

"Step Twelve. Once you get to the bottom of the stairs, stare at the crack in front of you. Feel homesick and alone."

Murgatroyd groaned. The crack was easier to find from here. It was almost four times the size it had been in the Known World and was indeed right in front of him. But he really didn't feel like feeling homesick and alone. He felt itchy. So very, very itchy. In fact, that was all he could feel running through his mind—an itchiness, as regular and resounding as a heartbeat. *Itchy. Itchy. Itchy. Itchy. Itchy. Itchy.*

No. If you want to get out of here, you have to concentrate. Murgatroyd gritted his teeth and tried to think back to the scene from his childhood that Ann had used to get him to see the More Known World during their first meeting. Then he thought of how he had felt all last night—the doubt and mistrust and dissatisfaction and isolation . . .

He was back. The man in the suit was still sitting in his armchair, doing his crossword, but Murgatroyd barely registered his presence as he sped past him and burst out the back-room door.

Ivan was standing there to receive him, a green plastic bottle in his hand. "Stretch out your arm." Murgatroyd obeyed, his eyes watering. Ivan drenched the arm in lotion and vigorously rubbed it in. The pain and heat vanished instantly. Murgatroyd looked at his arm. It looked like its pale, non-inflamed self again.

"Is it better now?" Ivan asked.

"Much better."

"Did you like them? My pets?"

His mind less clouded with pain, Murgatroyd reflected. "Yes, I did."

"They're a very rare variety of mosquito and very sensitive. Ann got them for me from a new Territory she'd been exploring. They don't do well in the Known World, so that's why I keep them there. They can live for much longer and I don't have to feed them as often."

"Why mosquitoes?" Murgatroyd asked.

"It sounds a bit funny, but I like them." Sighing, Ivan shook his head at his own silliness. "I don't know why. They probably don't even know or care about me. Or what a pain it is to feed them. Literally. Luckily, I do have this lotion." Ivan jerked his head towards the back-room door. "My older brother invented it."

"That's your brother?" Murgatroyd exclaimed.

Ivan nodded. "He's a little eccentric, but he's very clever. He's not really as bad as he seems."

Murgatroyd smiled.

"Thanks for dropping by," Ivan said, tugging on his eyebrow rings, this time as if it were his way of smiling. "I have to start taking inventory right now, but it was nice to meet you. I hope your father gets better."

"Thanks."

"Sorry you can't go on the Quest."

"Yeah," Murgatroyd rubbed his neck and looked at his feet. There was a moment of silence, as if they both were mourning the missed opportunity. "Ann did say she'd still be there, in case I changed my mind, but I don't think I'll be going."

"Yeah. It's a shame," Ivan said.

The bell above the entrance door tinkled. Both Ivan and Murgatroyd looked up to see who had come in, but nobody had.

"Must be the wind," Ivan said.

Murgatroyd nodded. He felt reluctant to leave this new unexpected acquaintance he had made. "It was nice to meet you," he said.

"Nice to meet you too. Oh, wait a second. I almost forgot." Ivan handed him a paper cup of vanilla soft-serve ice cream. It had a little blue parasol stuck in it. "Have a Mister Softee. Free of charge. If you do see Ann, tell her I said hi. Here's a spoon."

Feeling shy all of a sudden, Murgatroyd took the little plastic spoon, said thank you, and left. He looked at his wristwatch. It was a lot later than he thought. He had to report for work. As he walked towards the bus stop, he ate the ice cream and thought about what he had just experienced. So that was what travelling to the More Known World was like. And he now knew what Ann meant about feeling most at home while doing so. Now that he was back in the Known World, he felt the deep despair and confusion he had been experiencing lately beginning to wash over him again. To delay this reality, he thought about the wondrousness of his visit to feed Ivan's mosquitoes and grinned to himself. He felt hope and joy welling up within him—and a curious, renewed yearning for these sensations, so new to him, to remain with him always. Was this what going on the Quest would be like?

His meeting with Ivan Ho and his brief visit to the More Known World had given Murgatroyd great joy indeed. These were the exact results Ann had hoped the visit would produce when she had arranged it. Unfortunately, Murgatroyd's third visit to the More Known World also had other consequences—ones that neither Ann nor the One, the Other nor Yusuf, nor any other soul living or dead could ever have foreseen. For although new knowledge was being gained every day, there was still much about the worlds that nobody knew.

For example, nobody knew that, technically speaking, Oddfits didn't adapt to the Known World; the Known World adapted them. It was a small distinction that hardly made any difference when it came to the day-to-day business of existence; but it did imply that the Known World was capable of exerting more power than its inhabitants tended to ascribe to it. Another interesting thing that nobody knew: oddfittingness wasn't just a matter of quantity, but also of quality. There was a type of oddfittingness that the Known World could never diminish, never eradicate, and therefore, could never tolerate. An unadaptable Oddfit couldn't be allowed to live: it was an inalterably foreign element that had to be purged in order to preserve the healthy functioning of the whole.

A third of all Oddfits conceived possessed this type of oddfittingness, and a third of all Oddfits conceived met their demise before they ever took their first breath.

Murgatroyd should have died before he was ever born.

And yet, he lived. At the risk of attributing to the Known World sentience, unified thought, and feeling, one might even say that the Known World spared his life. It certainly had intended to eliminate the foreign being, as it did with all the others; but there was something different about this one. This one loved.

All the others emitted hate—hate pure and blind for the world they found themselves in, and understandably so. They were creatures out of their element—birds in water, fish in air. With every act of cellular proliferation, with the formation of each new type of cell, each new organ, and each new appendage, every burgeoning nerve and sinew and blood vessel of these rapidly growing beings screamed silently in protest, consumed with an instinctive hatred for an environment to which they could never belong. The reaction was mutual: the Known World felt their presence as a burning, festering rash across the skin, a thick splinter in the foot's sole, the sharp sting of an angry wasp. They were as incapable of tolerating the Known World as the Known World was incapable of tolerating them.

Then there was this one. This one who, against every inclination of every growing fibre of its being, struggled to love the world in which it now found itself gaining form and consciousness. Love in spite of it all.

The Known World was confused. Could it be that this being was, in some way, one of its own? Or maybe this one just needed more time. Could it be adapted later?

Improbable, but there was still a small chance . . .

The Known World made its decision with great trepidation. The being could live, but the adverse effects of its presence had to be suppressed in order to be made endurable: in lieu of getting rid of the illness, the Known World treated the symptoms. In exchange for its life, the being had to be kept in a weakened physical and psychological state.

So it was done. The being was born and it grew, after a fashion. And it reached adulthood, of a sort. And it bore the weakening that was inflicted upon it admirably. It still loved. In response, the Known World remained wary, but also gracious. When the being departed the first time, returning pungent with the aroma of the other world and slightly stronger than it should have been, the Known World dismissed this as a fleeting lapse, resumed its suppression of the being, and let it continue to be—for the being still loved.

When the being did this a second time, the Known World was alarmed and pained, but took no action—for the being still loved.

This time, it could not be abided, no matter how much the being still loved. Aside from the fact that this third departure was simply excessive—a clear sign of the being's wavering determination to endure the Known World—the being had come back far too robust. Upon its re-entry, the Known World had groaned in agony. The being called Murgatroyd had become a cancerous tumour, a deadly virus. There was no alternative. It had to be destroyed.

Murgatroyd was blissfully unaware of the aggravation his actions had incited from the world in which he now sat, waiting for the bus to take him to work. He was also unaware that he was being watched. The watcher was someone who had also been in the 7-Eleven at the same time as Murgatroyd, and whose stealthy departure had caused the little bell above the door to give a cheerful tinkle. It was the Duck Assassin, lurking in the shadows of a nearby banyan tree, dutifully carrying out the work assigned to him by Mrs. Vithani.

The Duck Assassin was a quiet young man. Or perhaps "silent" would be a better word, since one associates "quiet" men with innocuous activities like library-frequenting and chess-playing and stamp-collecting. He was a silent but dangerous sort who had nothing personal against Murgatroyd Floyd Shwet Foo. Nothing but the nameless dull contempt he felt for everyone and everything. At least, that was what he had always felt. Until now.

Crouching very still behind the tree trunk, dressed in his usual black attire, with the lower part of his face concealed, the Duck Assassin watched Murgatroyd at the bus stop. The little *ang moh* wasn't doing anything very interesting—sitting, standing, sitting again, standing and stretching, walking in circles. Finally, the *ang moh* pulled out a little blue paper parasol from his pocket and, twirling it about between his hands, seemed to lose himself in happy contemplation. Yes, the *ang moh* hadn't really done anything, and wasn't really doing anything now, but the Duck Assassin was beginning to feel much more than mere contempt for Murgatroyd. *Much* more. As he watched Murgatroyd, he felt his contempt blossoming into a searing hatred, intensifying exponentially with each second Murgatroyd was passing alive under his surveillance. He didn't know why. The *ang moh* had never caused him offence. There was no explanation for it.

Or was there? Yes. Yes, there was an explanation, now that he thought further on it. It lay in everything—*everything* he had observed about the *ang moh* as he had followed him over the past few days: the pathetic grin that lit up his whole pathetic face every time he encountered some insignificant reason to rejoice in his pathetic little life; the innocent, misplaced faith he so stupidly and stubbornly had in everything and everyone around him; the way the world kicked him as if he were a mangy roadside dog and the way the stupid little *ang moh* kept trotting back for more, tail wagging, eyes bright. It was positively infuriating.

And now, this pitiful, idiotic *ang moh* had an opportunity to embark on some sort of "Quest"—one that would enable him to leave this place forever and go far, far away. On Friday at seven p.m., he could meet that one-eyed woman in green and leave for good. The assassin wasn't quite sure what the *ang moh* would eventually decide to do. From the conversation he had just overheard while hiding in the corner of the 7-Eleven, it appeared that he wasn't going after all. But there was something incomprehensibly annoying about the way the *ang moh* glowed happiness whenever he had talked about that stupid Quest. He recalled his first day on this assignment: he could always tell the *ang moh* was thinking about the Quest whenever he smiled or whenever his eyes twinkled without reason. He recalled how unnaturally hopeful the *ang moh* had been when sharing the news that night with his best friend. And even now, when he was apparently being prevented from going on the Quest, the yearning and wonder in the way he had spoken of it in the 7-Eleven made the Duck Assassin burn with rage.

How could that miserable little creature be so oblivious? So trusting? How dare he hope? How dare he dream? How dare he hobble towards the open horizon of freedom and gaze at it with such awe and longing even when he found his path blocked?

The Duck Assassin was still stewing in his hate and pondering it when, unexpectedly, a memory surfaced, long sunken and forgotten. As a child, he would often escape into the jungle that surrounded the wooden shack in which his family lived. There were no people in the jungle. Nobody to scold him or pull his ears, nobody to burn him with cigarette butts, or throw beer bottles at him, or slap him for misbehaving or not doing his chores properly. Just the dark, cool shadows of the forest floor, the nooks and crannies of giant tree trunks, the soothing rustle of the dead leaves crunching underfoot. He would capture all sorts of animals and put them in jars and boxes. The little snakes he would look at only for a few minutes before releasing them back into the wild. Ants he had often tried keeping as pets, but they always sickened and died, no matter how well he fed them. Lizards were usually too quick for him to catch. But one time, he came across a few moth cocoons hidden under some dead leaves and twigs. He brought one of them home and kept it in an old jam jar covered with some soft netting he had found among some rubbish in an alleyway. He set the jar amidst stacks of old newspapers and bottles on the rickety old table in the corner of the main room and waited for the cocoon to hatch. Several days passed, and he began to give up hope, but one afternoon, he came home and noticed something moving in the jar. It was a moth, all right—a fat, furry body on six hairy little legs, scuttling around in the small space of the jar. But something had gone wrong. The moth hadn't been able to climb the slippery glass sides of the jar to hang upside down and properly unfurl its wings. Now it was too late. Its wings were permanently damaged.

He put his finger inside the jar, letting the moth clamber onto the palm of his hand, and he stroked it for a while with the back of his finger. It was trembling, and so soft and fuzzy. Gently, he set it down upon the table and let the deformed creature waddle about. It might have been a handsome moth—its body and wings were a bright green rather than the usual brown of most moths he had seen, and the wings were adorned with shades of black, dusky purple, and rose pink. But the wings were crumpled, misshapen, and awkwardly angled, sometimes tripping their owner who half-limped, half-flapped about in circles, attempting to take flight.

The young boy had felt an overwhelming sense of empathy for the moth, for he understood it—understood it even more than he himself knew. And with this profound empathy came an inexplicable rage. The moth was stupid. It would never fly, but it still tried. It tried again and again. With the bare heel of his hand, he smashed it to death.

Stupid moth.

***

By the time Murgatroyd's bus had arrived, the Duck Assassin was speeding away on his motorcycle to the Vithani residence, where Shakti had been expecting him. Upon hearing the Duck Assassin's report, Shakti's eyes blazed with contempt and wounded pride.

"So he is leaving me," she murmured under her breath. Leaving her. And of all things, he had *lied* about it. "On Friday evening, you say? You're positive about this? Absolutely positive?"

If Shakti had been watching the black-clad figure standing before her more closely, she would have noticed that the figure hesitated—just for a moment—before it nodded in the affirmative.

But she wasn't paying any attention to the minutiae of his movements. All her attention was directed inward, focused on herself: her humiliation, indignation, and wrath. In a paroxysm of fury, she picked up a small porcelain statuette on the table next to her and hurled it against the wall. Its shattering calmed her a little. Just a little. She turned the matter over again in her head. Little Shwet Foo was leaving *her*—Shakti Vithani. Possibly the most influential and charismatic woman in Singapore. She who had deigned to spend her own precious time grooming that hunchbacked caterpillar into a beautiful butterfly. All for some one-eyed woman and a preposterous mission. And he had dared to lie about it. To her face. She never would have thought him capable. She never would have thought that he had the guts. But he had. It was a brazen act of deception that she would have admired if she hadn't been the object of deception. *Heartless guttersnipe*. Shakti Vithani always had a tendency to overreact, but something that day prompted her to overreact even more than usual. As the Duck Assassin stood dutifully before her, awaiting her next order, Shakti had this to say:

"Kill him."

CHAPTER 19

"Hah? Say again?" Murgatroyd exclaimed to the manager of L'Abattoir.

"We're letting you go," the manager repeated. His tone was cool and firm, although he himself was recovering from surprise. Mrs. Vithani had called only fifteen minutes ago with the order to fire Shwet Foo.

"But—but—" Murgatroyd stammered. "How come?"

"Well . . ." the manager began tactfully. Managing three different restaurants belonging to the temperamental Shakti had given him a lot of experience in firing people. He launched into one of his five standard replies for this kind of question. "Although you're not a bad worker, we feel that you aren't invested seriously enough in this job. It just doesn't seem to suit you."

Murgatroyd attempted to laugh. "Eh, you must be joking, right? Does Mrs. Vithani know about this? Can I talk to her?"

"Sorry, Shwet Foo, but Mrs. Vithani is not in at the moment. She told me to wish you the best of luck on her behalf, and that she's sorry that she has to let you go."

So Shakti not only knew, but Shakti *herself* was firing him. The expression on Murgatroyd's face was that of a dog struck by its master for no reason.

On his way out, he passed Ahmad who thumped him consolingly on the shoulder. "Sorry, man. I just heard the news."

"Erh, thanks," Murgatroyd mumbled before stumbling through the front doors into the hot afternoon sun.

Ahmad called after him. "Eh, Shwet Foo! You gonna be all right or not?"

"Yeah . . ." Murgatroyd answered faintly, walking on.

Perhaps it was because he was in such a state of shock and despair that he didn't see the motorcycle roaring down the street towards him as he made his way to the nearest bus stop. He could have sworn that he had looked both ways twice. But however it happened, Murgatroyd had been crossing the road when he looked to his right and became aware of two things: one, that a large black motorcycle was advancing towards him at breakneck speed, and two, that these were to be the last moments of his life.

Startled by this double revelation, Murgatroyd's feet screeched to an abrupt halt and lost their balance, sending him tumbling backwards out of the street and, just barely, out of the path of the motorcycle. There was a flash of warmth in his feet—the friction of the motorcycle's wheels grazing the soles of his sneakers as it sped past. Lying on the pavement, flat on his back, Murgatroyd lifted his head and watched as the motorcycle zoomed away, turned a corner, and disappeared out of sight.

A young woman and her little boy ran up to him. "Are you all right?"

Murgatroyd looked upwards and saw two anxious faces against the backdrop of the blue sky. "I think so," he answered faintly.

"You can walk or not? You need me to call triple nine?"

"No, no. No need. I think I'm okay."

She helped Murgatroyd to his feet.

"Are you sure?"

"Yeah, yeah. Thank you."

"Okay," the woman said doubtfully, before taking her son's hand and continuing on her way. "See, Kiang Hong?" she said to her son. "This is why Mummy always tells you to be careful when crossing the street."

Thoroughly rattled by this brush with death, Murgatroyd decided it would be best to return home. After spending ten minutes steadying himself, Murgatroyd wobbled to the bus stop. His bus arrived. He stepped aboard and sat down. He pushed the signal button for his stop and disembarked. He walked back to his flat. He pushed the button for the lift.

Murgatroyd did all of these things mechanically and instinctively. Like a homing pigeon trained to always return to a specific location, Murgatroyd had made his way back to where he lived. Soon he would make his way to the kitchen, make himself a cup of Milo, add a heaping tablespoonful of salt, and sit there disconsolately. This was what he always did whenever he felt particularly morose. As for his thoughts, he hadn't really had any since he left the restaurant. But now, as he waited for the lift, his brain began to recover from the traumatic incidents he had just experienced, and with the return of its processing powers came misery. He had lost the one thing in his life that he was actually capable of doing well. So much for looking forward to the rest of his life in the Known World. On the other hand, he was grateful that the motorcycle hadn't run him over. But it was difficult to be enthusiastic about his narrow escape when his enthusiasm for the life he was living was beginning to wilt.

What's happening to me? Finally, the lift arrived and the doors opened. Something in Murgatroyd felt like doing something a little different. Something in him felt like taking the stairs. And so he walked up the stairs, all the way to the eleventh floor. As he did so, he remembered how just this morning he had been climbing up stairs in the More Known World, and he smiled a little on the inside.

Murgatroyd reached his floor, walked to his flat, and unlocked the door. Just as he closed the door, a crash sounded in the distance somewhere. Murgatroyd didn't even register that he heard anything out of the ordinary. With so much construction work going on in the area, he heard sounds like that all the time. What he had actually heard was the lift he had almost taken splintering to pieces at the bottom of the shaft.

Once inside, Murgatroyd surveyed the flat he had lived in for all his life. It was clean and tastefully furnished, but now he knew what home truly felt like and this wasn't it. Sighing deeply, he headed to the kitchen to make himself his usual consolatory cup of salty Milo. But as he reached for the Milo powder, his arm stopped. Something in him felt like having something else. He wasn't sure why. He almost never drank anything else, especially when he was agitated, or melancholy, or just plain upset. Salty Milo had the inexplicable power to soothe him, blunting the sharp corners and prickles of any anxieties that were niggling at him. In the warm drowsiness that would spread out from his stomach to the very tips of his toes and fingers and ears, all his worries and doubts would simply melt away.

Today, the very thought of salty Milo, and even its aftereffects, was unappealing. Instead, he poured himself a glass of apple juice, seated himself at the empty dining table, and began to think on the events of the past few days, letting them tumble out of his memory in a confused, colourful heap. Onto this heap, he added the childhood memories he had so long packed away and forgotten about: his first visit to the Tutti-Frutti Ice Cream Shop, the kindness of Uncle Yusuf, his first ice cream sundae, the Freezer in all its frozen splendour, his taste of the ice cream that had set his breath afire and made him feel so warm and alive. These memories were a little faded, a little creased, but as he brought them out of the dark recesses of his mind and into the light, they regained some of their original colour and glow.

Here they were: all the memories—from so many years ago, from a few days ago, and from only a few hours ago. They lay spread out before him in a splendid, multicoloured mess. But now what? Since he wasn't going on the Quest, were the events of the past few days destined to eventually be put away and forgotten too?

Of course, he could always change his mind about not going on the Quest, couldn't he? Ann had said she would still be there. Tomorrow at seven p.m. at Bedok Jetty in East Coast Park. Bring a toothbrush and a change of underwear, nothing else. Kay Huat had offered to give him a ride and see him off. He could call him now. It would be as easy as that. Nothing simpler.

What did he have left here? What could he look forward to? He felt like a castaway stranded on a deserted island, watching helplessly as a ship appeared on the horizon, chugged its way tantalizingly close to the island's shores, and continued on and away, leaving him still alone, still unrescued, looking after it in desperate longing. Now what?

"Now, I have my parents. And I have my best friend," he told himself out loud. The sound of his own voice startled him. It continued speaking. "What is wrong with you, Murgatroyd? You do remember that your father has *cancer*, don't you? You do remember that they love you, and that they bought you that wonderful bed in your room, and they fixed your hot water, and they make dinner for you every night, don't you? You do remember that you're staying because you're going to help them through this and return their love?

"And you do remember, Murgatroyd, that you have a best friend who understands you and loves you like a brother and looks out for you, don't you? Where would you find a better friend than Kay Huat?

"You do remember how fortunate you are, Murgatroyd? Don't you?"

Murgatroyd clapped his hands over his mouth in surprise. But now that he had said it all out loud, he felt somewhat reassured. *Yes*, he thought (silently this time). Eventually, he would get over the disappointment about the Quest and move on. Hadn't Ann herself told him that he would eventually adjust to the Known World and become a Sumfit like everyone else? Then the Known World would become his home.

Murgatroyd realized that he was sitting in the dark. Afternoon had slipped into evening and the sun had gone down. He glanced at his wristwatch: it was already half past seven. If he hadn't lost his job, he would be waiting tables at L'Abattoir. But not tonight. He wondered when his parents would be coming home. Surely they must have left work by now.

He stood up, turned on the lights, and used the phone in the kitchen to dial his mother's mobile number.

"Hello?" his mother's voice answered. He could hear a lot of voices in the background.

"Erh. Hallo? Mum?"

"Oh it's you, Murgatroyd. What is it?"

"Just wondering if you and Dad are coming home for dinner. I . . ." he gulped. "I got fired today, so I can cook something."

"What did you say?" his mother asked. "You got fired?"

"Erh. Yes."

"Hold on for just a second." Murgatroyd heard something that sounded disconcertingly like muffled laughter. "Sorry, I'm back. Oh dear. That's terrible news. Would you mind repeating it again?"

"Huh?"

"Your news about getting fired. Could you repeat it again? It's a bit loud here in the . . . office. I just want to make sure I heard it properly."

Murgatroyd sighed and repeated the bad news: "I got fired today." Saying it a second time felt a little more painful.

"Oh dear. Yes, I did hear it properly," Olivia said. "You really liked that job, didn't you?"

"Yeah . . ." Murgatroyd sighed again. "Yeah, I did."

"And you were actually good at it, weren't you?"

"Yeah . . .yeah, I was."

"Come to think of it, that was the only job you've ever been good at."

Murgatroyd winced. "Yeah . . .yeah, it was."

"Yes, that is a real shame." Olivia was silent, but only for a few seconds. "Are you sad?"

"Erh. Yeah, of course. How come you're asking?"

"No reason. Just wondering. But just *one* more question, dear boy. If you had to rate your sadness on a scale of one to ten, one being 'slightly sad' and ten being 'extremely sad,' how would you rate it?"

Murgatroyd was beginning to feel that this was getting downright strange. Still, he tried to answer truthfully. "Erh. A nine, maybe?"

"A nine, you say? Not a ten, then?"

"Well . . . I *was* feeling really, really sad just now. But I tried to think of how lucky I still am to have you and Dad and Kay Huat."

"I see," Olivia said. "Yes, I suppose so." For some reason, she sounded slightly disappointed.

Murgatroyd tried to change the subject. "So, are you and Dad coming home for dinner?"

"Actually, no. I have to work late in the office tonight. And your father told me he has to work late in his office as well."

"Are lots of people working late in your office? It sounds very busy," Murgatroyd said.

"Yes, yes. Lots of people working late. We're working on a big project. Yes, the sushi platter is for me."

"Sushi platter?"

"Sorry about that, Murgatroyd. Just talking to a coworker. She just brought back Japanese takeout for the office. For all of us here in the office working on the big project."

"Oh right. I'll give Dad a call then and tell him the news."

"The bad news, you mean? About you getting fired?"

Murgatroyd winced again. "Yes. About me getting fired."

"Ah, yes. Don't worry about that. I've told him. I mean, I'll tell him. I'll call his office and tell him. About the firing. You just get some rest. You must feel absolutely terrible. We'll see you when we get back from dinner . . . and from the office. Because we're both working late and have to eat dinner in the office. Our respective offices, that is."

"Okay. How late will you be getting back?"

"How very sweet of you to ask, dear boy."

She hung up.

Murgatroyd too hung up the phone, and resumed sitting alone at the dining table. Perhaps it was just as well they were both working late. To be honest, he didn't really feel like cooking or eating. Perhaps he would just take a shower and go to bed early. But first, he would think a little more about things.

Sitting alone at the dining table, continuing to mull over his thoughts, his life, the Quest, Murgatroyd hadn't the faintest idea that his own little insignificant self was occupying many other people's thoughts as well.

As he sat alone at the dining table, his mother and father were sitting across from each other at their favourite Japanese restaurant—the one they used to frequent all the time, back when it had just been the two of them. James and Olivia Floyd hadn't eaten at that restaurant for years, but they were there tonight to celebrate their success at foiling their son's pursuit of genuine happiness.

Olivia snickered to her husband as she pressed the "end" button on her mobile phone. "He thinks we're both working late. I told him you were still in your office too."

James laughed and took a sip of sake. "So, he got fired today too, eh? Perfect."

"When it rains, it pours," Olivia said. And they both laughed.

"We haven't had this much fun in years," James said. It was true. This last concerted effort to prevent their son from escaping, from leaving them stranded in their otherwise joyless marriage, had enabled them to regain some semblance of the passion they had once felt for each other. Tonight, in the pleasant glow of romantic lighting, amidst the hustle and bustle and clatter of the restaurant, it felt almost as if they were in love again.

James raised his cup of sake. "To Murgatroyd!"

"To Murgatroyd!" Olivia repeated.

And together they drank in honour of their dear boy.

***

Elsewhere on the island of Singapore, a little over six kilometres away, Murgatroyd was on someone else's mind. Seng Kay Huat was in his flat, eating dinner with his father. This was unusual, as Hong Low never took a break from running his char kway teow stall. Never. Ever since he had opened it, he had been there every day without fail. Until today. His son had insisted so strongly, ferociously even, that they should—*must*—have dinner together, that he had consented to close the stall and come home early. In fact, Hong Low had never seen Kay Huat act the way he had acted yesterday when he had asked his father to take the following night off. The boy had first pleaded, then began shouting, and finally burst into tears. His son had never been so hysterical before. All for an impromptu dinner? He wasn't sure what to make of it. Reluctantly, he had consented. Something was wrong.

Even now, as he sat across from Kay Huat, picking at the pasta dish his son had made (Hong Low had never really liked the taste of western food) he wondered and waited for his son to tell him what all the fuss was about. But Kay Huat too was picking listlessly at his own food, absorbed in thought.

Hong Low cleared his throat. "Ah-Boy. Is there anything wrong?"

Kay Huat looked up, his face the very picture of innocent confusion. "Hah? Why would there be anything wrong, Ba?"

"Well, you know. You telling me to take the night off. This dinner. Just thought I'd ask, lah."

"No, no. Nothing wrong. Just wanted to spend some time with you."

"How come? Are you going somewhere?"

"No, no," Kay Huat lied. "I . . . I feel like I've been taking you for granted. That's all."

Hong Low narrowed his eyes in suspicion. "Are you sure?"

Kay Huat nodded.

"Ah-Boy, you don't lie to me. You're sure nothing is wrong?"

Kay Huat shook his head.

"You sick or something? No bad news?"

Kay Huat shook his head.

"You're sure, hah?"

Kay Huat nodded. "Yes, yes, I'm sure, Ba. I just wanted to tell you . . ." Kay Huat reached over and touched his father lightly on the arm. "That I love you very much. You're the best father anyone could hope for."

Hong Low grunted shyly and feigned renewed interest in his pasta. Kay Huat smiled because he knew that he had gotten the message across, and that had been the purpose of this entire dinner.

Tomorrow evening he would be off—setting out to accomplish whatever the Quest required him to do, and at long last, achieving the greatness that he had always been destined for. (His father didn't know the details, of course. Explaining would have been far too complicated, and it would be easier for both of them this way.) Kay Huat had always wondered exactly how he would become great. All the activities he had engaged in, hobbies he had taken up, knowledge he had acquired, had all been efforts to prepare for this point in his life. His academic excellence, his musical proficiency, his literary talents, his athletic abilities, and even his abstention from any bothersome romantic relationships: it had all been for the sake of this predestined greatness. The certainty that he was meant to achieve it had ripened in his mind over the past several years into a sweet, juicy peach hanging pendulously from its bough. And finally, the opportunity had arrived. His patience was now going to be rewarded.

Yet, lurking in the background of Kay Huat's meditations on his future greatness was a small, skinny, scraggly silhouette. It was Shwet Foo. The unobtrusive, unremarkable, unassuming, and ever-trusting Shwet Foo. Kay Huat tried to tell himself that he wasn't doing Shwet Foo any wrong. After all, now that his father had breast cancer, Shwet Foo had decided himself not to go on the Quest. He was simply supporting his friend's decision not to go. And didn't somebody have to take his place?

Do you honestly believe that Mr. Floyd has cancer?

Well, no, he admitted to himself. But just as it had never been any of his business to interfere with the Floyds' dislike of their son, neither was it his business to interfere with what they chose to tell their son. Besides, even if Shwet Foo knew the truth about his parents, then what? He'd go on the Quest? Puny little Shwet Foo? It was too dangerous for him. Even if Shwet Foo had intended to go, it would have been Kay Huat's duty to prevent him from doing so, to keep him safe and sound in Singapore.

As much as Kay Huat told himself that he was doing nothing wrong—told himself again and again in every way imaginable—the silhouette still haunted him, attending his every thought. For despite himself, Kay Huat really did love Shwet Foo like a brother, almost as much as he loved his father.

Sacrifices had to be made for greatness. There was no alternative.

Kay Huat and his father finished their dinner without another word. Gently nudging his father in the direction of the television, Kay Huat cleared the table, stored the leftovers in the refrigerator, and washed the dishes. Then he retired to his bedroom to make sure all the preparations were in place. Laid out on his bed were two envelopes. One contained a letter for his father, bidding him goodbye and explaining the arrangements he had made regarding finances. Effective two days from now, all of Kay Huat's assets and investments would be transferred to his father's name. The other envelope was addressed to Shwet Foo: a letter of apology and farewell.

Tomorrow would be his last day at work, Kay Huat reflected. He would leave the office a little early. He would drive to East Coast Park and park his car. Then he would depart forever.

I've done nothing wrong, Kay Huat repeated to himself. Still, he couldn't help but murmur out loud, "Shwet Foo, I'm sorry."

***

"Murgatroyd, I'm sorry."

In a faraway Territory of the More Known World, Ann was sitting on her dock, bathing her legs in the water. Something had compelled her to say that, although she wasn't sure what. She felt that she had failed Murgatroyd somehow. She should have pleaded his case more convincingly to the One and the Other. She should have figured out what was going on earlier. It was ironic that despite her remorse for what she had failed to do, she remained ignorant of the adverse effects that Murgatroyd's third visit to the More Known World was having on his continued safety in the Known World. Aware that Murgatroyd's wellbeing was under threat, yet utterly unaware that Murgatroyd's life was now in danger, Ann hoped fervently that Murgatroyd would show up tomorrow. What she didn't know was that now his very life depended on it.

***

Back in the Singapore of the Known World, eleven storeys below Murgatroyd's lighted bedroom window, stood a young man who was also contemplating Murgatroyd's life—contemplating how he would end it. It was the Duck Assassin, crouching in the shadows of the building, seething quietly with rage. He had failed twice. The next time, he wouldn't fail again.

Craning his neck upwards, the Duck Assassin never let his gaze shift from Murgatroyd's bedroom window. Not when the lights were turned off at nine thirty. Not when they were turned back on for a few minutes. And not when they were turned off again for the rest of the night. The little *ang moh* was sleeping, but he had to leave the flat at some point. And when he did, the Duck Assassin would be ready for him.

The Duck Assassin had seen Murgatroyd's bedroom light turn on and off, and he had wondered, briefly, why. *Probably a trip to the toilet*, he had thought. Actually, Murgatroyd had gotten out of bed not to empty his bladder, but to make a phone call. Just as he had lain his head down on his pillow with the intent of going to sleep, he remembered what Ann had asked him during their last phone conversation.

Do you believe everything your parents tell you?

He had turned on the lights and gotten out of bed to look up a number in the address book his parents kept in the kitchen. He had called the number and left a message. And then, he had gotten back into bed, switched off the lights, and tried to lose himself in the world of dreams.

CHAPTER 20

"Twelfth floor," announced the automated female voice. The silver lift doors parted, revealing what they did every time Dr. Loy alighted on the twelfth floor: a very large pleasant painting of a lake, done in watercolour, framed in burnished bronze. Occasionally, Dr. Loy would have the satisfaction of having the lift doors open to reveal someone looking at the painting—usually a patient of his, or one of the other medical practitioners whose offices were housed in the same building. Sometimes, he thought he saw admiration and appreciation in their faces as they looked at it.

The reason Dr. Loy took such note of the painting and its beholders was that it was he who had painted it. It had taken two years of Sunday afternoons at the Botanical Gardens, but he had finally finished it six months ago, and decided to display it in the hallway outside his office. It made him feel like a real artist. If only he had time to paint more. But he didn't really have any regrets; he was very satisfied with the career he had made and the life he had fashioned for himself. Someday, someday, it would be *that* time. *That* time would be the time to paint. Now was a different time.

Still, he often wondered what would have happened if he had become an artist instead of an oncologist. He had never seriously entertained the notion—after all, you can't support your parents or start a family on an artist's income. He had always reasoned that he could paint in his spare time, but these days the practice was thriving so much that he never had time to spare. He rather liked being a doctor, but he also dreamed of the retirement awaiting him many years down the road—of spending his twilight years travelling around the world, sketching water lilies in Monet's garden and painting giraffes lumbering across the African savannah; of the exact tints and brushstrokes with which he would recreate the peaks of the Andes, enshrouded in morning mist.

He strode into his office. "Good morning, Betty. Any messages for me?"

The receptionist looked at her notepad. "Got three. Mrs. Kwee called this morning to ask if you can issue her another prescription. She lost the one you gave her."

"What for?"

"Posilex."

"All right. Next message?"

"The son of James Floyd left a message last night asking for more information about his father's breast cancer."

"Say again?"

"The son of James Floyd wants to know about his father's breast cancer."

"James Floyd?" Dr. Loy's eyebrows lifted in astonishment. "I haven't seen or heard from him for over two years! He has *cancer*? Oh dear."

"He left a number. Should I call him back?"

"No, no, I should talk to him. His son, you say? Didn't know he had one. I'll call him right away."

"Here's his number." She handed him a slip of paper.

He thought for a moment. "*Breast* cancer?"

Betty shrugged.

"Oh dear. You know that's very rare—breast cancer in men."

Betty shrugged again.

"And what's the third message?"

"Dr. Matthews wants to know if you're still on for racquetball this evening."

"Oh, that's right. I'll call him too. Thanks, Betty."

"Eh, wait. One more thing." Betty hefted a large stack of files from under the desk into his arms. "You asked for these yesterday."

"Oof. Thanks."

Loy staggered into his office and sighed. Somehow, the sight of his desk covered with medical journals, documents, and files never ceased to overwhelm him. Clearing a small space, he unloaded the slip of paper and files with a heavy thud. Then he rang up Dr. Matthews to confirm their racquetball game at the club.

Betty's voice came over the intercom. "Dr. Loy, Mr. Stanley Ng is here for his appointment."

He sighed. "Send him in." He was very happy that it was Friday. He was looking forward to getting some painting done on the weekend.

***

James and Olivia Floyd sat side by side on the sofa in their living room, the coffee table covered in novels, magazines, newspapers, and empty mugs containing soggy tea bags. As Olivia typed busily on her laptop, James flipped through magazine after magazine.

"Damn it, Olivia, I'm bored," James complained, tossing aside his two-year-old issue of *The Economist*.

Olivia rolled her eyes. "Just treat it like a lazy Sunday afternoon."

"But it's *not*. It's a *Friday* afternoon, and I am intolerably bored."

"Do you want more tea?"

"No, damn it. I don't want any more damn tea."

"Well, you needn't be so grumpy."

"I'll be as damn grumpy as I please. I don't see why we have to stay home all the damn day long."

"James, I told you," Olivia said, lowering her voice. "We can't risk him leaving."

"Look, he already said he's not going on the Quest. The boy may be stupid, but he doesn't lie!" James stood up and began pacing around the room. "You know, I have a lot of work at the office that I could be doing right now."

"You know, James, it's not my fault that you forgot we agreed to stay in today. *Some* people brought their work home." Olivia gestured at her laptop and documents.

James paused midstep and coldly eyed his wife. "Damn you."

"Damn yourself. I'm going to make more tea."

"Damn the tea too. And damn that boy. What's wrong with him anyway? It's four thirty in the afternoon and he hasn't even gotten out of bed."

"Who knows? Depressed, I suppose."

They both cackled with glee.

Murgatroyd was indeed depressed. He was lying in bed staring at the ceiling, the sheets pulled up to his chin. There was a sharp rap on the door, followed by the sound of his mother's voice.

"Murgatroyd, dear. Do you want me to make you a cup of Milo?"

"No thanks, Mum. I'm all right."

"What? I can't hear you."

"No, I'm fine."

"What?"

"NO, I'M FINE."

There was a pause. He heard his mother's voice again. "Well, you needn't shout. It's bad enough that your father has cancer without you screaming at me."

Murgatroyd rolled over onto his side and pulled the covers over his head. He knew that he should feel guilty for yelling at his mother.

He also knew he should feel guilty about the resentment and exasperation which sat in his stomach like a ball of lead. But he didn't. He felt unashamedly resentful and exasperated. And sick to his stomach. And ungrateful for the very bed he was lying in, and the hot water running through the pipes in his bathroom, and the miserable existence that his mother and father had given him. And he wanted to get away from this place, and he wanted to run away and meet Ann on Bedok Jetty. And he wanted to travel in the More Known World where it felt like home. And he hated stupid cancer and his stupid father and this stupid, stupid life.

And he felt selfish and childish.

And he felt trapped.

Trapped. He pulled the blankets around him tighter and began to feel drowsy with despair. *Trapped . . . trapped . . .*

The next thing he knew, there was a faint ringing sound in his ears and a voice yelling at him through the door. He must have dozed off.

"Murgatroyd! Can you get the phone?"

Even though it was never for him, even though the phone was in the kitchen, closer to *them*, and he was in his bedroom, it was *his* job to answer the phone. With the exaggerated sigh of a melodramatic teenager, he threw off the covers and got out of bed.

"Hello?"

"Ah, hello. May I please speak with . . . erh . . . Murgatroyd? Murgatroyd Floyd?"

"Yes, that's me."

"The son of James Floyd?"

"Yes."

"This is Dr. Loy, returning your call. Unusual name, Murgatroyd."

"Oh. Hello, Dr. Loy. Yes, I just called about—"

"Sorry, I meant to call earlier today, but I was busier than I thought, and then your number got lost on my desk, and then—"

"It's okay. I just wanted to know about my father's—"

"Ah yes, your father's—oh dear, oh dear. Let me just say, I was so shocked when the secretary told me. I *am* sorry. How is your father, by the way?"

Murgatroyd felt confused. "Erh . . . he's okay, I guess?"

"Oh good. Give him my best. We should really play racquetball sometime."

"Erh. I don't play racquetball."

"Ha ha. Sorry, I meant your father, not you." Dr. Loy paused. "Oh sorry, I didn't mean to sound rude. You . . . you could play too, if you like."

"Oh . . . okay."

"Dear me. Sorry, again. I didn't mean to sound insensitive. Perhaps racquetball might not be the best, given your father's condition."

"Oh."

There was silence, which was eventually broken by Dr. Loy's voice.

"So . . . why did you call me?"

"Huh? Oh. I wanted to ask about my father's cancer."

"Yes, breast cancer. Very rare in men, you know. I *am* sorry. How is he taking it?"

Murgatroyd peered through the open door into the living room where his father was sitting, eating vanilla ice cream straight out of the container with a spoon.

"Erh. He seems okay. He was very sad a few days ago, though."

"Yes, I can imagine. That's terrible. Do you know how advanced it is?"

Murgatroyd frowned. "Sorry. Say again?"

"I said, 'Do you know how advanced it is?'"

"What? Don't you know?"

"Why would I know?"

"Didn't you know?"

"Know what?"

"He has cancer?"

"Yes, you told me."

"No, no." Murgatroyd took a deep breath. "He said that *you* said he has cancer."

"Come again? I'm very confused. He *does* have cancer, doesn't he?"

"Doesn't he? I thought you knew!"

"I only got the news when you called. I haven't seen your father for two years!"

"What?! But he said *you* told him he has cancer."

"What? I never told him he has cancer."

"I—"

A wave of dizziness swept over Murgatroyd. Leaning against the wall, he peered again at his father comfortably ensconced on the sofa, contemplating his spoon. A rivulet of melted ice cream dribbled slowly down his chin. James looked up and glanced in his son's direction.

"Ah, dear boy! Glad to see you're up and about, finally! Could you look in the fridge and see if we have any chocolate syrup?"

"I—"

"Who are you talking to?"

Murgatroyd stared at him. "You. You—"

"Yes, I *know* you're talking to *me*," his father said impatiently. "But who are you talking to *on the phone*?"

"You . . . you . . ." The phone fell from his hands and clattered onto the floor. Dr. Loy's voice sounded faintly over the receiver. "Hello? Hello?"

Murgatroyd took a step in his father's direction and pointed a trembling finger at him. "You don't have cancer."

James lowered his spoon. "Who told you that? Who was that?"

"It was Dr. Loy. You don't have cancer."

A look of panic crossed James's face. Eying his son as he might a hungry wolf, James slowly set the ice cream carton down on the table. He called out to his wife. "Olivia!"

"I'm in the loo! What is it?"

"Olivia, just get out here now! Hurry!"

There was a flushing sound, and Olivia emerged, hands unwashed, from the bathroom. "James, what is it?"

James looked at his wife, then again at his son. "He knows."

Olivia was quiet for a while. "How much does he know?"

"I don't know," James answered. With apprehension, they both regarded their son.

Murgatroyd couldn't believe it. And yet, he could. He believed it, and moreover, somehow, he had known it all along. Staring at his mother and father's faces, taking in their expressions of shock, dismay, nervousness, and a certain *something else* that had always been present but that he had never been able to quite figure out, Murgatroyd realized that he knew everything. He felt out of breath, lightheaded. As if the air around him had become thinner, as if his body were only barely anchored to the ground beneath his feet. Weightless. Stretching out his arms, he steadied himself against the kitchen door frame.

When he tried to speak, he choked, and tears sprang to his eyes. He tried again. The voice that came out of his throat was thin, small, pathetic. He knew what the certain something else was. And he wanted to know why it was.

"Why do you hate me?"

Much to their surprise, James and Olivia too felt the warm saltiness of tears running down their own faces. James answered truthfully.

"We don't know."

"You *don't know*?" Murgatroyd repeated. He was panting, sucking at the air in long, painful draughts. "How . . . how long?"

Olivia answered this time, as gently as she could, for it seemed as if the boy was going to collapse.

"Ever since you were born."

Ever since you were born. The words astounded him. And somehow, he knew that too. *Ever since I was born.*

"So everything. Everything . . . sleeping on the floor . . . the salt . . . the games me and Dad used to play . . ." his voice gave out as, mentally, he penned an interminable list, a list with no end. The toilet incident at the YMCA. The food poisonings. The girls who never spoke to him again. The persistent, mysterious rash on his buttocks. The cheese problem in primary six. The terrible smell that lasted for three months. The haircut. The accident at the orthodontist. And how many more? Was it *all* of them? Where did it begin and where did it end? How had they done it all?

"We're sorry, dear boy," Olivia said. "We just can't help it."

With frightened eyes, they watched their son stand there for what seemed like an eternity, his scrawny body stretched out and suspended in the doorway like a delicate, trembling spider web. What could they have done differently? They couldn't help it. He had to understand. They couldn't love him. They could never love him.

Then, without a word, he went to his room. Half a minute later, he re-emerged, carrying a little plastic bag. He picked the phone receiver off the kitchen floor and dialled a number.

"Hello? I need a taxi. Goldenview Towers, 349 Stamford Lane. Going to Bedok Jetty, East Coast Park. Yes, I need it now. Okay. Thank you. Bye."

"Murgatroyd, wait," Olivia cried as he hung up the phone. "You can't leave us."

Standing in front of the door, he refused to look his mother or father in the eye. He stared determinedly at his feet, clenching his plastic bag in front of him with both hands. "Why not?"

"It's true we don't like you. But—"

James finished his wife's sentence: "—we need you."

Murgatroyd kept his eyes downcast. "You need me?"

James answered. "You're the only reason for us."

"'For us'?" Murgatroyd asked. "What do you mean?"

James tried to explain. "Making your life . . ."

". . . a living hell," Olivia finished, bluntly. "It's the only thing keeping us together."

James chimed in again. "It's the only thing that keeps us happy."

Murgatroyd didn't speak.

Cautiously, James walked over and placed his hand on his son's shoulder. Murgatroyd didn't move away. James hesitated, then continued. "We . . . haven't been good to you. We really tried, dear boy. We tried hard. But we couldn't stop hating you. It was terrible for us."

"Terrible . . ." Olivia murmured.

"Do you think we *wanted* to be like this? Do you think we *wanted* to hate our own child?" James gave his son's shoulder an affectionate-like squeeze. "We can't help who we are, Murgatroyd. But you—"

He searched for the right words to express what he truly felt. "But you've been good to us. More than good to us. You *loved* us, when you had no reason to. And . . . I know it's true that we can never love you back—"

"We just *can't*," Olivia explained.

"But we appreciate it." James nodded firmly to emphasize just how much he and his wife appreciated Murgatroyd's love. "And we would appreciate it . . . appreciate it *very much*, if you stayed around. Even though we don't deserve it."

"Without you, we'll fall apart."

Still staring at the floor, Murgatroyd lifted his father's hand from his shoulder, and held it in his own. James was right. He did love them. He loved them very much. Even after all that they'd done to him, he couldn't help it, the anger and love and pain all tearing at his chest at once. It seemed ridiculous, but he didn't want to hurt them, didn't want to leave them alone, miserable, in the shambles of their love for each other.

He gave his father's hand a short squeeze, and then he slipped his feet into his orange flip-flops and left.

CHAPTER 21

"Uncle, can drive faster, please?"

"Young man, I drive as fast as I can, okay?" the driver snapped. "You want to get speeding ticket, is it? Then how?"

Murgatroyd glanced nervously at his wristwatch. Six forty-five. They would make it just in time. To relieve his anxiety, he began to count the hairs sprouting from the shiny dome of the taxi driver's head. After counting seven, he couldn't contain himself anymore.

"Uncle, how much farther?"

"Don't worry, lah. Not very far."

Murgatroyd twiddled his thumbs. This time, the driver spoke.

"Eh, young man. How come your accent like local one?"

"I grew up here."

The driver contemplated this.

"So . . . your mother local, is it?"

"Erh, no. I went to local school."

"Ah. I see." There was another pause, as the driver mulled over this additional piece of information. "So . . . your father local, is it?"

"No, no. They're both from England."

The driver took a few moments to digest this.

"Ah, I see. From England, is it? British, is it? You know something? Between you and me, you British, not so bad, lah." Briefly checking over his shoulder before exiting the freeway, the driver continued. "What's past is past, right or not? Now we're independent, not colony anymore, can be friends, what!" The driver chuckled to himself. "Eh, you British, right? You like football? I'm *big* Manchester United fan. You British play damn good football, what!"

"Uncle, stop here! Stop here!"

"What, here?"

"Yeah. Right here."

Murgatroyd hurriedly thrust three ten-dollar bills into the driver's hands and opened the door.

"Wait, wait, young man! Got change one!"

"Can keep the change!"

"Wah! Cannot! Too much!"

But Murgatroyd was already sprinting across the grass in the direction of Bedok Jetty, the plastic bag in his right hand flapping against his leg. In the distance, beyond the paved pathways for bicyclists and joggers, beyond the stone picnic tables and benches, he could see the concrete jetty extending out into the ocean, lined on each side with bony, dark-skinned old men leaning against the railing, tugging their fishing lines hopefully and casting new ones out into the blue sea. Squinting ahead into the cloudy horizon of the sea, which was darkening with the setting sun, he thought he could make out the figure of a woman, standing quite still against the railings. He was almost there. He was almost ther—

"SHWET FOO!"

Murgatroyd only had time to register a violent blow to the right side of his body before he found himself sprawled on the grass. He opened his eyes in a daze. It was Kay Huat. And he was clutching at his T-shirt and barking something at him in a loud voice.

"Kay Huat? What are you doing here?"

"GET OUT OF HERE!"

"How did you know I was com—"

"RUN!"

"But—"

Confused still, Murgatroyd looked around to see what had thrown his friend into such a panic. His eyes came to rest on a knife, plunged point first into the ground just a few metres away. Its blade was still quivering.

"GO UNDER THE TABLE! UNDER THE TABLE!" Kay Huat ordered, picking Murgatroyd off the ground.

"Wha—?"

"GO! NOW! GO!"

As Murgatroyd scurried under a stone picnic table, Kay Huat yanked the knife out of the ground. "You want to kill my friend, is it?" he bellowed. Passing bicyclists and Rollerbladers stopped to gawk at the crazy young man: very handsome, but obviously crazy. He appeared to be addressing the cluster of palm trees that stood between him and the sea beyond. "Coward! Show yourself!"

A thin figure clad in black stepped out from behind one of the trees, an ugly gash across his lower face. The gash curled upwards into a smile.

Kay Huat remained undaunted. "You got a problem with my friend, is it? IS IT?"

In reply, the Duck Assassin reached behind his shoulder, unsheathed the sword slung across his back, and held it at the ready with both hands.

"You want him, hah? Hah?" Kay Huat gestured at his best friend, who watched wide-eyed from underneath the table. "COME GET HIM!"

Letting out a great yell, Kay Huat charged at his opponent. The Duck Assassin remained perfectly still. Kay Huat was almost upon him, his knife poised to impale the Duck Assassin in the stomach. Kay Huat braced his arms for the impact.

At the very last second, the Duck Assassin stepped aside, sending Kay Huat stumbling past him. Kay Huat regained his balance and spun around just in time to see the Duck Assassin's sword come sweeping towards him to cut off his head. Kay Huat ducked, losing a few centimetres of hair to the flashing blade. Crouching close to the ground, Kay Huat attempted to stab the Assassin in the calf, only to have the knife kicked out of his hand. He yowled in pain as the foot came into contact with his fingers, then with his mouth, sending a bloody tooth flying onto the grass.

Dazed and desperate, Kay Huat hurled himself against the Assassin from behind, butting his head into the back of his legs. The Assassin stumbled forward, falling to his knees. Regaining control, the Duck Assassin arched his body backwards and brought his left elbow down sharply onto the nape of his opponent's neck. With a cry of pain, Kay Huat fell onto his belly, releasing his hold on the Assassin, who sprang up and twisted round with the intent of plunging his sword into Kay Huat's body, prostrate on the ground.

"KAY HUAT! WATCH OUT!"

Roused by his friend's cry, Kay Huat mustered enough strength to flop to the left, the sword blade nicking his right arm as it plunged into the ground. Blood oozing from the wound, the weakened Kay Huat attempted to raise himself on his left arm. Over him stood the Duck Assassin, savouring his opponent's pain.

Kay Huat grunted and lifted his face to squint at his foe, dark and faceless against the cool blue of the evening sky.

"You," he gasped. "You leave Shwet Foo alone."

The Duck Assassin smirked. In reply, he lifted his sword over his head to deliver the final blow.

And then, something hit the Duck Assassin with a light *pok* in his right armpit. He looked down. It was an orange rubber flip-flop followed by a thin little voice.

"Don't you dare!"

The Duck Assassin lifted his head to look at the skinny, barefoot *ang moh* standing by the picnic table, wielding the other flip-flop in his hand as if he were going to squash the Assassin like a cockroach. It almost made the Assassin smile. Almost.

"That's my best friend. Don't you dare!" the *ang moh* repeated.

So it has courage after all, the Assassin thought to himself. There was no more time for fun and games. The real job had been delayed long enough. He spat on Kay Huat's face and turned his attention onto the *ang moh*, advancing towards him like a predator to its prey.

Kay Huat sat up weakly and watched as the Assassin approached Shwet Foo, who backed away with every step the Assassin took towards him. *I must save him*, he thought. To his complete surprise, another thought entered his head. *Why? Just let him die*. He shook his head vigorously, as if to shake the thought away. He made to stand up, but his body felt as heavy as a sack of lead. What was wrong? *Just let him die.* A sudden wave of apathy washed over him, as if some outside power were exerting some sort of pull on him, trying to prevent him from saving Shwet Foo. It was a strangely calming force. *He's not one of us*, it seemed to be saying. *Not one of us at all. He must die.*

"NO!" Kay Huat roared. Letting loose a low bellow, he drowned out the voice and staggered to his feet. It felt as if he were defying gravity. How long had it taken for him to stand up? It seemed like ages. He looked over to see the Assassin stepping closer and closer towards his friend, who was now motionless, paralyzed with fear. He wasn't too late. He could still save Shwet Foo.

The Duck Assassin was now so near to the *ang moh* that he could see the arm holding the flip-flop aloft was trembling. The Duck Assassin was pleased. Quick as lightning, his left hand shot out and seized the *ang moh* by the neck, making his little blue eyes bulge in fear and pain. *Just like a duck*, he thought to himself. He grinned. At the sight of the cruel smile, the *ang moh* whimpered and tried desperately to free himself, slapping at the arm that held him prisoner. It was useless. He wasn't strong enough.

The Duck Assassin spoke. It was a voice dry, harsh, and raspy from lack of use. "You think it's so easy, is it? To escape your life?"

He strengthened his grip on Murgatroyd's neck, lifting him off the ground a little so that he had to scrabble around on the tips of his toes, gasping for air. The Duck Assassin leaned his face close to Murgatroyd's—so close that their foreheads were almost touching. "Guess what?" he whispered. The sword in his right hand swung up high, ready to make its descent. "It's not so easy to escape after all."

"NO!"

The Duck Assassin felt his feet flying out from under him. The force of whatever had barrelled into him caused him to lose his grip both of the *ang moh* and his sword. He flew sideways towards the table under which Murgatroyd had cowered only moments before. He flailed his arms but couldn't stop. The side of his head met the cool, unyielding stone. Everything went black. Everything went quiet.

Murgatroyd ran over and struggled to lift Kay Huat off the Duck Assassin, who lay slumped atop one of the stone benches with his head on the table. It looked almost as if he had fallen asleep while picnicking, save for the small trickle of blood running down his forehead. Kay Huat had saved his friend's life.

"Walau, Kay Huat! Are you okay?"

Kay Huat grunted and roared in pain as Murgatroyd's hands pressed against his upper arm.

"Oops! Sorry!"

Shaking off his well-meaning friend with a shrug of his shoulder, Kay Huat got to his feet, only to collapse seconds later onto the grass. With a heave of his lungs, he spat out some blood.

Murgatroyd stared wide-eyed in appreciation and admiration at his friend. "Kay Huat," he began, almost choking on his tears. "How did you know?"

"Know . . . know what?" Kay Huat gasped, still breathless from pain and exhaustion.

"That I was going on the Quest after all? Why else would you—" his voice trailed off. Lying about five metres away on the grass were two plastic bags. One was the one he had brought, containing his toothbrush and his pair of clean underwear. He walked over and peered into the other one—a toothbrush and a pair of grey Calvin Klein briefs.

Murgatroyd's hands trembled slightly as he turned to his friend and held up the plastic bag that wasn't his. "Kay Huat?"

Weak and in pain, Kay Huat could only meet his friend's heartbroken gaze with fatigue. His mighty chest heaved a great sigh.

"Shwet Foo, I was only trying to protect you."

Murgatroyd stared again at the contents of the plastic bag.

Kay Hat tried again. "Come on, Shwet Foo. Understand, lah. You think you're strong enough to go? Smart enough?"

Murgatroyd didn't answer.

"Shwet Foo. You know I'm speaking the truth, right? The Quest is too much for you." Kay Huat added weakly, "Besides. I didn't think you were going on the Quest. You said you weren't going."

Murgatroyd looked at Kay Huat, drenched in sweat, blood still trickling from the corners of his mouth and the wound on his arm. He didn't feel shocked anymore, or even angry. Instead, he thought about what good friends they were. He even managed a faint smile. After he had picked up his plastic bag and retrieved his flip-flops, he shuffled over to his best friend.

"Goodbye, Kay Huat. I'll miss you."

"What?" Kay Huat sat up. "So that's it? You're just going to leave me now? I just saved your life! I protected you all those years! Don't you remember how we first met? Does our friendship mean nothing?!"

"I'm sorry, Kay Huat."

Murgatroyd turned away and began walking towards the jetty. With tremendous effort, Kay Huat got to his feet, grabbed his friend by the shoulder and spun him around.

"You can't go, hear me? You can't go! Why are you so stupid? The Quest is too much for you! Let me go! I'm the one who's supposed to go!"

A woman's voice interrupted them, clear and firm. "And who are you to decide who gets to go on the Quest?"

The two friends looked up. Walking towards them from the direction of the jetty was Ann. Her long green skirt billowed in the wind, and her emerald eye blazed bright in the light of the setting sun.

To their surprise, she walked right past them to the Duck Assassin, still lying prone and unconscious on the table. She examined the wound on his head.

"He's alive," she sighed with relief. "Good. We've just started keeping a file on him."

"A file? What for?" Murgatroyd asked.

Ann turned to Murgatroyd, but didn't answer the question. "Murgatroyd, are you ready to go? We're late."

"No, he's not!" Kay Huat snarled. "He'll never be ready. Why *him*? Look at him!" Kay Huat gave Murgatroyd a light push on the shoulder. It sent him tumbling to the ground. "Is this the one you chose? What about me? Look at me!"

Ann surveyed him with a scornful eye. "And what *about* you?"

"I was *born* to go on the Quest! It's me you want! You made a mistake! Do you hear me? You made a mistake!"

Ann was silent, and Kay Huat too fell silent. "This isn't a mistake," she replied. She turned again to Murgatroyd, who had picked himself off the ground, and repeated her question. "Murgatroyd. Are you ready to go?"

"Yes," Murgatroyd answered enthusiastically. "Yes, I am!"

"No! No, he's not!" Kay Huat turned to Murgatroyd. "Shwet Foo, look at me."

Murgatroyd looked at the ground.

"Shwet Foo, *look* at me."

Murgatroyd finally raised his eyes to Kay Huat's and saw that there were tears in his friend's eyes. "Shwet Foo, I didn't mean to hurt you. Look, I just saved your life! How could I ever want to hurt you?" Murgatroyd felt himself begin to cry.

Kay Huat continued. "We're like brothers, you and me. I would never want to hurt you. But this is *my* Quest. This is for me. You know me. I've spent all my life preparing for this chance, waiting for my big break. It's finally come. Don't you understand?"

Wiping the tears from his friend's face, Murgatroyd then wiped his own and shook his head. "No, I don't, Kay Huat. Goodbye."

Kay Huat sputtered. "But what about me?"

Murgatroyd replied in a small, quiet voice, "This isn't about you." He turned to Ann and nodded, and turning their backs on Kay Huat, they walked towards the jetty.

Murgatroyd heard Kay Huat's voice call out after him. "Fine! Go on your precious little Quest! See if I care!" It was the shriek of a wounded eagle. Glancing back over his shoulder, Murgatroyd could see Kay Huat stalking away, clutching his injured arm. Turning around once again, he set his eyes on the faraway horizon of the sea. Ann and he were now on the jetty, walking towards it.

"Murgatroyd." Her voice almost bordered on gentle. Almost. "I didn't tell you before, but I'm glad you made it."

"Me too," he said, and gave her a half smile.

"That's some friend you have there."

"My *best* friend," Murgatroyd said defensively. "He just saved my life."

Ann nodded in respect, and they walked on in silence until they reached the end of the jetty. Ann noticed that the sea around them had gotten a little more restless in the last few minutes, lapping more vigorously against the concrete supports below them, sending up ocean spray into their faces. But never mind that now. Resting their elbows on the railing, they watched the cargo ships floating on the horizon.

"Ann, can I ask you a question?" Murgatroyd blurted out.

"Yes."

"What happened to your eye?"

"The missing one or the one that's still in its socket?"

"Erh . . . the missing one."

Ann's expression almost grew soft. Almost. "There's not much to tell, really. When I was asked to go on the Quest, my mother refused to give me her permission. I told her I was leaving. She was furious. She was holding a pair of very sharp scissors."

Murgatroyd gasped. "Your mother attacked you?"

"Actually, no. I was so exasperated that I grabbed the scissors from her, gouged out my own right eye, gave it to her, and left. If I couldn't live up to her idea of what a good daughter should be, I figured at least she'd know I made *some* sort of sacrifice for her." Ann reflected. "In hindsight, it was a rather silly and unnecessary thing to do."

They lapsed into thoughtful silence once more. A swell of water surged up surprisingly high and licked Murgatroyd's toes. He didn't notice; he was mustering up the courage to satisfy his curiosity on another point.

"Ann? How come your left eye is green?"

"Contact lens."

"Oh."

Silence again. But filling the silence was the ambient roar of the ocean, louder and closer than it had been a few seconds ago. Murgatroyd asked a third question.

"What now, Ann?"

A wave broke against the jetty's edge, soaking them from the waist down.

"We start walking." Ann gestured out towards the ocean. "That way."

"Where to? We've reached the end of the land."

"No, we haven't." She fiddled with something on the railing. "Aha. There we go."

Something clicked and a portion of the railing swung open like a little gate, leaving a narrow gap to walk through. Beyond that, Murgatroyd could only see the edge of the concrete platform, and the churning, angry water below.

"Are you ready?" Ann asked.

Murgatroyd nodded. Another wave—this time strong enough to have swept him off the platform entirely if he hadn't been hanging onto one of the railings.

"Don't let your eyes deceive you. Just keep your eyes on the horizon, keep walking, and think of leaving here and getting to go home." She motioned towards the horizon.

Murgatroyd nodded again. As he stepped towards the gap, he staggered a little. A sharp pain shot through him. He remembered waiting tables for Shakti Vithani. He remembered all the good times with Kay Huat. He remembered his father and mother. He did feel homesick, but for what lay behind him, not what lay ahead.

He legs felt weak. Ann grasped his elbow to steady him. She looked up. In the distance, she could make out a wall of water moving towards them, gaining height and force by the second.

"Ann?"

"Yes, Murgatroyd?"

"I feel terrible."

"I know. It's normal. Come on, let's go."

And so they went.

THE END
(and THE BEGINNING)

ABOUT THE AUTHOR

Photo © 2015 Leah Diprose

Tiffany Tsao was born in San Diego, California, and lived in Singapore and Indonesia through her childhood and young adulthood. A graduate of Wellesley College and the University of California Berkeley, where she earned a PhD in English, she has taught and researched literature at Berkeley, the Georgia Institute of Technology, and the University of Newcastle, Australia. She holds an affiliation with the Indonesian Studies Department at the University of Sydney. Her works include short fiction, poetry, literary criticism, and translations and have been published in *Transnational Literature*, *Asymptote*, *Mascara Literary Review*, *LONTAR*, *Comparative Literature*, *Literature and Theology*, and the anthology *Contemporary Asian Australian Poets*.

Tsao currently lives in Sydney, Australia, with her husband and son.